Bubba and t...

By

C.L. Bevill

Bubba and the Ten Little Loonies
Published by C.L. Bevill LLC
© 2014 by Caren L. Bevill

The order of the Bubba mystery series is as follows:

Ideally they should be read in order or bad things might happen. (Not really, but you never know. It's always better to be safe than sorry.)

Table of Contents

Chapter One

Bubba and the Lonesome Moment of Utter Solitude

Saturday, April 6th

Bubba cast the Fresh Water Jr. Baby Bass lure into the lake. (It was hand painted with a green- and silver-metallic sheen, just like the color of the fish he liked to catch most.) He reeled the lure slowly across the surface because bass were basically lazy fellas, and the water was a little cool even for April. This caused sluggish fishies. Sluggish fishies liked sluggish bait, so they wouldn't have to put out a lot of effort. Consequently, this made for more catches for Bubba.

The best of this was that he could reflect on the simplicity of the moment. The brief respite and feeling of complete contentment gave Bubba pause. If all was utterly well, then something bad was about to happen. It had happened this way too many times in the past to be pure happenstance. This made him want to ensure all was well.

Boat. Check.

Lake. Check.

Dog. Check.

Fishing rod. Check.

Lure. Check.

Balmy breeze out of the south. Check.

RC Cola. Check.

Moon Pie. No check. No Moon Pies. There were no more left because he'd eaten them all. Precious, his stalwart Bassett hound, had wanted to eat them too, but chocolate wasn't good for a dog, so she'd gotten two Milk-Bones instead. She hadn't complained. She'd eaten both treats and presently lay on the bottom of the boat with all four legs in the air, enjoying the sunshine on her belly. Even though she wore a specially made life jacket for dogs, she was comfortable. A loud canine snore ensued.

Moon Pies and Milk-Bones: it's what's for brekky.

Bubba leaned back and felt his back pop. Certainly, he needed a break. Not from his life, not from his mother, Miz Demetrice, surely not from the beauteous sheriff's deputy, Willodean Gray, and not from being in the great lone star state of Texas. No, none of those.

He closed his eyes, still holding onto his fishing rod, and took a deep breath. He needed a break from finding dead bodies. Specifically, he needed a break from finding murdered dead bodies, although he had recently found one that hadn't really been murdered at all. It had been four weeks since the last one (the non-murdered one) and all was good. Because all was good, he suspected that all was *not* good.

This had given birth to a new integral law of nature: if all is good, then all is truly bad. It should be the Snoddy family's new motto. If Bubba were inclined to have it translated into Latin, he would have it put on the coat of arms and then slap the sucker on the front gate. In fact, he should just shorten it to "Bad things will happen soon." Possibly he should add suckers to the end, but he was sure that wouldn't translate into Latin.

He cracked open an eye. No dead bodies. None in the air. None in the wind. And most importantly, none in the lake.

Bubba nodded. That was good, as good as redeye gravy on top of eggs and sausage on a homemade biscuit. As far as he knew, he was alone for the moment. Alone was good, too. However, Willodean's company would have been just as nice. She enjoyed a good quiet moment as much as Bubba. He was teaching her how to fish, although the last time when she'd attempted to gut a trout, she'd vomited all over the fish. That really wasn't her fault because Willodean was vomiting all over a lot of things lately.

In fact, Miz Demetrice had made the mistake of calling Willodean "The Vomit Comet" while within the hearing range of Celestine Gray, Willodean's mother. It ended acrimoniously with the two women banned from touching any kind of edged weapon or gun while within fifty feet of each other, which was difficult because both women liked their guns. Also, since Celestine was staying at the Snoddy Mansion, the mandate was somewhat limiting. On the good side, the two had settled into a friendly détente.

Bubba opened the other eye and gazed at the lake. No one was complaining about murdered fish. Generally, Bubba didn't even keep the fish he caught. On the contrary, the enjoyment was in the serenity of the lake and the thrill of the hunt. He caught the little slippery fish and then gently admonished them not to eat the weird thing that looked like a baby fish before tossing them back into the depths. The fish largely did not say thank you. In fact, they swished their tails at him in a highly derogatory manner before vanishing into the green murk.

Yes, Bubba did need a break from ugly murder poo. He also needed a break from what he privately called WWWA, otherwise known as World War Wedding Armageddon. He had, in fact, proposed to Willodean Gray. His timing was a little off. Regardless, she had said yes. They told the families. (It might have been the other way around; the families might have told Bubba and Willodean. He couldn't really recollect.) Then Miz Demetrice and Celestine had gotten rabid cases of weddingitus. It was an ugly condition, largely not discussed in popular venues, but well known to those who had experienced it firsthand.

Bubba might have thought that his mother and Willodean's mother had been listening to Lloyd Goshorn's frequently escalating tales of their "wedding." (Wayne Newton had presided. Two former presidents had attended. Willodean's train had been longer than Princess Di's. One version had tuxedoed robots holding the lengthy train off the ground. Lloyd was required to take off his shoes and two someone else's shoes too, in order to count all the bridesmaids and groomsmen involved.) However, the immediate situation was not truly attributable to Lloyd Goshorn. It was all weddingitus of the maternal kind.

Willodean, in her delicate condition, didn't really want to be bothered by planning a wedding. Miz Demetrice having only had one child – Bubba, wished to have an event of epic proportion no matter what Bubba and Willodean wanted. Celestine Gray had taken time off so that Willodean would not be overly stressed. She had other children who were married, but she still caught the dread condition.

Willodean had mentioned that her blood pressure was up, and the horses at the gates were off. She also mentioned that she was given medication, and it was now under control, but no one wanted to hear that part. Bubba had listened, although he had also spoken to Doc Goodjoint about it and had been thusly reassured. The reassurance hadn't stopped Bubba from making certain guarantees on his part. He could only hope that Willodean didn't cotton to some of them, or she would be very angry.

If Willodean did find out, Bubba would be forced to move to an uncharted Indonesian island or someplace where he could hide from her until she calmed down.

Using a smooth motion, he reeled the lure in a little more. Bubba didn't feel like concentrating on fishing, which was a shame. He'd been warned that sleep was going to quickly become a valuable and limited event, and fishing might be put off for a year or two. Who knew when he was going to be able to make it out here again? He wanted to enjoy it, but there were so many other things to think about. His free hand went to the seat, and he thumbed through the book lying there. He happened upon the J's, which was just about where he'd left off.

Jasper. There was a fine name. It was old French and meant the jasper stone. Bubba didn't know what a jasper stone was but it might fit. It sounded right when accompanied by Snoddy.

Then there was Jayson, which was just like Jason except with a y thrown in. It was another old French name meaning gracious gift of God. Bubba nodded. A child was always a gift from God.

He flipped a page. Jesus was the name on the top. Bubba shook his head. No, he wouldn't name a child after the Son of God, nor after a man who thought he was Jesus Christ and wore a sheet wrapped around himself like a toga. Bubba would never do that to a child.

Another page turned. There was Jibben which was English Gypsy and meant life. There was Jing, which was Chinese and meant pure. There was Jock which was a familiar short form of Jacob or John, and those two names meant something else altogether. There were Joel, Johar, and Josiah.

Bubba grimaced. He tried one out, "Jory." Precious, still asleep, snorted loudly and then farted. "Jonte. Jovan. Julius." He frowned. "Ain't none of them sound right."

He brought the lure in, set up his line, and cast it again. "Might be a girl, too," he said to himself because Precious wasn't listening. "Don't mind a girl. I bet they make little life jackets for babies. A girl might like to fish." His mother didn't mind casting a line on occasion. He considered. "I'd have to get a shotgun ready on account that the little one will come out as good lookin' as Willodean."

He cast the line where he wanted it to go and then used his free hand to flip to the J's in the girl's section of the book. "Jacklyn. Jade. Jessie. Jetta. Jillian. Joline." Bubba pursed his lips. "Don't I know a gal named Joline? Mebe I'm thinking about a song. Jolene, not Joline. Right. She was poaching on another gal's territory. We don't need to name a child after a man-stealing gal."

Bubba let the book close by virtue of simply removing his hand, and the pages fluttered shut by themselves. "This name thing is *hard*," he muttered. Willodean hadn't said anything about names. They had gone to an obstetrician in Tyler a week before, and they'd both seen the sonogram. When the doctor asked if they wanted to know the sex, both had said "no" in unison. Bubba had been gratified that Willodean was on the same page of the same book.

Willodean. The most beautiful, gracious, wondrous woman on the face of the planet. She could also use a can of mace like a pro. Her lovely green eyes didn't even get watery when she used her police-issued defensive weapon. The local bar Grubbo's had bronzed her last can and mounted it over the bar. A visit to Grubbo's wasn't complete without law enforcement coming in to break up some issue or other. The locals all cheered when Willodean came through the front door.

Willodean could toss her sooty hair over her shoulder in slow-motion and look like a million bucks while spraying errant perpetrators; she was that good.

Bubba reeled a little bit, perked up when he saw it jerk once, and then sighed. The fish had done a drive-by. Even the fish didn't want to mess with him on this particular day.

He looked around. He was on the east end of the lake in his favorite fishing spot. When it got hotter, he would move the boat over to the shade of the cottonwoods on the other side. At the moment he was all alone, but it was a large lake, and there were lots of good fishing holes for the early birds.

His hand touched the other book. *What to Expect When You're Expecting* was what someone had left on his front doorstep one day the previous week. He didn't know who but he suspected it was some sympathetic individual who'd had a pregnant significant other in the recent past. He deftly opened the book up and held it open with an index finger. He looked at the pictures while holding onto the rod with the other hand.

Bubba knew about changing a baby's diaper. He could sterilize a bottle and burp a baby with aplomb. He'd had practice as a youngster and more recently with the babies that had flowed through the Snoddy Mansion like water over a dam. His mother and Miz Adelia Cedarbloom, their housekeeper and longtime friend, had been up to hijinks again. That time had involved a series of orphans from a Latin American country. He shuddered, not because of the babies involved, but because the DEA, local law enforcement, bags of flour, and lots of mystery had been included.

Bubba also suspected that the DEA was still sporadically following him. (A white panel van with a set of graphic donuts on the side parked at the end of the drive beside the gate. Sometimes it was a black panel van with a Hormel advertisement for processed meats on the side. The folks inside wore dark glasses and stared endlessly at the Snoddy properties.)

The point was that while Bubba knew about babies, he didn't know bupkus about pregnant women. There were things in the second book that Bubba had never dreamed about. Mucus plugs, hyperemesis gravidarum, nesting instinct, pregnancy brain, mood swings, and the linea negra.

"Great glomping goose bumps," Bubba muttered, using his pinkie to turn the book so that he could see the photograph a little better. "Why does *that* happen?" He turned it the other way, and it didn't become more readily comprehensible.

Clearly, Bubba realized he didn't have an appropriate grasp of the matter. He was sorely uneducated on the issue.

The line jerked once. Bubba lifted his head. He let the book go, and the pages fluttered in a light morning breeze. He put both hands on his rod and pulled it just a tad. The line was caught on something. He twirled the reel experimentally. Something tugged on the other end.

Fish. Bass. Striped? Largemouth? Spotted? Bubba smiled to himself. Or maybe it was something else. *A bluegill or a redear? There's a few others it could be. A carpsucker or a gar or mebe a logperch. Not a catfish. They don't usually swim up to the top for the twinkling lures.*

Bubba slowly and methodically began to bring it to him, all thoughts of pregnancy, weddings, and dead bodies forgotten in the moment of highest tension. Would the fish slip the hook, or would he belong to Bubba, heart and fishy soul?

His heart beat a merry tune. Catch-the-fish, catch-the-fish, catch-the-fish. Bubba kept a steady pull on his line, lest his prey find a way to get away. As the end of the line began to draw near, he leaned forward so that he could see the silver glint of scales as they breached the surface of the lake.

Instead, he saw...leather.

"What in tarnation?" he muttered. Bubba jerked hard once, and whatever he'd caught came with the line. It bumped into the side of the boat, and he pulled it out of the water.

There was a long instant of purest introspection.

The item in question twirled leisurely in the morning sun, blue droplets falling away in slow motion. A spiritual guru would have giggled at the clarity of the moment. Realization was an abrupt slap in the face.

Bubba had caught a boot. A leather boot. A large-sized boot that was likely a man's. It was covered with muskgrass, and the laces flopped about. The lure had caught the tongue of the boot.

Bubba thought about coincidences and probability and froze in place. He'd caught some odd things in his life of fishing. (Once a toilet seat cover and another time a plastic lei, its faded flowers dripping with algae.) Folks used the lake and streams that fed into the reservoir for all kinds of things. Once, he'd heard that someone caught a steering wheel and swore it was part of Bayou Billy's Model-T Ford that had gone missing in a hurricane. (Supposedly that Ford came complete with Bayou Billy's missing corpse, but some stories were too tall to be believed.) Bubba resisted another shudder. He didn't need to think about *that*.

Precious snorted again and flopped over to her belly. Her head came up, and she wearily eyed the boot swaying in the breeze. She didn't seem to be impressed.

The canine didn't mind a little fresh fish now and again, but that didn't look like fresh fish at all. On the other hand, she didn't mind gnawing on a little footwear either. Regardless, it wasn't appealing to her at the moment. She whined once and put her head down on her paws, closing her eyes with an alacrity that surprised even Bubba.

Bubba had a sudden vision in his head. He would tilt the pole toward him at the same time he reached for the boot with his left hand. The water would spill out of the boot and reveal someone's rotting foot that had been separated from the rest of the body. He had inadvertently come across another nasty murder where someone had dumped the body in the lake and left it to decompose. With all of the karma that seemed to afflict Bubba on a regular basis the last few years, it would be he who discovered it.

Bubba couldn't seem to help himself. He tilted the pole toward himself. The boot sloshed, and water spilled back into the lake. The fingers of his left hand touched the slimy edge of the leather and pulled it toward him. He craned his neck to see, moving the boot so that the sun was shining directly into the shadows within. He saw...

A small turtle. It looked at Bubba and then his head whooshed back into his shell. Bubba tilted the boot a little more, and the turtle took a trip back into the lake. The rest of the boot was...

Empty.

There wasn't even a corroded sock, much less putrid flesh and rattling bones. Bubba sighed with heartfelt relief. He hastily shook his head and unhooked the boot. He tossed the footwear back into the lake and watched as it sank into the blackness below.

Bubba put the rod down. He reached for the small aluminum cooler and flipped the lid off. He retrieved a bottle of RC Cola and deftly removed the bottle cap with his beefy fingers. He took a long pull and looked around him. He wasn't supposed to be anywhere in particular on this day, so he could take it easy.

Willodean was working. He reckoned that if she threw up in the sheriff's department they might send her home, but she was getting pretty good making it to the bathroom or to a bush, so maybe not.

The Snoddy Mansion was full of interlopers, which made Bubba happy that the caretaker's house was finished, and he was living in it. He was further happy that Willodean was in the process of moving into the house with him. They'd agreed that it was better than her duplex apartment, and there was convenient babysitting available.

The mansion was full of...visitors. Wedding-related visitors. Celestine Gray was located in the red room. Then there was the— Bubba had to take a reassuring breath to finish the thought— wedding planner.

Bubba very nearly growled. He was an easygoing individual most of the time, but the wedding planner was an irritating tall glass of sour lemonade with a distinct lack of sugar. The person wanted things. They wanted to know what colors the napkins would be. They wanted to show samples, and they had samples of everything. (Why did their names need to be printed on the toilet paper that went in the bathroom? Why did the little candy- coated almonds need to go in little white baggies on the tables? Why were all the flowers so danged important?) The person didn't quit.

Bubba had a suspicion that the wedding planner was on crack. The person was like a small annoying dog that zipped around peeing on every tree and bush in sight. He apologized mentally to Precious.

Relax, Bubba told himself. *Just a weddin'. How hard kin that be?* He closed his eyes and listened to the quiet of the lake. Although it was a Saturday morning, it was as quiet as a grave...*stop that.*

Without opening his eyes he took another shot of RC Cola. The caffeine would hit his bloodstream soon and perk him right up. He didn't have to be anywhere, but there was always something that needed to be done around the Snoddy Estate. His afternoon was spoken for, and he wanted to make Willodean a very nice evening meal for just the two of them, preferably something that wouldn't make her gag and run for the bathroom. He had a follow-up plan that involved rubbing her feet with baby oil.

A faint noise disturbed Bubba's reverie. It sounded like several cars screeching to a stop. It was followed by engines being cut off. Then distantly someone shrieked, "Look, there's his truck!" The noise began to increase in volume as it came closer to him.

Bubba frowned. He cracked open his eye again. No dead bodies. No fish either. Just a dog at the bottom of the boat who had just cracked an eye in a way remarkably similar to Bubba. Precious lifted her head, opened the other eye, and looked toward the shore. Bubba didn't want to look toward the shore.

"Mebe if we row to the other side of the lake," Bubba muttered. He started to feel for the stowed oars.

It was too late. He opened his other eye and saw a group of people explode out of the brush and pause just before falling into the lake. One teetered at the edge before someone else yanked him back.

"I told you he was here," one proclaimed. "I get the reward. Fifty bucks, right?"

15

"Where is he?" another one asked. "Oh, out there. Fishing. O.M.F.G. How provincial."

"I need him more than you do," said another one. Bubba squinted. That one looked like…

Sherlock Holmes, complete with a tweed deerstalker cap, Inverness coat, and a long-stemmed calabash pipe.

Bubba decided to row for any place on the lake furthest away from the group of people on the shore staring at him. To be perfectly precise, he wondered if he could row down to the Gulf of Mexico and across to a Central American country where he could take up as a sheep herder or sell clay pots to tourists.

It was worth a damn good shot.

Chapter Two

Bubba and the First Loony

Saturday, April 6th

"Watson!" Sherlock Holmes bellowed. "Come here! I need you!" It must have been difficult to yell with a fake British accent because the end product wasn't even close to being British.

Sherlock wasn't really Sherlock Holmes. Bubba knew that even while he thought about acceding to the demands of the various onlookers. For the moment he sat in the boat with an RC Cola in one hand and scratched Precious's head with the other. The next time he came out on the lake, he vowed to bring earplugs and possibly blinders, too. He glanced at the crowd to ascertain his chances for escape. Once he hit the shore it would be like running a gauntlet.

Bubba thought about it. He wasn't in bad shape. He'd been jogging a couple times a month. He could make it. Feint left, and go right. Duck and cover. Yep.

The wedding planning was there. Sherlock Holmes was present. Bubba squinted. Was that Jasper Dukeminer to the right side of Sherlock? Jasper was a friend of Tom Bledsoe, a local pickpocket, and Laz Berryhill, the son of the woman who owned a junkyard. Both men hadn't been seen much in these parts since an unfortunate event that involved both Bubba's cousin's son, Brownie, and chemicals mixed in the proper proportions. (It had been truly fortunate that the junkyard hadn't blown to smithereens.)

Jasper was on a level par with the two would-be kidnappers, Tom and Laz. Jasper stumbled through life and expected people to part before him or things to fall into his lap with minimal effort on his part. Once, he'd tried to steal Jeffrey Carnicon's Dodge Challenger, but Jeffrey had a sign on the side of the Challenger that said it was guarded by Vermicious Knids, and Jasper had freaked out, calling 9-1-1 to tell them that Vermicious Knids had escaped and were going to devour the town. Mary Lou Treadwell, the receptionist and 9-1-1 operator, had to look up what a Vermicious Knid was before she hung up on Jasper. When he wasn't trying to steal cars, Jasper worked at the manure factory when they had extra work that needed to be done. Mostly, he went around changing letters on signs so that they said something offensive. *Jasper? Dang. Now I can't use that name. I would think of signs that said Flick with extra lines drawn in and possibly Vermicious Knids.*

Wait. Reward? Who offered a reward? A reward for what? For finding me?

"The game's afoot!" Sherlock called.

"Is everyone in this town cracked?" the wedding planner asked.

"I deduce that you are a former smoker," Sherlock said to the wedding planner, "based on your yellow nails."

The wedding planner glanced at the fingernails in question. "I have a French mani in canary yellow," came the protest. "It's all the rage in Paris this season. Yellow is in. Yellow should be in your wedding, Bubba." There was a significant pause. "Is your name really Bubba?" No time was given for an answer. "No one should be named Bubba, even in— " a big sigh followed — "Texas."

"It's a fine Southern name," Jasper protested. "Where's my fifty bucks?"

"I'll write you a check," the wedding planner said. "Or better yet, I can credit you with fifty dollars of Pure

Love Weddings, LLC trade. Pure Love Weddings, LLC is the name of my company, by the way. I am, needless to say, the owner and proprietor. When your wedding comes up, fifty dollars can get you well on the way to the wedding of your dreams."

Jasper glowered. "My girlfriend left me last week for a plumber."

"*No*," the wedding planner said, eying Jasper's denim overalls. "I can't imagine that. I'm sure the girls will be lining up."

"Mebe," Jasper admitted. "I do cut the fine figure at Grubbo's, especially on ladies night. Ladies drink free that night, you know?"

"See. Problem solved." The wedding planner turned back toward the lake. "Bubba Snoddy! Your tuxedo fitting is awaiting you. We can't decide to go with royal blue or dignified distinguished black."

Bubba glanced at his t-shirt. It had been a gift from someone after the news had gotten out about the impending event. "Bun in the oven" was displayed over an arrow that pointed down to his stomach. Willodean giggled every time he put it on, so he put it on as often as he could get away with it. It wasn't royal blue or even dignified distinguished black, but creamy lemonade cake yellow with black lettering. Even though it was yellow, he knew it wasn't really wedding material.

Another voice came, "BUBBA!" Bubba sank down into the boat, wishing it was a bigger boat or that he was a smaller man. (Most boat makers didn't account for a man who was six feet four inches tall and weighed in the neighborhood of 240 pounds.)

Even Precious winced at the sound of Bubba's name being called. It was Miz Demetrice, his mother, the not-so-saintly matriarch of the Snoddy clan, and her mother-voice was both shrill and commanding.

Abruptly, with a thought that profoundly disturbed him, Bubba sat straight up. "Is everything all right?" he yelled across the water, meaning Willodean.

"No, everything is not alright!" Miz Demetrice yelled back. She stood there in her lavender skirt set and brushed an errant white hair away from her forehead. She might have been attending a PTA meeting or planning to steal artwork from the Louvre. *"That woman* wants to serve caviar at the reception! Have you ever heard of such a thing?"

"I have," said the wedding planner smugly. A hand fluttered as a mosquito was shooed away.

Bubba relaxed. He looked over the side of the boat into the gray waters. Maybe a dead body had appeared in the few minutes since all the people had arrived. That would be a tremendous distraction. Then he briefly felt ashamed of himself.

"Should I shoot him?" came another voice. Celestine Gray had arrived, AKA *that woman.*

"The boat might sink," the wedding planner pointed out.

"Precious's got a life jacket on," Miz Demetrice said. "You know that reminds me of the time I drowned Elgin, my late husband. I put his feet into buckets of cement while he was drunk. He thought I was giving him a fancy pedicure. It was funny when he sobered up just as I shoved him out of the boat. One of his hands ripped a board off the side of the boat. That boat was never the same."

"Pa had a heart attack, Ma," Bubba called.

"Pshaw," Miz Demetrice said.

"What's wrong with caviar?" asked the wedding planner. "I'm thinking boiled eggs with a little salmon

caviar and orange roe on top. Very elegant. It's a stylish hors d'oeuvre. Then mini ramekins of macaroni and cheese. Possibly with goat cheese. I was thinking of a middle display of little bags of grits with the bride and groom's name and wedding date on it. The guests could take those home. Grits. Tee-hee-hee. You know that country singer did that at her wedding reception last month. There was an entire photo shoot of the reception in *Weddings Today*. She wore a Mauro Adami gown. It had platinum thread. *Tres chic.*"

"Willodean all right?" Bubba asked.

"The last I heard she threw up in the department's Bronco," Celestine said. "But that nice receptionist, what's her name, Mary Lou?, was cleaning it up. I don't think anyone would have done that for me. I usually managed to puke out the side of the patrol car, except the one time that I threw up in the sergeant's hat." She laughed. Then Miz Demetrice laughed. They laughed together. Bubba didn't laugh.

"Seriously, Bubba," Miz Demetrice said. "You have to come in and make some choices. Get your fitting and all that. You belong to us until you say 'I do.'"

"I choose to stay in the boat," Bubba stated adamantly. Precious woofed in adamant agreement. The boat was likely adamant, too. It was difficult to say for certain.

Miz Demetrice stared at Bubba over fifty feet of water, clearly weighing her options. "Celestine, dear, do you think you could shoot a few holes in the bow of the boat? If it's sinking, then he has to come in."

Celestine was a tall woman, the opposite of Willodean. Other than being Willodean's mother, she was also a police sergeant in the Dallas Police Department. If she said she could shoot something, she probably could. After all, Willodean had mentioned that it had been her mother who had taught her how to shoot. She expertly appraised the situation. "I could do that," Celestine said.

"No holes in the boat!" Bubba protested.

"Watson!" Sherlock cried. "Shall I create a diversion for you? I shall disguise myself and cause these malingering miscreants to divert their attentions. I do a smashing milkmaid."

Bubba looked at Sherlock. Sherlock appeared a little shorter than Basil Rathbone. Other than height and general build, it would have been hard to tell who he was beneath the deerstalker cap, the Inverness coat, and the oversized pipe. However, Bubba had a sneaking suspicion. "David Beathard? Is that you?"

"Is that the one who used to dress all in purple?" Celestine asked, looking at Sherlock. She said out of the side of her mouth to the wedding planner, "Even his underwear was purple. With sequins, or so I'm told. I didn't really see that."

"I'm Holmes now," David said with his best British accent, which really was dismal, "Sherlock Holmes. The detective."

Celestine appeared unimpressed. "Sherlock Holmes was a fictional character."

"Madam!" David protested. "I can deduce all simply with expert observation. For example, you recently stopped chewing your nails, and you've lost five pounds."

"I never chewed my nails," Celestine said, "and I've gained three in the week I've been here." She glanced at Miz Demetrice. "Miz Adelia is a very good cook."

Miz Demetrice nodded. "David, whatever are you doing out here?"

"I need Watson!" David barked. He turned his head toward Bubba and yelled, "Watson! I have need of your medical expertise and keen eye! You may not be up to my level of investigatory proficiency, but it needs to be done!"

"David," Miz Demetrice said softly, and Bubba had to lean closer to that side of the lake to hear what she said, "you haven't been doing cocaine, have you?"

"Madam! It's none of your business," David protested. "Watson!"

Bubba sighed. "I'm coming in." He put the empty RC Cola bottle into the cooler, and then removed the oars from their slots. It took him a minute to settle the oars into the rowlocks.

Nearby, a fish jumped out of the water, and the Basset hound leapt to her feet and bayed accordingly. The fish had likely overheard Bubba planning to come in and jumped for joy.

"Listen!" David yelled. "It's the hound of the Baskervilles! Beware!"

Bubba thought the warning was a little too late.

•

Everyone helped pull the rowboat out of the water, even Miz Demetrice with her smart skirt set. The wedding planner touched the side of the boat and winced. "Is that algae on the side? Don't you scrub it off or anything? Don't they have those flesh-eating microbes down here? Does anyone have any antibacterial wipes?"

Typically, Bubba would have carried the boat himself, but Jasper, David, and Celestine helped him lever it into the air and place it on the trailer hooked up to his truck. Bubba gave the boat a little shove and seated it in the trailer. Then he removed the ratcheting tie-down straps from the bed of the truck and made sure the boat wouldn't fly into the car behind him while he was driving home. While he was doing that David put his cooler and the two books into the truck bed. Celestine carried the fishing pole and tackle box and placed them beside the cooler. She gave the *What to Expect When You're Expecting* book a double look.

Bubba pulled and ratcheted the last line into satisfactory tightness. He had that irritating feeling of being watched while he did this. It was likely because everyone *was* carefully watching him.

After all, everyone was still there. David Beathard chewed on the end of the pipe and appeared nervous. Bubba's mother smoothed back her hair and appeared distinguished. Celestine wore a baseball jersey and jeans and appeared as though she was just along for the ride. Jasper scratched at the top of his head and appeared to wonder about his fifty dollar reward. Precious sat on her rump near the 1954 Chevy truck that belonged to Bubba and appeared to snap at a fly. The wedding planner anxiously paced back and forth and appeared...just weird.

Bubba was used to weird. There was all kinds of weird in his life. But the wedding planner was new and unusual weird.

"Say, Peyton," Bubba said.

The wedding planner turned. Longish hair that was streaked with three different colors of brown was tossed over a shoulder. Blue eyes studied Bubba.

"I reckon the reason you got hired was to man this shindig," Bubba said.

Peyton nodded. An iPad appeared as if by magic and fingers began swiping and tapping.

"Ifin there's some decision to be made, I'm an easy fella," Bubba finished. There. It had been said. But then he thought about it. "And if I ain't about, then Ma there— " he indicated Miz Demetrice— "can make that decision. Or mebe Miz Celestine. You won't hear a complaint pass my lips."

"Just Celestine is fine," that person interjected.

"But what about the bride's desires?" Peyton asked. Fingers smoothed over one eyebrow. It was finely plucked. Eyeliner had been applied expertly under the arched brow. A light coat of lipstick was skillfully apportioned and outlined the lips in a way that Bubba didn't know could be done. "A bride will probably only do this once, and that lady needs to be involved."

"Willodean's...occupied," Bubba said.

"I'm aware of her condition," Peyton said with a chipper tone. "This isn't my first wedding rodeo, you know." There was a wave of fingers as insects discovered the aroma of freshly unmolested skin. "Are the bugs always around here? I need a can of Raid. Do they do designer Raid?"

"Okay, then," Bubba said. "Ifin you go on inside the Snoddy Mansion, there's a dearth of bugs in there."

"Silence, darling," Peyton said imperiously. "I must take you to the tailor. The fitting has to be today. No one can guess the size of your massive shoulders. My goodness, have you ever measured your biceps?"

Bubba looked at Peyton nervously. "I'm straight. My biceps are only for Willodean."

The other man rolled his eyes. That was the primary reason Bubba was uneasy. Peyton was a man. He was a man who wore makeup and flicked his wrist and his shirt was silk. Willodean had instructed Bubba that Peyton was not gay, but metrosexual. Bubba hadn't told her that he had to look the word up, and he hadn't told her that he wondered how she knew the fact.

"So am I, dear dimwitted redneck person," Peyton said patiently. "I have a girlfriend." He flipped the iPad around and expertly pushed an app button without even having to look at it. A redheaded woman in a bikini popped up. She would have looked good on the cover of a mechanic's weekly magazine.

"Was she always a woman?" Bubba asked, and Miz Demetrice popped him in the back of the head.

"Provincial idiots," Peyton said. "This is just who I am, and yon yokels will have to get used to it. I shall follow you to your...mansion, and then I'll take you to the tailor. I had to dredge for a shop in the area, but there's a remarkable lady two towns over. She was mentioned in *Bridesmaids and More* a year ago. We're very fortunate to get her." He flipped the iPad back, clutched it to his chest, and swished his way over to a Dodge Charger. "One could slap a saddle on some of these bugs and ride them!"

"Ma, ifin he can call me a redneck, then I kin ask if that gal was always a woman," Bubba said to Miz Demetrice. "He don't come from Texas?"

"He came from New York City," Celestine said.

"Oh," Bubba said. That would probably explain it. The folks in New York City probably thought the people in Texas were just as weird. "Is that a girl on that pad or not?"

"I can hear you!" Peyton sang. He continued to sing the rest, "Her name is Ginger, and she does my eyebrows!" One hand flapped in the air.

"I don't want my eyebrows plucked for my wedding," Bubba snarled only for his mother to hear.

"Well, then," Miz Demetrice said, "it's a good thing Ginger isn't here, isn't it?"

Bubba watched Peyton climb into the Charger and sighed. He turned to his mother. "And why are *you* chasing me down?"

"Bubba dearest, do you really want me to make the decisions for your wedding and your reception?" his mother asked calmly.

"I-uh-oh, crap, I mean carp," Bubba said. He looked at Celestine. "And you?"

Celestine shrugged. "Wills is at work. The wedding planner threw a hissy fit because you weren't around for the fitting. He got all the people at the house to go looking for you because he offered a reward. Jasper was trimming some of the Spanish moss and said you had a boat on your trailer when you lit out early. So he got the reward. And there isn't anything to shoot at the house except this one guy who was out back earlier with a shovel and a metal detector."

That explained why Jasper Dukeminer was present, as well.

That left Precious and David Beathard. Bubba knew why Precious was around because she was his beloved dog, and she went just about everywhere that Bubba went. Fishing wasn't her favorite pastime, but the Milk-Bones made for a satisfying morning.

However...

"David," Bubba said, "last time I saw you, you were plain ol' David Beathard, former United States Postal Service employee and graphologist."

"You know very well the post office doesn't want me back, and the store went under," David said. He adjusted the deerstalker hat. "And the game's afoot. Afoot, I tell you, eh what?"

"His accent just sucks," Celestine observed. "That's like when Kevin Costner tried to do it in *Robin Hood: Prince of Thieves*."

"Low blow," Miz Demetrice said. "Why is it okay that David is a psychiatrist, the Purple Singapore Sling, a pirate, or Sherlock Holmes, and it's not okay for the wedding planner to be metrosexual?"

"David spends half of his time in a mental institution," Bubba explained slowly as if he was speaking with someone a quarter of his age.

Miz Demetrice shrugged. "Celestine, dear, I know a wonderful place where they serve coffee and tequila, not together of course."

"Do they allow weapons?"

"Naturally."

"Let's go." They quickly went to Miz Demetrice's Cadillac, which was parked next to David's Smart car, which still had its Jolly Roger wraps on it. Bubba supposed finding Sherlock Holmes-related wraps was next to impossible.

That left Jasper, Precious, and David. Bubba stared at Jasper until he scuttled to his 1973 Ford Courier. It started up with a roar, and a cloud of gray smoke bellowed from the exhaust. Precious licked her hind leg and ignored them.

"David," Bubba said gently. "You seem a mite put out."

"Watson," David said insistently, "you must come with me. The game, as I've said, is afoot."

"I think I liked the PSS more, or maybe Black Dog McGee."

"Bad Black Dog McGee," David corrected. "Arr. Er, I mean, jolly good, what."

"What's going on?" Bubba asked.

David glanced around as if he was ensuring that no one could be listening. "It's a crime of epic proportion. Clues abounding. Bodies bouncing off the floors. No man or woman is safe." He looked directly at Bubba, and his warm eyes caught Bubba's. "It's murder, Watson. Dastardly, despicable *murder*."

Chapter Three

Bubba and the Coping Mechanism

Saturday, April 6th

Bubba watched David Beathard climb into his little Smart car. David seemed unhappier than Bubba was, albeit for reasons that Bubba couldn't understand as David had not informed him of the specific causes of his melancholy. His deerstalker hat perched on his head in a distinctly dismal angle. His Inverness coat drooped. The sleeves appeared disjointed under the cape part of the garment. The calabash pipe had vanished into a deep pocket. Even the Smart car seemed depressed. Was the Jolly Roger grimacing sadly?

Bubba had simply told the former Bad Black Dog McGee that he couldn't come with him, as Dr. Watson or anyone else because he was otherwise spoken for.

"Is he all right?" Peyton the wedding planner asked. He sat in the Charger with the door open and watched as David closed the door of the Smart car. "I mean, other than dressing up as Sherlock Holmes, which is an interesting fashion statement, especially out here in the sticks." He waved his hands around at the wobbling trees, the buzzing insects, and the swaying lake. "You don't see that kind of panache every day of the week. It takes a little— " he snapped his fingers— "to carry that off."

Bubba cast Peyton a quick glance. He wasn't paying for the wedding planner. That all came from Miz Demetrice and Celestine Gray, who had come to an unholy agreement straight from a hellish dimension concerning the nuptials of their children. That agreement had led to the hiring of a "professional."

However, Bubba had agreed to it, which was quickly becoming a fact he was starting to sorely regret.

"Ain't rightly sure," Bubba said. He looked back, and the Smart car started up. David didn't look back as he turned around in a sharp circle. The vehicle accelerated in the widest part of the turn, and the end fishtailed for two seconds. Then it plowed down the double rutted road that led to the main road.

Bubba wasn't sure if David was all right at all. The other man had the whole Sherlock thing down pat. Where he'd gotten the hat and coat Bubba didn't know, but the former Purple Singapore Sling was in full-blown new persona, to include wanting his sidekick, Dr. Watson, at his flank. How Bubba had been transformed into Dr. Watson was a dubious event at best.

"Snap. These bugs are going to carry me off. Can we go now?" Peyton asked with a tiny quality of whining that made Bubba want to grind his teeth together.

"Shore," Bubba said. With that he dismissed his uneasy feelings, ushered Precious into the cab of his truck, and clambered in.

•

An hour later, Bubba was being measured, poked, and prodded. The suit didn't look like a suit because it had a pattern pinned to it, and the tailor was making noises that made Bubba uncomfortable.

The tailor, a woman in her late fifties named Sachi, said, "Can you not slouch?" She touched the top of his right shoulder. "Oh my, that's all muscle, isn't it? No padding for you, nosiree."

Bubba straightened.

Peyton sighed loudly. He held up a book of fabric swatches. "This one is grayish greyish gray," he said.

"Very somber. Gray is always in. It looks great with a white boutonniere. Perhaps a lily."

A pin sank into the hardest part of his bicep. "Ouch," Bubba said.

"Sorry," Sachi said. She withdrew the pin with a sly smile. "It's unlucky if that doesn't happen at least once. I'm just used to people who have a little fat there." Her eyebrows went up. "Not like you."

"Then what does it mean ifin you do it four times?" Bubba asked sourly.

"It's going to be a very lucky wedding," she said cheerfully, rubbing a hand across the breadth of his other shoulder in a way that made Bubba want to take a hot shower. "There, all done. Just take that off for me, will you, sweetie pie?"

"Kin I go back to fishing?" Bubba asked Peyton.

"Of course you can*not*," Peyton said. He flipped several multicolored locks of hair over one shoulder and shut the fabric book with a note of finality that was not final at all. "You have several decisions to make." He glanced at his iPad. "We have an hour and twenty minutes to get back to Pegramville and meet with the blushing bride to be."

Did Willodean blush? Bubba nodded with a smile. She did. Mostly it was when other people weren't around. "Dint we discuss who was making decisions?" *That means not me. Not me. I need to do other stuff. Any other stuff. Believe there's a toilet in the mansion that needs worked on.*

"Naturally, we run it past your mothers," Peyton added. He blew kisses at the tailor who also blushed. Bubba declined to blow kisses at anyone, except possibly Willodean, and only when other people weren't looking. He considered. *Well, mebe then, too.*

"I need food," Bubba said. "Let's stop at a restaurant."

"A restaurant? Here?" Peyton asked as if something distasteful had touched him.

"Are you...a vegan?" Bubba asked. The previous year, he'd had a whole lot of experience with a vegan Buddhist by the name of Daniel Lewis Gollihugh. Dan was a very tall individual who had a lot of experience with offending the police, the sheriff's department, and law enforcement in general. He'd discovered Buddhism in prison the last time he was there, and he'd turned himself around. However, he kept turning back. Courtesy of Miz Demetrice and Willodean, Dan had been Bubba's shadow when there was a chance someone had been trying to kill Bubba. Consequently, Bubba had gotten to know Dan a bit. Dan wasn't really a vegan because he didn't quite get the whole gist of the concept, but it was a fearful notion overall.

"A vegan," Peyton giggled. "Gracious no. I love meat, cheese, and eggs. I especially like bacon. I couldn't live without bacon." His voice lowered to a whisper. "Don't tell Ginger. She worries about my cholesterol levels. She likes a lot of salad."

Bubba nodded. "There's a barbeque place on the way back. The last time I was there the DEA arrested me for having flour in my truck. But they got dang good food. If there's something vegan or low-cholesterol on the menu, I don't know about it."

•

"Did David Beathard seem odd to you?" Bubba asked after he swallowed a large piece of sausage. The Hogfather's was busy, but they'd found a table quickly. Peyton had clapped with glee when he'd gotten an eyeful of what was on the menu. Truly the man had *clapped* like a six-year-old child after Santa had departed up the chimney at Christmastime. He might have said, "Yea!" too, but Bubba made himself forget that part.

"Sherlock Holmes?" Peyton said. "Like I said, he's wearing a Sherlock Holmes getup in rural Texas. I don't think that's normal. But it is such a kitschy overcoat. I love the cape part." He smiled at his Vito Corleone special which towered over the plate it sat upon. It had everything meat available in the restaurant sitting upon toasted and buttered sourdough bread. There was an obligatory piece of lettuce and two slices of tomato, but they were strictly for show. The wedding planner had been made an offer he couldn't refuse. His fingers wiggled enthusiastically in anticipation. "Oh, I'm going to gain five pounds while I'm here. Yippee!"

"He seemed depressed," Bubba said as he went after some okra with his fork. They were deep-fried bites of perfection. "Try the okra."

"I don't think I've ever eaten okra before," Peyton said and helped himself. "Mmm. Yum poo city."

"They have a Southern fried-chicken meal on Wednesdays," Bubba said. "I think it's the Sonny Special. On account of it gets you when you're not looking. The owners are real particular about their recipes. They don't share nothing."

Peyton drooled from the side of his mouth and quickly wiped it away with a napkin. "I'm beginning to see the appeal." He grasped the sandwich with both hands and gave it his best shot. After several minutes he put it back on the plate and daintily dabbed at the corners of his mouth with the napkin. "This is going to take some effort, but I'm game. Did you really get arrested by the DEA here?"

Bubba pointed out the window. They sat two booths down from where he had sat with Willodean.

"That's the spot. My mother put a ten-pound bag of flour in my truck and called the DEA with a burner phone. She wrapped the flour up like you see drugs are done in the movies. I don't ever recollect seeing a ten-pound bag of drugs in real life. I guess I'd have to ask someone ifin that was like the real thing."

Peyton stabbed another okra before he paused. "Your mother planted...flour in your truck."

"Yep."

"And called the DEA."

"Yep."

"Because...?"

"She wanted a distraction," Bubba said and went after the quarter of chicken that came with his combination platter. He waved a leg in the air. "Ma's a sneaky sort."

"And your fiancée is okay with that?" Peyton appeared confused. "She's a sheriff's deputy. I was speaking with her at the station the other day. She threatened to shoot some man in the parking lot but only after she maced him. Her mother thought that was terribly funny. But then her mother's a police officer, too. I was trying to show her fabric swatches, and she wanted to match one to the color of mace as it's sprayed." He clicked his tongue. "That's a first for me."

"Celestine's in the Dallas Police Department," Bubba confirmed. "Should be an exciting wedding with all of the guns about. Willodean has sisters who are in law enforcement, too."

Peyton mumbled something that sounded like, "And they think New Yorkers are weird." He went back after the sandwich with a sound of digestive approval. "Barbeque meat, good," he muttered.

"You know, Bubba didn't really deal in drugs," came a voice from behind them. "Everyone in Pegram County knows that's just a plain ol' falsehood." The booth there contained Rodney Fosdick, who was a parole officer, and Rosa Granado, who used to work for George Bufford. Bubba had once worked for George Bufford, as well, but in a purely mechanical capacity, where Rosa's employment had been more varied. George had fired Bubba on account that everyone thought he had murdered his ex-fiancée, but that had been cleared up. Later on, Rosa had decided that George was never going to leave his wife for her and left him, and his employment.

Rodney grinned at Peyton and then blinked when he saw the make-up. "Just a big misunderstanding, am I right, Bubba?"

"Big misunderstanding," Bubba said, but it wasn't exactly agreement. "Miz Rosa," he added.

Rosa nodded and daubed at her mouth with a napkin.

"Say, you haven't seen those two fellas, Tom and Laz, have you?" Bubba asked, as Rodney Fosdick was known to be their parole officer.

"Lit out for places unknown," Rodney said blackly. "Someone will pick them up sooner or later. I hear tell it had something to do with that boy, Brownie." He frowned. "Not sure how that child ain't in the federal system already."

"Brownie...Snoddy," Peyton said. "I didn't know you were related to him. You know he..."

"We know," Bubba said darkly. He'd seen it on the news. It was all over the Internet, although it had died down. Folks were apt to show him on a weekly basis, which was bad enough. It had been once a day. Those smart phones could do anything including playing videos from YouTube. Matt Lauer was said to still have a restraining order against Brownie. Brownie was supposed to carry a tape measure around in case Matt was ever in the vicinity.

"This place is getting more and more interesting," Peyton remarked. Then he took another bite out of his sandwich. He even got most of it into his mouth.

"It's about to get a lot more interesting," Rodney said. He nodded toward the exterior.

Bubba turned and expected to see the DEA or perhaps someone else coming to arrest him. However, it wasn't the law enforcement he was expecting.

The lights on the Bronco were flashing red and blue. It skidded to a halt behind Bubba's truck, and he swallowed convulsively. "Is it too late to hide?" he asked.

Peyton glanced over and he said, "Is that...?"

The doors to the restaurant slammed open a moment later, and Mamie, one of the waitresses, winced.

Bubba sank down into the seat. Perhaps it was a case of pregnancy brain? Perhaps something happened with her mucus plug, which Bubba had failed to read further about. Perhaps there was the number one spot on the FBI's Ten Most Wanted list sitting two tables over from him. A serial killer or someone who specialized in securities fraud or possibly a politician.

"BUBBA!" Willodean Gray yelled.

The sun came out from behind a cloud and shown down on her glossy head. Of course, then the doors juddered shut and blocked out the sun, leaving her in shadow.

Several people helpfully pointed at the booth that Bubba was attempting to hide within.

Willodean stomped over to them. Peyton took another bite of his sandwich and appeared fascinated with the show.

"Bubba Nathanial Snoddy," Willodean said as she came to a stop beside the table. Bubba couldn't but admire her fine figure encased in a Pegramville Sheriff's Department uniform. On another woman khaki would have appeared bland, but on Willodean, it made her skin luminous, and her green eyes as large as could be. He couldn't help the obvious comparisons. Her lips were as red as an International Harvester tractor. Her eyes were the green of a 2010 Camaro Synergy Special Edition. Her curves were like Lombard Street in San Francisco. Did he need to mention that she could shoot off the head of a mosquito from fifty feet? (It wasn't really good for the mosquito, but she didn't really do it all that often.)

"Willodean, darlin', looking at you is like when I open a toolbox first thing in the morning," Bubba said and sat up straight. "A feeling of exhilaration just runs right through me when I see your beautiful face." He fluttered his hand over his chest. He wasn't lying. He didn't have to lie.

Willodean's glower faded just a teensy bit before she clearly remembered what it was that had brought her here to where she had tracked Bubba down.

"A toolbox?" Peyton said. "I wouldn't have thought that line would have worked."

Willodean shot Peyton a glance, and he took another bite of his sandwich.

"Bubba, when I went to pick up Jim Biggerstaff at the five and dime an hour ago, he told me that he couldn't resist me," Willodean said.

"You are a lovely woman," Bubba said. "No man could resist you. Ain't that right, Peyton?"

Peyton nodded, still with a full mouth.

"Jim didn't mean it that way," Willodean said. "Is that okra?"

Bubba pushed the dish of deep fried-okra toward Willodean. She motioned for him to move over and slid in, adjusting her tool belt as she did so. She removed her police baton and put it in the center of the table.

"You want some sweet tea, Willodean?" Bubba asked and slid the baton away from him.

Willodean stuffed three pieces of okra in her mouth and nodded. When she swallowed thirty seconds later, she said, "This doesn't mean you're off the hook."

"Who's Jim Biggerstaff?" Peyton asked, taking a break from the Vito Corleone special.

"He's a fella that works in Tyler but lives in Pegramville," Bubba said. "I think he's a boat mechanic."

"He's delinquent on his child support, is what he is," Willodean said, reaching for the remainder of Bubba's chicken. "And I followed him from his house, which is not in Pegramville but in Pegram County, which is why I have the papers for him. When he stopped to go in the five and dime, he told me he could not...my gosh, that chicken almost melts in your mouth. Don't tell Miz Adelia that this recipe is almost as good as hers."

The two men waited while Willodean chewed. Bubba motioned at Mamie, who appeared afraid to come much closer than five feet away. "Sweet tea, and mebe a combo plate for the lady," he ordered. "We'll talk dessert later."

"Some mood stabilizer, mebe?" Mamie asked.

Willodean showed her teeth to the waitress. Mamie retreated for the kitchen. "It's not like I pulled out my service revolver," Willodean said nastily. "My fingers didn't even get close to the mace."

"God forbid," Peyton said.

"How do you get those wings above your eyes?" Willodean asked. "I would have thought you'd poke your eyes out with the wand."

Peyton smiled. "You wouldn't believe the bridezillas I have dealt with. They make you look like a cranky little five-year-old princess singing a song from *Frozen*. Something about making a snowman, perhaps."

Bubba pushed his plate at Willodean before she developed a notion to pull out her leather sap and use it on the wedding planner. "Here. Go ahead while we're waiting on yours."

"I'm going to get fat," Willodean complained.

"Never. You haven't gained a pound. It's all going to the baby. You're like a svelte goddess with a gorgeous teensie-weensie baby bump."

Willodean's hand briefly wavered over a piece of sausage before plucking it up. "This won't work, you know."

"Of course not," Bubba said. "I could never fool you."

"That's right," she said, waving the sausage at him. "Jim Biggerstaff said that he wasn't allowed to resist me. In an official capacity."

"Wasn't allowed?" Peyton asked. "Whatever do you mean?"

The sausage came around to point at Peyton. "That's right. I asked him the very same thing, and Jim clamped his mouth shut tight." The sausage came around like a gun turret and settled its business end on Bubba. "Like he'd been warned not to try anything around me. Do they have the corn casserole today?"

"No, but they have a broccoli one," Bubba said. One hand waved at the owner of The Hogfather's. "Add a broccoli casserole on to that order, Jethro!"

"Sure, Bubba," Jethro called back. "Got some cornbread muffins on the way out, too."

"Cornbread muffins," Willodean sighed. "I don't know where it all goes." She patted her stomach. She was about three months along, and nothing but the slightest curve was showing. However, she could eat and eat and eat. She probably wasn't gaining weight because she could also puke and puke and puke. Bubba would have been concerned, but the obstetrician said she was doing fine except for that little bit of blood pressure that was completely being controlled by medication.

Peyton steepled his fingers together in a thoughtful fashion. "So what you're saying is that you think that Bubba warned all of the local populace off messing with you while you're on duty."

Willodean mumbled something in agreement.

Bubba glowered at Peyton. Bubba had a plan. If he could distract Willodean enough, then he wouldn't have to lie to her about doing that very thing that she wasn't exactly accusing him of. The truth was that Willodean's boss, Sheriff John Headrick, otherwise known as Sheriff John, was doing something similar. Sheriff John thought of Willodean as the daughter he didn't have, and to Southern males, there was something profoundly uncomfortable about Willodean doing her patrols while she was pregnant.

Bubba knew that Willodean could take care of herself in 99% of the cases, but there was always that pesky 1% that haunted him.

"Eat some more, baby," Bubba urged.

Peyton slammed down a book of fabric swatches. "Then we can choose some fabric, right?"

"Bubba, where was he hiding the book?" Willodean asked with her hand full of a cornbread muffin.

"I don't want to know."

Chapter Four

Bubba and the Helpless Urge to Be a Stand-Up Joe

Saturday, April 6th

It was proved true for a second, or perhaps a third time, that Willodean was easily distracted once she was served her food. Peyton the wedding planner became dreadfully insistent on interjecting his needs into the communication arena. Five kinds of flowers were discussed along with twenty-three swatches of fabric, fifteen potential appetizers, and several types of almonds. Thoughts about whether Bubba would have gone behind Willodean's back in order to keep her safe went bye-bye for the moment.

Bubba focused on what Peyton was discussing, or rather was broadcasting. Types of almonds. "Blanched, nonblanched, nonpareil, Mission, California, and Carmel. Carmels are good because they can be both blanched and roasted."

"What if someone has a nut allergy?" Bubba asked. He hadn't known there were so many different types of almonds. (He could think of only two. There were the kind that you ate out of a bag and the kind that went into a candy bar.) "Ain't there some kind of allergy whereby a fella just touches the dust made from nuts and swells up into a watermelon? Hate like hell to have to call an ambulance to the reception. But maybe we should just have one on call. Then again, mebe we should just invite them, too. Ifin there's going to be liquor and spirits on hand, it would be the safest call."

Willodean snickered.

"Then they shall eat cake," Peyton proclaimed, with the wings above his eyes going as far up as they could.

Bubba interpreted that as "How dare some plebian soul have a nut allergy at a wedding reception that I have arranged? The arrogance of those simple-minded heathens."

Willodean put a half-eaten cornbread muffin on her plate, clearly having reached her gastrointestinal limit, and sighed. She sat up a little and said, "That feels pretty good. I don't think I'm going to ralph. These days any time I don't feel like I'm going to blow chunks is good.""

Bubba put his hand on her abdomen and smiled at her. "Ain't nothing like The Hogfather's to make it right."

Peyton eyed the remnants of his Vito Corleone special. "I'll have to come back to Texas just for this place. Ginger would just *die*."

"Say, Willodean," Bubba said, "you know anything about the Dogley place? Anything unusual going on?"

Willodean adjusted herself. "We're still inviting the loonies, right?"

"Loonies?" Peyton repeated.

"They ain't that loony," Jethro said as he picked up an empty plate from the table. "Just folks with some problems."

"That gal who does the Shakespearean insults is a loony," Ruby Mercer said from two tables away. She sat next to her sister, Alice. The Mercer sisters owned a mutt named Bill Clinton who had previously been very friendly with Precious. Too friendly if one asked Bubba, but one hadn't asked Bubba.

That train of thought led Bubba to Precious who'd been left at the Snoddy Estate with his mother. Precious didn't really get along with tailors or new Dodge Chargers that wedding planners insisted on being driven instead of a perfectly good 1954 Chevy truck.

"That's her way of communicating," Alice said. "Ain't so bad. She bluffs like a...I mean, she helps out with the Pegramville Women's Club something fierce."

Jethro snorted. Everyone knew what Alice meant. One of Miz Demetrice's hobbies was the Pegramville Women's Club, which was a euphemism for an illegal gambling ring that she and Miz Adelia ran. It usually went on Thursday nights, but the previous evening Willodean had barfed on one of the round felt tables, and it had been postponed until the smell could be removed or a new table could be obtained or when Willodean agreed not to attend anymore until the pregnancy culminated in a happy event. (Uninviting a pregnant law enforcement officer to an illegal event was precipitous at best. In fact, it might be the beginning of WWIII. It simply wasn't done.)

"So do you," Ruby said. "*Four tens.* That's like asking if a frog's tushy is watertight."

One day Bubba would like to go to a place to eat and have a "private" conversation. His mother would probably say then he should eat at home by himself in a dark room with the curtains pulled and the telephone turned off.

"What are you saying?" Alice demanded. "That I cheat? I spit on you. May the fleas of a thousand camels lay eggs in your armpit."

"Cheat," Ruby repeated. "That's one way of putting it. And you've got to stop reading *1,001 Arabian Nights*."

"That makes me madder than a legless Ethiopian watchin' a donut roll down a hill," Alice declared, obviously leaving *1,001 Arabian Nights* behind in favor of a more ethnic insult.

"Oh, my," Peyton said, clearly having forgotten about almonds in any form. "Will they fight?"

"Sheriff John took away their grandpa's shotgun last week," Willodean said. "They'll just say nasty things until they start to cry."

On cue Ruby began to cry. "My only sister," she sobbed. "She hates me because I don't know a full house from a straight flush." She ran for the door, and Alice rolled her eyes before following.

"So Dogley," Bubba said to Willodean.

Willodean patted Bubba's hand. "Not much going on there. They've got a few famous people going through thirty-day programs. One suicide last week. Then there was a lady who had a heart attack the week before. There's always been a higher incidence of deaths when it comes to that population."

Bubba didn't really like the way Willodean sounded when she said it like that. He knew she didn't really mean it. Police officers tended to be jaded. Willodean had a touch of it herself.

"A suicide and a heart attack," Bubba repeated. He thought of David Beathard. The phrase wandered through his mind, *"It's murder, Watson. Dastardly, despicable murder."* It made for a bad taste in Bubba's mouth. In fact, his stomach did a little rebellious roll. "Did Doc Goodjoint look at them dead people?"

Willodean covered her mouth and burped the most delicate burp possible. She slowly cast her lovely green-eyed gaze upon Bubba, then her eyes narrowed suspiciously. "Why do you want to know?"

"David Beathard came to the lake this morning," Bubba said. "So did my mother, your mother, and Peyton."

"Also that guy who was trimming the yard," Peyton added helpfully. "I don't think he'll really get married, do you?"

"Ifin he does, he probably won't use fifty dollars of your services," Bubba said. "That's Jasper Dukeminer," he added, "which means I have to strike Jasper off the list."

"What list?" Willodean asked. "You know he got caught adding an X to the men's room sign in the BuyMeQuik. Then he added a little Wolverine head to the man figure and drew on claws with a silver Sharpie."

"The name list," Bubba answered, ignoring the part about Jasper and his penchant for creating sign vandalism.

"You're thinking of baby names," she breathed, as if she was completely bemused by the fact.

See. Easily distracted.

"I'm in the J's now," Bubba said. "Judd, Julian, Julius. I don't reckon naming a child after an orange juice place or a Roman leader would be a good thing. Of course, it could be a Julia, Justine, or Junella, too. I've eliminated Jasper on account that Jasper Dukeminer ratted me out to Peyton this morning."

Willodean sighed. "No, Doc Goodjoint didn't look at them, you goober. The doctor at the hospital did. Doc Goodjoint looked over the medical reports and said it was pretty open and shut. Steve Simms looked over the suicide, and it was a done deal."

Steve Simms was another sheriff's deputy. He wasn't Bubba's favorite because he liked to target tourists for speeding tickets. It gave Pegram County a bad name. However, Steve wasn't all bad, if one disregarded the corn cob that was placed in a strategic part of his anatomy. He had taken to dating Penny Sillen after her common-law husband had been murdered, and by all accounts even her kids liked him. Also he was sporting a basketball-sized gut thanks to Penny's cooking.

Bubba shook his head. "He's got a new him now."

"Who? Doc Goodjoint?"

"No, David Beathard," Bubba said. "Now he's Sherlock Holmes."

Willodean blinked at Bubba. "No shizz, Sherlock." She laughed at her own joke. "Wait. Does that make you Dr. Watson?" She giggled and then snorted. Then she laughed when she snorted.

Bubba glowered but only momentarily because Willodean was so danged cute when she snorted.

"It *does* make you Dr. Watson," Willodean said. "Ma always wanted me to marry a doctor. Now I can finally retire and be a lady of leisure. Bring on the bon bons."

"It's temporary."

"So you're suggesting that these people were murdered and that David is onto it before anyone else," Willodean concluded.

"He said it was murder," Bubba said quietly. "Dint say who, what, when, or why."

"Oh, my God," Peyton said, "I didn't connect it before. This is *that* place! That place! There were the murders by the people looking for Civil War gold. Then the Christmas Killer business. The missing sheriff's deputy." Willodean cast Peyton a pained glance. "The murder mystery festival with the real murders. Then the zombie movie thing. I loved that movie. But hey, the director wasn't really murdered, was he? That was all *here*? O.M.F.G. I might tinkle." His fingers fluttered excitedly in the air.

Bubba glowered some more.

"Wait until I tell Ginger," Peyton said with a little giggle that made Bubba distinctly uncomfortable. "I'm going outside to make a call. Excuse me."

Willodean brought her gaze around to rest on Bubba. He almost removed his hand from her belly upon the change in mood. "You're just asking about the Dogley Institute because of a certain affection for the loonies, right, Bubba?"

"David looked...scared," Bubba said. His stomach said some bad words.

Willodean's expression changed. "I love you, Bubba. I love you like the earth loves the rain. Nothing will change that. But you know David's not right in the head."

"Lots of folks around here are like that," Bubba said. "He's helped me, and he ain't all bad. In fact, he ain't bad at all." His stomach said some more bad words and then twisted abruptly in a way that could never be considered good.

"I know that," Willodean said. She lifted her wrist and glanced at her watch. "I'll ask Doc Goodjoint again, and I'll make a few calls, okay?"

Bubba nodded. "That's just fine." He liked that. That meant she would stay in the office and not patrol the streets. Sheriff John had mentioned that he was about to restrict her to desk duty anyway, but he told Bubba he wasn't ready to tell her yet.

Willodean abruptly swallowed, and her normally creamy flesh started to change into a light green. "You know what, ulp?" She tried to swallow again. Then she looked around frantically. "I— ulp. Ulp. Ulp."

Bubba's eyes went wide. "Bathroom's back there," he pointed. Bubba watched as Willodean rushed away. People scrambled to get out of her way. Then his stomach started feeling even more odd. He stood up as

48

it rumbled dangerously and muttered to Jethro, "Be right back," and rushed to the men's room himself.

•

Doc patted Bubba's head and said, "They call it Couvade Syndrome." Doc Goodjoint was a tall man of an undeterminable age. He was old. His hair was white, and he had degrees from Johns Hopkins and Harvard. He was a general practitioner in the area and a lifelong family friend of the Snoddy's. He often dined with Miz Demetrice at the Snoddy Mansion.

"Am I dying, Doc? It was all the times Ma dragged me to protest nuclear plants, wasn't it? Radioactive infection, right? I probably glow in the dark."

Bubba had lost his lunch in the restroom at The Hogfather's. Then as he'd watched Willodean get a to-go bag, he'd felt nauseous and a bit of back pain. Unlike Willodean, he wasn't inclined to go for seconds at that moment. Peyton had driven him to the doctor's clinic, and fortunately for all involved, the doctor was in.

Doc grinned at Bubba. "It'll probably last as long as six months. There might be a little weight gain, some labor pains, and such. It might hurt."

"Labor pains?"

"Sympathetic pregnancy, boy," Doc answered, slapping Bubba's knee. "A fella sometimes gets the same kind of symptoms as the lady."

"I'm not pregnant," Bubba said darkly.

"Some studies suggest it's a hormonal issue," Doc said genially. "You live with Willodean now, and you're impacted. Some folks say it's all in your heard. But you've got a pretty clear noggin, boy, if we discount all the times you've been hit there."

"Don't tell Willodean that," Bubba snapped.

"Of course not, dear boy," Doc agreed. "I'm simply glad that you haven't had a concussion for coming up on a whole year, isn't it? Just the shotgun wound."

"I cain't remember exactly," Bubba admitted and then almost bit his tongue for saying that.

Doc nodded sagely as his shock of white hair bounced in time.

"It ain't like that," Bubba said. "I'd have to look at the hospital bills or something. I've had my mind on other things. Ain't nothing wrong with my brain. Ask me what the equation is for Moser's worm problem."

Doc began to list things. "Items that would stress out any living soul. Then there's weddings, babies, people wanting invites to the biggest event in Pegram County's recent history."

"It is not."

"You say potato, I say po-ta-tah. Also tater tots. Tatos. Patty poo cakes."

"You honestly serious, Doc? You think I got some kind of likeminded syndrome that makes me have symptoms like Willodean?"

"No fever. No diarrhea. I've checked your blood work. Looks good. You said you ate after you threw up and felt just fine."

"I think I threw up my toenails. It's no wonder that I needed something to et. It wasn't right after I threw up that I had such an empty stomach. It was about ten minutes later as that wedding planner fella was bringing me here. We ran through Jack in the Box. But Willodean had her hand in the Styrofoam box as she was walking out to the Bronco."

"And how do you feel right now?"

"I feel fine," Bubba said, honestly perplexed. Sympathetic pregnancy symptoms. He loved the woman, he loved that she was pregnant with his child, he loved that they were going to get married no matter how difficult everyone was being with the planning, but...

"Really?" Bubba asked. "Couvade Syndrome? Seriously?"

Doc nodded.

"Okay," Bubba said with finality, "I kin live with that. Don't tell anyone."

"I have an oath," Doc said. "Please let me tell your mother."

"Oh, hell no."

"Pretty please with sugar on top?"

"Ma will tell everyone within a radius of 200 miles."

"I'll give you free medical checkups for the next six months."

"Wait. Mebe. No. No. Doc," Bubba shook his head, "keep it zipped."

Doc shrugged.

"Okay, what about the deaths at Dogley?" Bubba asked before Doc could shoo him out the door.

"You're not going to let me gossip about your sympathetic pregnancy symptoms, but you want some inside information on some other deaths?" Doc shook his head sadly. "There were two there in the last four weeks. It's certainly noticeable but hardly abnormal."

"You're the county coroner, so why dint you look at them?"

"There's three medical doctors on staff at Dogley, Bubba," Doc said. "I only had to rubberstamp their findings. There was very little to indicate anything but what they had reported. Likewise Steve Simms reported on the suicide. Sheriff John was the one who looked at the heart attack, and I don't second-guess him. It's simply not necessary."

Bubba frowned. "There ain't any other deaths out there?"

"Not that I'm aware of," Doc said. His expression became curious. "Why would you be asking about this?"

"David Beathard," Bubba said.

"David said there were other deaths there at Dogley?"

"No, he said there was murder."

"Bubba, David is, in my professional opinion, a nutjob."

"That's not very nice, doc."

"Most of the residents of Pegram County are nutjobs," Doc added cheerfully. "In fact, I'm probably a nutjob, too."

"What about patients disappearing?"

"I wouldn't be privy to that, Bubba," Doc said. He sighed and sat on his doctor's stool. "All this chattering is making me tired. You know, Mrs. Greenjaw is next door, and she's got an abscess in a place that I shouldn't even imply anything about." He shuddered. "Oh the challenges of a medical professional never cease."

Bubba sat up on the examining table. His stomach felt just fine, as he'd told the doctor. He didn't feel dizzy or sick or anything. He definitely didn't feel like there was a baby growing under his heart. No, Doc had to be wrong. Maybe it had been a very sudden virus. The two-hour kind. Yeah, that sounded much better than sympathetic pregnancy symptoms. There certainly wasn't a need to tell anyone else.

"I haven't heard anything new about Dogley at all," Doc went on. "There's a new guy out there who's a social worker. I think they finally found someone to replace Nancy Musgrave. Did you hear that she's going to try to plead out?"

Nancy Musgrave was the woman who'd wanted a little something along the lines of bloody revenge and had been willing to go through half of Pegramville in order to get it, Christmastime or not. Bubba didn't know why she was so mad at him; Brownie Snoddy, his cousin's precocious son, had been the one who'd thwarted her gory vengeance via the homemade stun gun method. "I ain't heard that. They keep putting off the trial date. Sometimes the prosecutor remembers to tell me."

"Well, this fella is named Blake Landry," Doc said. "Came from um, let's see, Georgia, I believe. Came in to get a prescription for allergies."

"It wasn't a nut allergy, was it?"

"No, pollen."

"I guess he kin come to the wedding reception then." Bubba straightened his shirt. "We're having several kinds of almonds there. The fabric for my tux will be grayish grey grayed grayity grey or something. The Blue Angels might be attending. Ma knows some Air Force general."

Doc blinked. "Dear boy, if you don't want a big wedding and reception, then run off to the county courthouse."

"That wouldn't work," Bubba said sourly. "I think Willodean's mother would shoot me. Then Ma would shoot me. Luckily, Willodean wouldn't shoot me."

Doc shrugged. "There is one thing that's lucky," he added.

"What?"

"You haven't actually found a dead body, have you?"

"Day ain't over yet."

Chapter Five

Bubba and the Impending Sense of Doom

Saturday, April 6th

Doc Goodjoint gave Bubba a list of dos and don'ts. Bubba wasn't inclined to do or don't anyway.

"Keep hydrated. I don't want to see you fainting at the altar and then see it on *America's Funniest Home Videos* over and over again. Drink lots of liquid. Not beer or liquor, not that you do that, boy. Gatorade is good. Water is better. If you start showing other signs that are problematic, come back and see me. I won't tease much. Otherwise you might expect some sleeplessness, a need to urinate frequently, especially at night, possibly some swelling, headaches, and a few other things I cain't be bothered to list." Doc went, "Tee-hee-hee," under his breath, then added, "I won't say you'll be needing maternity clothing or that you might get a mite moody." Then he tittered again.

Bubba nodded while grinding his teeth together and kept his head down as he left the clinic. Peyton was waiting for him with the Dodge Charger. "I have just three more things for you, Bubba," the wedding planner said, "and then we're done." He paused and then added, "For the day."

"Home, James," Bubba said, climbing into the Charger's passenger side.

"I met the most interesting person," Peyton said. "Her name is Kiki something or other. She does the dreads, you know. She says you and she are best buds."

Kiki Rutkowski lived next door to Willodean or used to live next door to Willodean until the beauteous sheriff's deputy had been persuaded to move in with

54

Bubba. Kiki was a perennial college student and found employment at the oddest places. The last he knew she was one of the professional murder victims of the First Annual Pegramville Murder Mystery Festival. But before that she'd worked at a fortune cookie factory and for a process server. She'd also helped Bubba with valuable internet intelligence on events that had caught him up. She was good peoples.

"All righty then," Peyton said and buckled up. He started the Charger and pointed it in the direction of the Snoddy Estate. Bubba was impressed that he'd gotten the lay of the land so swiftly, but of course the GPS unit in the dashboard helped mightily. "Home and then we have to talk venues. Miz Demetrice is discussing the grand staircase, and I know the photog is happy about that, but what if the bride trips down the stairs when the music is playing? I wouldn't be happy about that at all. I noticed a pergola in the back that could easily be transformed into a wedding extravaganza galore. I see white flowers and vines flowing over it. I envision little twinkling lights at dusk. I picture globed candle holders glittering in the evening as the reception occurs. I hear elegant music playing like the softest notes of angel's wings flying into a heathery sunset. I predict wedding brilliance." He let go of the wheel to clap his hands together before he casually grasped the steering wheel again.

Bubba's stomach said another nasty word. He told it to stand down. "That pergola will likely fall down if a fella leaned against one of the supports," he told the wedding planner. "Been meaning to chop it down and burn it with the fall leaves for the last two years. Them termites said they wasn't done with it yet."

"I have a handyman fixing that right now," Peyton said smartly. "His name is Lloyd Goshorn. He's a rough individual, but he has a recipe for gout that involves tea bags, chamomile, and exotic spices from the orient. My grandmamma will be ecstatic!"

"Did he charge you for the recipe?"

"No, but I did give him credit from Pure Love Weddings, LLC. $100 worth."

Bubba chuckled at that. Clearly, Peyton was cleverer than he had previously let on.

Peyton began to discuss all things wedding and all things wedding reception. Twenty minutes later Bubba wished he could plug his ears with his fingers and yell/sing, "I AM NOT LISTENING! I AM NOT LISTENING!" However, he tuned out the other man by thinking that the event would be over soon, and the world would probably not come to a flaming, explosive end.

"...piano with a white cover versus a quartet of violinists playing selected music from Bach. Cellos would be interesting, too. The musicians could be dressed in the same gray as your tuxedo. They would be cordoned off with white ribbon and flowing flowers and vines. It'll be so extraordinary."

Bubba thanked God when the Charger parked next to Ol' Green. He got out more quickly than he wanted. He gently herded Peyton toward the big house, saying, "Ma will want to hear all of this. I'm shore she's got some ideas on this. Miz Celestine will want to put her stamp of approval on it. I'm perty shore Miz Adelia might want to put a nickel's worth in, too."

Peyton gathered a bundle of books, albums, and notebooks and headed toward the house. Precious exploded out of the kitchen door and charged toward Bubba with a plaintive howl. The wedding planner stopped to consider the canine. "We could have the dog carry the rings. It would be absolutely adorable. A cushion tied to her neck with ribbons. I remember when she was a zombie dog in that movie. You know I once did a zombie-themed wedding. Oh, the fake blood went everywhere! He went inside with a chirpy, "Cheerio!"

"Precious would et the cushion and probably the ring, too," Bubba said with no little amount of certainty. The canine bumped into his leg and he grunted. She did a fancy-toed trot around his legs, looking up at him lamentingly. Then she nipped his ankle.

"Sorry I left you, Precious," Bubba murmured. "Wasn't a place for a princess like you. Although you might have liked the barbeque place quite a bit. Willodean got a to-go bag, and you know she always saves some ribs for you."

Precious stuck her nose in the air and turned away.

"Who's my widdle wooby dooby?" Bubba crooned.

Precious presented him with her tail end. Her tail flicked once and drooped. A dog knew when to play hard to get, especially when the aforementioned to-go bag wasn't front and present.

"Who wants to play ball before we go to the mental institution for people who have big problems that they cain't really deal with like some folks can? Them folks loves dogs. One of them thinks you're the second coming of the messiah, which really ticks Jesus Christ off. The Jesus who thinks he's Jesus, not the real one, of course."

Precious glanced over her shoulder at him. She clearly didn't follow except for the word ball. She knew that one very well. She lifted her head again and looked into the woods. The woods were very interesting.

Bubba strolled over to the little porch on the caretaker's house. It wasn't really the caretaker's house because the original caretaker's house had been burned, condemned, and then rebuilt, but everyone still called it the caretaker's house. (Bubba wasn't certain there ever had been a caretaker in it at all.) The original original had been a stable. Bubba's grandfather had thought to turn it into a rental house for soldiers from a nearby Army fort, but the Army closed the fort down, and no one wanted to rent an oddball house.

On the small covered porch sat a basket of dog toys to include a well-masticated, yellow tennis ball. Bubba held up the ball, and Precious gave up the ghost, baying with incipient excitement. She wheeled and ran toward him.

Ball! Ball! Ball! A dog's got to have a BALL! GIMME! GIMME! GIMME!

Bubba spent the next twenty minutes forgetting why it was that he was a little stressed. It wasn't that he had sympathetic pregnancy symptoms. It was that all these people wanted the wedding just a certain way. It was that Willodean was pregnant, and he was worried about her as well as the baby. It was that all the newfangledness was causing him to be off his feed; it was that he had a dreadful feeling that the other shoe was about to drop upon his unwary and unprotected head.

He watched with satisfaction as Precious fell over onto her side. Her tongue lolled out of her mouth, and she panted with pleased exhaustion. The saliva-drenched ball sat between her paws and had been subjugated to within an inch of its being.

Bubba gave Precious some extra water from the hose and made sure she was cooled down before he headed for his truck. He glanced around to ensure that he wasn't being followed. Doubtless Peyton had all of the womenfolk at the Snoddy Mansion under a hypnotic spell as he discoursed about wedding arrangements in lurid detail.

It was Bubba's big chance to get away. As he headed for his truck, Precious tight on his heels, an orange Ford Pinto circa the seventies and the era of fatal rear-end collisions, pulled in behind him and parked. A tall man in his early forties got out of the Pinto and smiled broadly at Bubba.

"Hey," he said. "Looking for Bubba Snoddy."

Bubba glowered and looked him over in the way that he looked over most strangers these days. (Is this person a potential victim or murderer? Does he take his coffee with cream or sugar or icky Sweet 'n Low?) The man was about six feet tall with graying brown hair buzz-cut in a way that would have made a drill sergeant happy. His eyes were blue, and his smile was expansive and inviting. (He showed at least twenty teeth in that smile; predators everywhere would be proud, or possibly envious.)

The result of Bubba's estimations was anticlimactic. The man didn't look like a process server, and he wasn't someone from the government, as Bubba was certain the DEA didn't drive Ford Pintos, and if they did, they wouldn't be orange. Dressed in a blue button-down shirt and faded Lee jeans, he didn't look like someone who wanted to provide an as yet unknown and unwanted service for the wedding and/or reception. He might have been a politician, but it was only April, and things didn't usually get geared up until around Halloween in Texas. He might have been a treasure hunter, but he didn't have a shovel and a metal detector, so that left a limited set of roles he could have fulfilled.

"I'm Bubba," Bubba admitted reluctantly.

The man held out a hand. Bubba shook it and the man said, "I'm Blake Landry. I've heard a bit about you."

Bubba had to think about where he'd heard the name and in what context. It hit him at the same time that Blake added, "I'm the new social worker out at Dogley." He had a soft Georgia drawl that only someone from the South could appreciate. Bubba always thought the gentile and graceful Georgians could tell someone to go to hell while sounding like they were inviting them to an evening of canasta and canapés.

"You ain't a friend of Nancy Musgrave by any chance?" Bubba asked. To be sure, there was a chance that the two social workers were acquainted with each other. Bubba didn't feel like taking chances.

"I have never met the lady," Blake said with a smile. "I'm not likely to meet her since I'm sure they're not going to let her out of the prison for the next fifty years, isn't that right?"

Bubba didn't begin to understand how the legal system was working. Nancy should have been tried and convicted by this time, but her impending trial, as well as those of Donna Hyatt, Noey Wheatfall, and Morgan Newbrough, lingered on and on while the government got all its legal ducks in a row. It was even possible there might be an actual trial one day.

"Not unless she can get them same lawyers who represented O.J. Simpson, I reckon not."

Blake glanced around. "That little boy, Brownie, isn't about, is he? I heard all about him."

"Boy's in Louisiana," Bubba said, "but he and his family are coming for the wedding." Bubba's cousin, Fudge, his wife, Virtna, and baby Cookie, would be coming for a few days before the wedding and then scooting back to Monroe because Brownie was in school. Brownie had sworn that he would not bring any weapons of mass destruction, and supposedly the school had been gleeful to be rid of him for even a brief period of time.

"Lately, I've heard rumors about how he managed to get the best of two fellas who tried to kidnap him," Blake said. "He's a right pistol."

"Oh, don't say that," Bubba said. "You might give the boy an idea. Kid's got enough ideas without adding firearms to the equation."

"Well, then I expect you're a busy man these days, with impending nuptials and all."

"Word gets around, I suspect," Bubba offered. Was he supposed to invite Blake Landry, too? The reality was that he didn't know if he was supposed to invite anyone. There had been rampant discussion about the number of people coming to the wedding and to the reception. Apparently, every invitee was to be vetted by Miz Demetrice, Celestine Gray, and Peyton.

"Even out to Dogley, we've heard about the big event," Blake said. "I'm somewhat concerned about David Beathard, and that's why I'm here."

"David," Bubba repeated. It wasn't a question. He himself was somewhat concerned about David. "I saw him this morning. He wasn't happy."

Blake shook his head. "I can't go into details about Mr. Beathard, as I'm his social worker and therapist, but I wonder if there's anything you can tell me about him that might help."

"He's gone Sherlock." Bubba supposed that Sherlock Holmes was better than the Purple Singapore Sling persona and the dread pirate, Bad Black Dog McGee. But there had also been a psychiatrist and possibly a first lady, too. However, this was the first time Bubba had been required to take on a persona, as well.

Blake nodded. "Another manifestation of his disorder."

"Don't seem like a real disorder like that gal Sybil, do it?"

"That's dissociative identity disorder," Blake said. "It's characterized by two or more distinctive personalities. The personality controls the person to the extent that the original might have a gap in memory during the time another personality is in control. Sometimes it's called 'missing time.'" He shook his head. "It's actually very rare. Authors love it a little too much."

Bubba thought about it. "David doesn't really do that. He remembers. Sometimes he talks about himself in the third person."

Blake shrugged. "Again, I can't talk about specifics."

"Obviously, something's bothering him," Bubba said. "Otherwise he would stay as plain ol' David Beathard." Something itched at the back of Bubba's neck. He reached up with a hand and scratched it. Alas, it was a metaphorical itch. "Why don't you ask him?"

"David hasn't been back to the institute since Wednesday," Blake said. "He's there voluntarily, of course, and I've been in contact with his family. You have no idea how glad I am to hear that you saw him this morning. I had a vision of that little car in a deep ditch somewhere."

"Healthy, no blood dripping, and dressed in a deerstalker hat with an Inverness coat, talking with what I think is the worst British accent ever." Bubba gestured with one hand. "That's how a fella like that asks for help. You know that gal, Thelda?"

"Another interesting case who lives in the halfway house now, although she's at the hospital a great deal, too. She's rather partial to the Pegramville area."

"That's on account that the folks here are half crazy, too." Bubba grinned wryly. "Makes us a mite more acceptin' and all."

Blake studied Bubba. Bubba didn't care for it much. He'd talked to people of the mental health care ilk before. The Army had made him speak to one of them for three weeks before he was discharged. There had been a lot of buzzwords about anger management, self-control, and self-actualization, but the man had been about as useful as a ball at a square dance.

"I think people are a lot more accepting than they give themselves credit for," Blake said. "Pegramville is a little canted to one side is all. That's a good thing." He paused. "I don't suppose David is staying here."

"Do you see a Smart car with Jolly Roger wraps?"

Blake smiled again. "He's not in trouble. I'm just concerned."

"Ifin I see him, I'll let him know." Bubba thought about what David said. There had been murder, despicable yucky murder and the game being afoot. He hadn't said where it was, and Bubba had assumed the Dogley Institute for Mental Well-Being was the locale of choice. Willodean had brought up the two deaths. Bubba hadn't heard of any other deaths, per se, and if there had been murders in Pegram County, people would have been talking about it. They would have been yelling about it. Bubba would have gone deaf listening to it.

Blake offered his hand again, and Bubba shook it. It was a nice strong grip but not too strong. A political grip. Three shakes, one firm squeeze, and then the release. He turned back toward the Pinto.

"Say, doc," Bubba said.

"Oh, I'm not a doctor," Blake said, turning back to Bubba. "I have an MSW. That's a master's in social

63

work. I have some extra credentials, too, but that's the gist of it. I get to put initials behind my name. Whoopee."

"You said you ain't seen David since Wednesday," Bubba said.

Blake nodded.

"That wouldn't be the day that someone kilt hisself out there at the institute, would it?"

The blue eyes turned solemn. "That's right. It happened either early Wednesday or late Tuesday. Half the patients had to be medicated." He slapped a hand over his mouth. "I didn't say that."

"Mebe David's just plumb upset and all," Bubba said. "There's a good chance he'll work it out."

Blake nodded. He went to the Pinto and opened the door.

"Hey, ifin you need some work on that Ford, bring it to Culpepper's Garage," Bubba called. "I kin rebuild a four cylinder in my sleep."

"I'll keep it in mind," Blake said.

As the social worker drove off, Bubba yelled, "Don't get into a rear-end collision!"

●

Bubba went in to see his mother before he went looking for one David Beathard. He supposed that David's disappearance couldn't be officially reported to the police department, seeing as how David had come to see him at the lake. There wasn't any real indication that David intended on doing himself any harm, other than becoming hot and sweaty from wearing the heavy Inverness coat.

"Bubba!" Miz Demetrice cried happily as he entered the kitchen with Precious at heels. "Open or cash bar?"

"Spring for beer and wine, Ma," Bubba said and turned right back around.

"Foreign or domestic?" Celestine asked.

"Mix it up," Bubba snapped.

"Where are you going, Bubba?" Peyton called.

"To the insane asylum! Also I feel like eting some pickles!"

Chapter Six

Bubba and the Dogley Institute and Also Some Loonies

Saturday, April 6th

The way to the Dogley Institute wasn't a difficult trek, but there was only one way to go. One simply left the greater downtown area of metropolitan Pegramville and headed north. After a few miles the farms disappeared into piney forests and great thickets that people had been known to go into and never come out. Eventually, there was a left turn onto a narrow two-lane road. That road cut through a deep ravine with the Sturgis River on one side and splintering red rock cliffs on the other. He drove over a narrow bridge and wound up on the top of a deeply forested mesa. Once, all the land had belonged to a distant cousin of the Snoddys who wanted to grow coffee beans, but he'd lost all his money during the Great Depression, sold the land to a developer, and moved to Argentina with his third wife, never to be heard from again. (It never failed to amuse Bubba that there was likely a line of Argentinian Snoddys who spoke Spanish and had never set foot in Texas.)

The developer who'd purchased the land tried to parcel it out but got into a financial dilemma with his bank which caused the land to sit undeveloped for nearly thirty years. Then a medical corporation bought it for pennies on the dollar because the developer gambled his fortune away on a franchise of mink ranches. Believing that the greater Pegramville area would develop because of the Army post and the bucolic attraction of cheap land, the medical corporation built a hospital on the location in the sixties. It wasn't the best place for a rural hospital, and it languished under different auspices for twenty years until it became a psychiatric hospital. Despite the Dogley Institute of Mental Well-Being being its fourth incarnation, it seemed to be doing well. It had been renovated, and all the employees praised its great perks. Its only failing was that it had inadvertently hired a sociopathic killer bent on revenge. However, Bubba had to admit that was water under the bridge.

Bubba had been to the Dogley Institute before but not in a professional affiliation. He had also come hunting on the mesa with one of his uncles, who assiduously avoided the hospital and its grounds whilst they sought squirrel and white-tailed deer out of season.

With a sigh, Bubba caught sight of his destination. It appeared as any regular hospital would. Whitewashed walls set the backdrop for a manicured lawn that spread far and away. There weren't any fences and especially not any with concertina wire mounted on top. The parking lot was close to the front entrance, and inside a nearby gazebo, a pair of nurses smoked cigarettes and chatted affably.

Déjà vu hit Bubba hard. He had been to Dogley to visit David Beathard in order to get his opinion as a pseudo-psychiatrist, and it was nearly the same as it had been before. At the time, David had been the only such individual that Bubba could think of to speak with. It had worked out even though David hadn't been Psychiatrist David but had been Purple Singapore Sling (or The PSS as it had been shortened to) David.

A handy formal sign on one side announced the name of the facility. Bubba slowed his truck to a crawl as he looked for the best place to park. With a little bit of effort he pulled in between a 1980something Mercedes Benz and a Volkswagen Rabbit of indeterminate age. He looked over the parking lot and thought it seemed light. It was a Saturday, and there should have been more visitors, but half the lot was empty. Additionally two cars pulled out and left just after he stopped the truck.

Most importantly, there was a Smart car with Jolly Roger wraps parked in one corner under the shade of an oak tree. Interestingly enough there wasn't an orange Ford Pinto about.

Bubba shrugged. Even a social worker had to have some time off.

He let Precious out of the truck to do some dogly business while he looked around. The nurses still chatted in the gazebo, and a lone gardener was clipping bushes with oversized shears. It seemed overly quiet for a place that usually had so much going on.

Without ado, Precious went to work sniffing grass and bushes alike in a great quest to mark as much territory in the little amount of time she had been allotted. Bubba often thought that Precious had an extra bladder to be used strictly for the marking of territory and to be held on reserve for such momentous occasions. When she noticed her master was getting away, she peed a final time and trotted after him as he wound his way up to the main door. The door had a sign next to it and a little button that begged to be pushed. After he pushed it, the door chirped open without anyone asking what his business was or wasn't.

Once inside, Bubba found the large-sized foyer about the same as it had been the last time. The floors were marble. The seats were metal and bolted to the floors. The desk sat in the same place. Surprisingly, the same red-haired girl sat at it and smiled genially at Bubba.

"Well, hi there, Bubba, isn't it?" she asked. His gaze dropped down to the nametag on her breast at the same time he remembered the girl's name was Cybil. It took him a moment to wonder if that was just ironic coincidence or the universe saying, "Gotcha," to Bubba. He decided it was ironic coincidence.

"Hey, Cybil," Bubba said. "They don't have you in the thrift shop no more?"

"It's closed two weekends a month, and we're having some renovation done next week so everyone who could arrange it got to go to a big company retreat at South Padre Island." Cybil smiled broadly. She was the type of girl who liked to smile. In fact, she was perpetually chipper. (Possibly she hadn't yet found any dead bodies in her lifetime.)

"You dint want to go to the beach?"

"Sand gives me hives," Cybil said, "and I get an extra two weeks off for working now. So I'm taking a month off to check off some items on my bucket list." She pulled out a logbook and pushed it at him. "You know the rules, right?"

"I sign in, no weapons, no fooling around, no causing drama," Bubba listed. He signed the log with the flowered pen she provided and pushed both book and pen back at her. Then he pulled out his keys, a Buck pocketknife, a spinner shaped like a cricket, and two pieces of Doublemint gum. "There ya go."

"Well that's just outstanding," Cybil said brightly, clearly meaning every word. "We just love visitors, although we don't get to see as many since half the people are gone."

"Gone?"

"That renovation, silly," she said. "The management's been planning this for months. All the patients were trimmed due to attrition and then put in the southern wing, so they can work on the northern wing. They hope all the noise won't bother the poor dears, but you can't have a building falling down on you, can you?"

"You cain't or I cain't?" Bubba asked, confused.

"You know what I mean, daffy doodle," Cybil chastised him. "The dayroom is the same as the last time you were here, if that was the last time. Goodness knows I might not have been here the last time you visited."

Bubba wasn't exactly sure how to respond to Cybil. She might talk to him some more and then call him a Happy Henry or a Dorky Doris. She gave him a visitor's badge and gently shooed him toward the double doors. "I'll buzz you through," she said. The doors made a sort of burping noise that made his stomach make a corresponding noise.

"Most of them just finished the last therapy for the day," Cybil called after him just before the doors shut, "so they'll be in the dayroom hanging out. A lot of them will be leaving pretty soon, but I think Mr. Beathard is staying, so no problem. Or maybe you're here to see Jesus."

Bubba didn't answer as he passed through the door and wondered why Cybil hadn't said anything about Precious. The dog kept to Bubba's heel and glanced around with cautious eyes. The last time she'd been to a place like this she'd lost a bunch of time and woken up with a sore belly, so she was naturally suspicious. "Don't worry," he told her reassuringly, "they don't do that sort of thing here."

Precious woofed softly. It sounded like canine contempt to Bubba.

The dayroom wasn't as full of patients as the previous time he'd been there. Three women dressed in hospital robes watched an old episode of *Starsky and Hutch*. Bubba couldn't remember which was Starsky and which was Hutch, but he did recognize Huggy Bear. One patient cheered on Starsky. "Go Starsky!" she cried. "Show them how it's done!" One of the other two women said plaintively, "I like Hutch better."

To Bubba's disappointment there wasn't a great reenactment of the crossing of the Delaware River by General Washington, but there was a courtroom drama going on in one corner. After watching for a minute, Bubba deduced it was a revisionist's view of the Scopes Monkey Trial. A man dressed in a skunk costume was

71

acting as Clarence Darrow and a woman with four sweaters was William Jennings Bryant. Sadly, Bubba recognized the William Jennings Bryant individual as Thelda, a woman who tended to speak in Shakespearean insults and the object of Ruby Mercer's pokerama-related derision.

"Thy vain, shard-borne moldwarp!" she accused Clarence Darrow. Bubba took that to mean that she thought he was contemptible.

"I object!" Clarence Darrow the skunk cried. His black and white tail bounced as he leapt to his feet.

The judge said, "Motion dismissed!" and hit the chair he sat in with the heel of his shoe. Bubba supposed it was hard to find a gavel in the vicinity.

The history buff inside Bubba wanted to watch, but what he really needed to do was to find David Beathard. He looked around for a pirate and saw nary a one, not even one that was vaguely like Johnny Depp. He looked for someone in purple and came up with zilch. Finally, he looked for Sherlock Holmes and not one deerstalker cap was to be located.

A man in a striped seersucker suit wandered past him. The man muttered, "Mechanical oscillators and electrical discharge tubes need to be connected to the high-frequency, high-power mechanism." Then a mad scientist laugh escaped his lips. "Bwahaha."

Bubba said, "Pardon me."

The man glanced at Bubba. "You don't happen to have an induction motor on you, do you?" he asked, adjusting the double lapel of his jacket.

"Ah, no," Bubba said. He patted his shirt, then

remembered he was wearing the same t-shirt he had put on for fishing. "Bun in the Oven" was still prominent, but it had no pockets for induction motors or any other kind of motors, for that matter. "You wouldn't know David Beathard, would you?"

"Is he related to Thomas Edison?" the man asked. He was about five feet ten inches tall and in his forties or fifties. Bubba didn't think he'd seen him before, although he looked vaguely familiar. He had an impressive hawk nose and a terrible scar snaking down his left cheek. "He stole all of my patents, you know."

"That's a dang shame," Bubba said, "but as far as I know, he ain't related to Edison."

"Perhaps one of the guards at this facility could tell you about Mr. Beathard," the man said. "If you happen upon an alternating current electric generator, come find me. I have inventions and electrical current to develop in diabolical ways. Bwaha."

Bubba pursed his lips as the man in the seersucker suit wandered off. He could check the cafeteria or David's room or many of the other places that a man dressed in a deerstalker cap could be hiding. A stout woman in a flowered dress and matching hat appeared next to him and made him jump.

"Ma'am," he said.

"I understand you're on the hunt for David," the woman said.

Precious bumped Bubba's knee. Bubba extended his hand down to scratch her head.

"And you've a hound for the hunt," the woman added. She wasn't that tall, but she made up for it in width. Her face was craggy and caked with makeup. The lipstick matched the poppies on her dress.

"She's a hound all right," Bubba said, looking at her suspiciously. "Do you know where David is?"

The woman leaned in, and Bubba nearly flinched. "Call me Cella," she said. "It was my grandmother's name, too."

"Are you a patient here or perhaps visiting someone?" Bubba asked.

Cella giggled and covered her mouth with a white gloved hand. "Oh, I'm a patient, too, if any of us are *really* patients."

Bubba's eyes narrowed. "Is that you, David?"

Cella abruptly stopped giggling. "You think I'm a man?" One of her hands fluttered in front of her chest. Her mouth opened, then shut, and then opened again. "I never," she said huffily.

Bubba felt he had come to a decision that was not made lightly. He could accuse the woman of being a man or pretend that the woman who wasn't really a man was a woman. It could very well be David under the caked makeup and the auburn wig arranged in curls that would have made a young Shirley Temple envious. Bubba was uncertain how David could have managed to temporarily shrink himself. "This ain't funny, David," Bubba said, going for the gusto. "I came all the way out here to see ifin you're alright."

Cella took in a deep breath and glared at Bubba in an exceedingly indignant fashion. That's what Bubba would call it, and he had seen it from his mother many a time. Indignant to the extreme. Bubba almost backed down, but he was starting to get a headache, and although he'd stopped at Jack in the Box for a Sourdough Jack burger, seasoned curly fries, and a vanilla ice cream shake, he was still a mite peckish. Pickles were sounding better and better.

"David," Bubba said again, "that social worker came to see me on account that you ain't bin out here since Wednesday. I'm sorry I couldn't come with you earlier. It's all this wedding bizness that's driving me crazier than a dog in a hubcap factory." He paused. "No offense intended."

Precious yipped, obviously offended.

"A wedding?" Cella repeated. Her demeanor abruptly changed. "I adore weddings. Can I come?"

"Of course you're invited," Bubba said impatiently. "I done sent you an invitation last week. Mebe you ain't got it yet. Jesus Christ is invited, too. Also Thelda. Wouldn't be a gathering without you folks."

Cella clapped her hands together.

"Dr. Watson."

She did a little jig. "I get to go to a wedding. I get to go to a wedding. I get to go to a wedding. Will there be a reception? With jumbo shrimp and cocktail weenies?" Her manner instantly turned serious. She stopped dancing to say, "I would *never* go to a reception without cocktail weenies." She glowered at him. "Swear there will be cocktail weenies."

"They ain't decided what they're serving at the reception," Bubba added sourly. "There was talk of caviar and macaroni and cheese. Not together, I hope. I would think there would have to be cocktail weenies.""

Cella smiled again. She resumed dancing.

"Dr. Watson."

"Okay, David," Bubba said to Cella. "Cain't you just go back to being Sherlock Holmes?"

Cella stared at Bubba. "I was never Sherlock Holmes. I was Mamie Eisenhower. Then I was Pocahontas in another life. I might have been kidnapped by aliens once. I'm not sure." She leaned in to whisper into Bubba's ear. "I think they did something to my brain."

"Dr. Watson!"

Bubba turned his head to look at the other person who was talking and saw the man in the seersucker suit with the scar on his face. The one who wanted an induction motor and to make sure relatives of Thomas Edison weren't there to swipe his patents related to electric currency. Who was that? Nikola Tesla?

Nikola winked at Bubba and leaned in toward him. "Dr. Watson, psst. It's me."

Bubba glanced at Cella who was still dancing a jig, although it had transmogrified into an electric glide. "Oh, carp, I mean, crap, I mean carp. Sorry, ma'am, I thought you were someone else."

Cella froze. "Does this mean I'm not invited to the wedding?"

"Uh," Bubba said. "No, you can come. I'll get the details to you later. Cella, right?"

"Cella Montague LaPierre Mitchell Blankenship," Cella said haughtily. "Get it right, or I won't bring a gift. Don't forget the cocktail weenies."

"Yes, ma'am," Bubba said obediently. He watched as

she danced away and then turned back to David Beathard. "Dang. I dint recognize you, David."

"Sherlock," David said. "Watson, I wouldn't have expected you to recognize me whilst in disguise. I am, after all, a master at the art of illusion and concealment."

Bubba inclined toward David in order to see the makeup better. "How did you do the nose and the scar?"

"Those people with the movie company were highly informative," David whispered confidentially. "There was one makeup girl who showed me pictures of herself dressed in a Lady Godiva outfit, not that there was much to it. She was wearing this wig with long silvery hair covering all the strategic spots. She told me she was going to a convention as a daisy this year with crystals glued to her body." He sighed. "What lucky glue."

"David," Bubba said, "don't you have a daughter not much younger than that makeup girl?"

"Silver wig," David explained, "no clothing. I'd have to be dead not to get that. I suppose you had to be there to appreciate it, Dr. Watson."

"Okay," Bubba said. "I talked to Willodean and Doc Goodjoint about the two deaths here."

"Murders," David corrected. He looked surreptitiously about and then tugged Bubba into a corner. "Remember I am still Nikola Tesla, famous inventor and eccentric Serbian American."

"You're David pretending to be Sherlock Holmes pretending to be Nikola Tesla," Bubba stated. "I ain't shore I kin follow this all the time, but I reckon I'll try."

"Good," David pronounced. "Try to remember to call me Nikola whilst I am in disguise. I cannot pretend to be a mad scientist if you call me David. Bwaha."

"I-uh-okay, Nikola."

"Walk with me, Watson," David said, pointing to the hallway. "I don't know why you brought the hound of the Baskervilles, but we'll adapt to it and possibly use the beast in the culmination of this quixotic conundrum."

Precious yipped sharply. Bubba blocked her with one foot as her sharp teeth were likely going for David's ankle. The dog knew when she had been insulted.

"Uh, Dav-Sher-uh, Nikola," Bubba said, "got any sardines around? I gotta hankering for some, mebe with chocolate poured over 'em."

Chapter Seven

Bubba and the Emergent Advent of Evil Intentions

Saturday, April 6th

To Bubba's abundant dismay, he didn't get sardines with chocolate sauce. He did, however, convince David to allow him to call him David instead of Nikola or Sherlock. "You see, you're really David here, and everyone knows you as David," Bubba reasoned. "Folks would be surprised if you wanted them to call you Sherlock once your gig as Nikola is up."

"By Zeus's electrical superconductors," David swore, "you're correct. Call me Nikola until I have undisguised myself. A truly intellectual man should keep to his masquerade no matter what the occurrence."

They walked down a long hallway. A man dressed in a hospital robe and ladybug slippers approached them and nodded genially. The antennas on the slippers bobbed in time with his slow shuffle. Precious moved as far away in the hallway as she could get from the bobbing slippers.

Once the man passed them, Bubba said, "So my contacts said one death was a heart attack and the other one was suicide. What makes you think they ain't just that?" It wasn't exactly what Bubba thought Dr. Watson would say, but it was as close as he was going to get being he wasn't British, a doctor, or cultured.

"The first victim, Mrs. Ingrid Ferryjig, was forty-two years old and in excellent physical health. The medical personnel performed a full physical examination upon her admittance to the Dogley Institute of Mental Well-Being." David glanced around. "This is what they do to all new patients upon her entrance. Personally, I think they're gouging the various medical insurances, but it's also a case of covering their bums. They wouldn't want a lawsuit to occur if a said individual died, and they were not thorough in their analysis."

Bubba frowned. "Why did they admit the lady?"

"Seasonal affective disorder, sometimes known as SAD," David said. He scratched at the fake scar on his cheek. A little edge peeled away, and Bubba resisted the urge to say, "Don't pick at that, you're making it worse."

"Some folks have something-like wrong with them, doesn't mean they don't have heart attacks." Bubba shook his head. "I would think forty-two was getting into the heart attack zone for a person. It's young, but it ain't unheard of."

"Key factors include family history, smoking, obesity, high cholesterol, high blood pressure, and blockage of the arteries. You see, Watson, a heart attack occurs when one of the oxygen-rich blood-filled arteries ceases to supply the heart. Coronary heart disease is the cause of heart attacks. What makes the artery become blocked is the curiosity." David glanced at Bubba curiously. "As a gentleman of medicine, you should know this already."

"You know my dad died of a heart attack, David." Bubba winced. "I mean, Nikola."

"Mrs. Ferryjig was a health food advocate. Her cholesterol level was exceptionally good. The levels of good cholesterol were high. The bad cholesterol numbers were low. She ran five miles four times a week. She weighed a mere one hundred ten pounds and was only five feet two inches tall. Her biggest problem was that she would break down and cry on a cloudy day. She would use an entire box of Kleenex in one sitting. It was most disconcerting. Gor Blimey."

"Sometimes there are factors folks don't know about," Bubba said. "A bad valve that ain't detected until after a soul is dead." His father's autopsy had revealed a lifetime of smoking, drinking, and eating fried foods had done him in; of course, no one was really surprised. Bubba himself could rarely resist fried food, but he also ate his fair share of veggies and forced himself to exercise several times a week, even if it was chasing a stranger with a metal detector and a shovel down the long drive that led to the main road. "Ifin you plant a tater, you get a tater," he added. Potatoes sounded good at the moment, covered with a chili sauce, parmesan cheese, and green olives.

"I'll grant you that, good man," David said. "All by itself, the death of Mrs. Ferryjig was not particularly doubtful. In fact, I was saddened by it initially but not suspicious. It was only after the second death that I began to look into it. All of Mrs. Ferryjig's medical records reflect that she was in supreme physical health. Her doctors must have been happy about that part. No family history of cardiac disease. No diabetes. She even had an EKG when she came into the facility."

"It's strange, all right," Bubba said, "but it ain't murder. Your docs here signed off on it."

"Then by process of deduction that means they are foolish and ill-bred or completely incompetent."

"Or mebe they don't want the hospital to have anyone in it that done got murdered," Bubba said and immediately regretted it.

"Remarkable process of reasoning, Watson," David proclaimed. "I had not considered that it could be a simple cover-up, which muddies the waters of indubitable investigation. We shall take that into account whilst we process all the myriad bits of information provided to us by the great human condition."

"Great," Bubba said, but he wasn't sure it was great because he didn't even want to venture a guess at what came next. "What about the other person who died?"

"Hurley Tanner," David said. "Mr. Tanner consumed barbiturates obtained from a source other than the hospital. He expired sometime in the early morning hours of the first of April."

"David, this ain't a belated April Fool's joke, is it?"

"Murder is never a joke, Watson!"

"Of course, it ain't," Bubba agreed. "You know I don't laugh at murder." He sighed and thought about cheese curds. Cheese curds suddenly sounded very good to him. Would a mental hospital have cheese curds in the cafeteria? Probably not. Deep-fried cheese curds with a ranch dressing dip and a side of cucumber relish. "What makes you think that Mr. Hurley Tanner did not commit suicide?"

"He was a recovering alcoholic," David said.

They reached an exterior door, and Bubba looked

outside. It had been a long afternoon and the sun was transcending into the area of evening. It would likely set in another hour or two. Precious made a hopeful canine sound as she pressed her long nose against the glass in the bottom of the door and created a nose print that wasn't going to be easily wiped away.

"Ain't shore ifin I see the distinction, Dav-er-Nikola," he said as he opened the door and let his dog outside. She trotted outside with a little prance in her step.

"Alcohol was his drug of choice. According to his brother, he never touched pills. The pills weren't from the hospital because the doctors testified to the sheriff that they weren't the same brand used in that regard. The only pills brought in with Hurley were antibiotics that he was finishing for a sinus infection, and those pills were accounted for."

Bubba thought about that and frowned. It wasn't exactly abnormal. An alcoholic man who he didn't know committed suicide by swallowing an overdose of barbiturates. However, the barbiturates weren't readily available from the hospital. Certainly, they had to have some kind of barbiturates around because it was that kind of hospital, but drugs like that were carefully monitored and kept under lock and key. Thus the man had gotten the pills from somewhere else.

The suicide had been investigated by Sheriff's Deputy Steve Simms, who wasn't exactly known for setting the woods on fire.

"Did this Hurley fella have visitors before he died?"

"His wife and daughter," David said, "who could have provided the pills. Or it was possible that the pills were acquired illegally. There is a booming business within the hospital of illegal chemical enhancers. Mostly marijuana. One can always tell when Ralph the Potman has been around by the number of people hitting up the vending machines in the middle of the night."

"What kind of place is this?" Bubba had a sneaking suspicion that Ralph the Potman was none other than Ralph Cedarbloom, Miz Adelia's cousin, who had a pot patch that he supplied Miz Adelia's mother with. Sadly, Miz Adelia's mother was dying from terminal cancer and used it as a painkiller. Ralph used the rest of the pot in his patch to make a living. The local authorities weren't exactly happy with him, but he hadn't yet been caught. Bubba would have thrown the DEA after Ralph but that would have made Miz Adelia readily unhappy, and Bubba couldn't stand the thought of taking the drug away from a dying woman, illegal or not.

"The people who are buying pot aren't here for chemical dependency, you daft halfpenny." David pointed toward the lawn where several people were playing lawn darts with foam missiles. They were a little hard to throw given that they weighed next to nothing. "There's quite a range here. Depression, schizophrenia, schizoaffective disorder, generalized panic disorder, which also can be generalized anxiety disorder. Disassociation disorders are common—" Bubba nearly snorted but bit his lip instead— "as well as bipolar, and I think we have two, no, three eating disorders. Of course, there are several people drying out here. Dogley is getting to be quite the destination facility for celebrities. The VIP suites are quite spiffy.

The shower has travertine tiles and multiple shower heads including one with a rain head on the ceiling."

"Were Hurley or Mrs. Ferryjig celebrities?" Bubba asked. He hadn't heard of them, but that didn't necessarily mean they weren't.

"Hurley is second generation oil man. Mrs. Ferryjig is the granddaughter of a very famous Hollywood director. They both inherited wealth."

Bubba shook his head. "I don't reckon I understand why you think them two were the product of foul play, David." How did a former postal employee afford to stay at Dogley, then? David was just that, but it was possible that there were things that Bubba didn't know about him.

"Nikola," David corrected.

"And I don't reckon I understand how you got to examine their medical records neither."

"That was simple, Watson," David said with imperious disregard, "I broke into the records department and took a look. It wasn't difficult. They write the passwords on the paper next to the computer. Horrific security in that regard."

They went out the door with Bubba wondering why getting buzzed into the front doors was a de facto security measure when someone could simply walk around to the side and come right through the open doors. They walked onto the lawn, and Bubba took in the spring air. It was still a pleasant day, albeit a strange day. He wasn't exactly concerned that people had been murdered. No, it was more likely this was an offshoot of David's latest persona.

Blake Landry hurried by them with a brief, "Hello." He added, "Can you believe I tripped coming from my car?" Bubba noticed that the man's shirt and jeans were a little dirty and immediately forgot about it as the social worker went inside.

Bubba glanced at David and hesitated. The reason Bubba had come to see David was because David had appeared scared earlier in the day. David took on a disguise to return and dig for clues to something he believed was wrong. But David still looked scared.

"What is it?" Bubba asked. "What's wrong?"

"I believe that—" the fractious British accent failed— "I'm being set up. You see I was the last person with both people. I played cards with Mrs. Ferryjig, and I had a rousing game of dominoes with Hurley. I was the last one with them, and they seemed very normal to me. In fact, I never would have thought Hurley apt to commit suicide. The doctors didn't explain the bruises on his upper arms that I saw later. Or the other bruises I noted."

Bubba tried to process all of that information. Being the last one to be with both people who died wouldn't mean much if their deaths truly were what they appeared to be. David wouldn't lie about how Hurley presented the evening before he committed suicide. However, there was something else that bothered Bubba. "How did you see bruises on Hurley's body?"

"Why, when I examined the corpse for clues, Watson," David said. The halfhearted British accent had returned. "It's what I wanted you for this morning, but you're so dratted busy with this wedding nonsense, I couldn't pry you away. Therefore, I beat feet back to the hospital and had a look at poor deceased Hurley myself. The bruises you see—" he put his hands on Bubba's biceps to demonstrate the location of the bruises— "were here and here."

Bubba looked down. David's hands were wrapped around Bubba's upper arms as if he was holding him in place.

"And there was this—" David paused to reach inside a pocket of the seersucker suit— "a few very sticky threads connected to the underside of one of Hurley's wrists, combined with some residual redness there." He produced a small plastic baggie.

Bubba leaned forward and looked at the threads. "That looks like duct tape," he said, touching the packet with a finger. The small plastic looked much more professional than the sandwich baggie he'd last used when he'd had a key piece of evidence.

"Very good, Watson. I have compared it to duct tape found in the handyman's shed. There is a dozen-roll package with one roll missing. It is the same color and consistency as this sample. I have examined it under a microscope and have determined it is so."

"Around his wrists," Bubba said. Duct tape was a handy piece of equipment to have around. He had duct tape in his truck. His mother had duct tape in several strategic locations in the mansion, but there would be some fierce argument about what her intention might be with such an item, especially if it was placed next to a shovel, a bag of lime, and an old rug. After all, his mother had once claimed to have buried Elgin Snoddy alive. Duct tape would have come in handily.

Precious trotted up to Bubba holding a foam lawn dart in her mouth. Several of the players cried out with protest. Bubba took the dart away from her and threw it back to the players. One picked up the dart with an index finger and thumb and watched with a disgusted expression as it dripped dog saliva. Precious tossed her ears back and presented Bubba with her back, clearly showing her displeasure with the rejection of her love offering.

Bubba thought about bruises, wrists, and duct tape.

"Finally, there's something terribly amiss," David said. He pulled an electric device from an interior jacket pocket. Bubba didn't know what it was, but it looked like a mini-sized computer about the size of a slender book. "This is my Motorola Xoom. It's an android tablet," he explained.

Bubba felt certain that neither Sherlock Holmes nor Nikola Tesla would have used a Motorola Xoom, but he wasn't going to point it out. While David was fiddling with the tablet, he peripherally noticed patients streaming inside. They appeared to be in a hurry to get somewhere.

"It's got both apps for Nook and Kindle," David pointed out as he pushed the button on the back of the device. The front lit up, and he swiped his finger across it. He turned it so that Bubba could see the screen. It looked like a very large android phone screen. The background had the Droid figure on it. There were a series of apps on the screen that David could access if he so desired. He tapped on one that looked like a globe.

"This one is an Internet browser." Immediately, Google appeared on the screen. Bubba brightened. He knew what Google was; he had used it before. It wasn't so bad, although he and computers tended to have a volatile relationship. They broke, and he didn't like it. Or possibly it was that he broke them, and they didn't like that. It wasn't really his fault that he tended to be fumble fingered with delicate instruments. Cell phones fell into the same category, and Bubba had no reason to think that tablets wouldn't be included.

David tapped a few more times. "I opened this on Wednesday morning, and it was already opened to a page. I had left it in my room and hadn't used it for a day or so. It was on the charger, but someone opened it and did a few searches."

Bubba shrugged. It was a hospital with people constantly coming and going for all kinds of reason. David was fortunate that no one had stolen the device.

"Here's the first search I saw," David said and tapped once. The screen came up with a website on assisted suicide with the search phrase "how to make assisted suicide look like regular suicide" in the box at the top.

Bubba's stomach made a noise. The search might as well have been "how to make murder look like suicide."

"Then there was this one," David said and tapped again.

Bubba looked. The website was plain and innocuous. He leaned his head in to read the first paragraph. David took the tablet and swiped the screen with his thumb and middle finger, which made the entire image larger. He turned it back so Bubba could read it.

It didn't make much sense but then Bubba gathered the gist of it as he read "making murder appear like a heart attack." He read a few more lines and understood that the author also believed in the men in black and aluminum foil caps. Apparently there was a sort of device that used radioactive waves to induce what would look like a heart attack in a person.

"Does it tell when that search was done?" Bubba asked.

David tapped again. He looked at the screen and turned it so that Bubba could see the history of the search. "The day that Mrs. Ferryjig had her 'heart attack.'" He shook his head sadly.

"And the date on the suicide one?"

David tapped again and then swiped with the same finger. "Tuesday morning," he said.

Bubba glowered. This was sounding worse and worse. He hadn't found a dead body this time. This time, the dead bodies had found him. Actually, David had found the dead bodies and then come to find Bubba, which meant that Bubba was like a great honking dead body magnet.

"Of course, the problem being that I didn't do these searches," David said. "Not on my Xoom, not anywhere. Bob's your uncle!"

Bubba's stomach made a viciously uncomfortable noise. It sounded like two corn dogs vying for kennel space in there. "Sherlock dint do these searches?" he asked. Corn dogs sounded very good at the moment, especially if they were dipped in Italian dressing mixed with peanut butter.

"No. Not Sherlock. Not Nikola. Not David," David said, and it was at that moment that Bubba truly became concerned. "I did not do these searches. Someone came into my room the day before each death and did these searches. Then they left the Xoom where they had found it. It was a case of jiggery-pokery to be sure."

"Are there any other searches on there?"

"Yes, and it isn't really wondrous news."

Chapter Eight

Bubba and the Mounting Evidence of Wrongdoing

Saturday, April 6th

"Kin you erase those searches?" Bubba asked.

"I could, but it's proof of something I dare not speak aloud. I would be totally gobsmacked."

"You already spoke it aloud. Someone's dropping a dime on you. Any minute and there'll be an anonymous telephone call that tells Sheriff John that them deaths aren't really what they think they are, that you were the last one with these folks, and then they'll start searching for stuff. They'll find your Xoom, they'll look at the history, and wham, you're in jail with Newt Durley down the hall trying to kill the toilet in a way that no one on the cell block will ever forget." Bubba shuddered. His stomach made another impatient noise. "I've got to get something to eat, David. Kin we hit the cafeteria?"

"But of course, my good man," David said. He punched a button on the back of the Xoom and slid the entire device back into the interior jacket pocket. "It's taco night. If we don't hurry, we'll miss the black bean surprise."

Bubba turned toward the hospital's exterior door, and there was a muffled boom. His head swiveled back. It sounded like the quarry was blasting again, but it hadn't been worked for twelve or thirteen years.

David said, "It sounded like a sonic boom. You know

I was in Dallas when the space shuttle Columba broke up. It sounded like three sonic booms. Or perhaps it was four. We didn't know what it was until the news people on CNN told us later." He had lost his British accent again. "You never know what you have until it's too late."

"Does Howdy Doody have wooden balls?" Bubba asked rhetorically.

David tilted his head. "I would imagine that he did."

"Food," Bubba told David. "Then we'll talk to the head guy in charge."

•

Taco night was an unqualified success. Everyone liked tacos. The sauce in the hamburger was just right. The tomatoes and lettuce were fresh. The cheese was cheddar and shredded. The shells were crisp and crumbled just the way Bubba liked them.

When he was done eating, he asked to borrow David's cellphone. He wanted to call Willodean and his mother to make sure they weren't worrying about him. (Willodean had given him a cellphone. It was a very nice one. It even had an app on it that was a flashlight, although it drained the battery dead in under two minutes. It was in his nightstand drawer because he often forgot to bring it with him. He also forgot to charge it which made it difficult to use when he did remember to bring it with him.) Furthermore, he wanted to tell Willodean that they might need to look into the deaths a little more. It seemed unlikely that anyone could really make someone appear to have a heart attack, but it wasn't unheard of to attempt to make a murdered person appear to have committed suicide.

It was most likely that someone was yanking David's neurotic little chains in a perverse manner.

David shoved a half of a taco into his mouth while reaching into his seersucker suit for the phone. He produced it and slid it over to Bubba. (How many electronic devices did David have on his person? Only God and David knew.)

Bubba took a whole minute to figure out how to turn on the cellphone. He would have asked David, but the other man was deep in conversation with a woman wearing a red silk robe and a matching headband. It took Bubba another minute to figure out that David was attempting to flirt with the woman but failing miserably because the fortysomething woman wasn't interested in how David could deduce her occupation and habits. It seemed odd that David was in the pursuit of female companionship while being framed, but possibly that was the way he compartmentalized.

Finally, Bubba punched in Willodean's cellphone number and put the phone to his ear. He didn't hear anything. He pulled it away and looked at it. He tried it again. Nothing.

"Cellphone coverage in this area is sketchy at best," a man across the table said.

"It ain't getting anything," Bubba complained.

The man shrugged. He pulled out a cellphone from his pocket. He was somewhat normal in appearance with a plain t-shirt, plain jeans, and a bland expression on his face. (Normal was something Bubba had learned was a sliding scale of epic proportion.) He punched and tapped. Ten seconds later, he said, "No signal. No surprise. Try out on the lawn. The north end. That's the end closest to the tower. I couldn't believe they only have one cellphone tower in this area. Every time there's a thunderstorm, we can't make calls. I can't make Facebook posts, and I certainly can't tweet. It's *horrible*."

Bubba bussed his own tray and wandered out to the north lawn with David's phone. Precious followed at a stroll. She'd gotten her fair share of hamburger. One of the chefs had come out to give her an unseasoned portion. The other patients had also oohhed and ahhed over the canine to the extent that she was about to bite the next hand that reached for her chin. Precious was unmistakably happy to escape with her master.

Bubba tried the phone again.

No signal. Bubba held it in the air and peered at the screen. No signal. He shook the phone. No signal. He went ten paces to the north. No signal. He went ten paces to the east. No signal. He did a little rainmaking dance that a Native American friend of Miz Demetrice's had taught him while they were protesting construction on a sacred site in Central Texas. No signal.

Abruptly, there was a muffled boom immediately followed by another one. Bubba glanced around. No space shuttles were apparent. But a few seconds later a cloud of blackness billowed up from the south, a mushroom cloud reminiscent of a nuclear blast.

"What the heck?" Bubba muttered. A few patients came out to see what was happening. A nurse followed.

They stared at the black smoke. The nurse tried her cellphone. She said, "Damn. No signal." She hurried back inside with a, "I'll use the landline to notify the authorities. Of what, I don't even want to guess."

Bubba eyed the smoke. He made a decision and turned toward the parking lot. He would get in the truck and go see what had just exploded.

"OH THANK all the gods of fashion and wedding design!" someone said as he stumbled out of the bushes to Bubba's right. It was Peyton the wedding planner, and his silk shirt was rumpled and torn. His slacks were dirty and ripped. He had part of a branch sticking through his hair. His makeup was askew.

"Peyton?" Bubba said unnecessarily.

"Bubba!" Peyton cried out unnecessarily. "The Charger got stuck just past the bridge. Did you know there's a cellphone tower that fell down? It's across the road. I mean, it's lying across the road. This would never happen in New York City. I mean, it's bad enough when you get a hot dog without mustard and relish. But this?"

"Did you go through the trees?"

"I have Gucci loafers on, man," Peyton said. "If I walk on the asphalt they'll need to be re-soled." He pulled the branch from his hair and tossed it. "Of course, it might be better than being chased by a horde of squirrels." He fanned himself with his hand. "I have no idea why the little rodents were so angry with me. I'm not into nuts except for almonds."

The downed cellphone tower explained why there weren't any signals. It also explained the first boom. He hadn't seen any smoke from that one.

Bubba sighed. There was always a time when he thought about coincidence and what that meant in relationship to what was happening. An overdose by drugs that a man didn't have wasn't a coincidence. Someone planting searches on a notepad wasn't coincidence. A muffled boom and then later someone saying that the cellphone tower was lying across the road weren't coincidences.

"Come on," Bubba said. Precious barked once, and Peyton shrugged.

Bubba found his truck without further ado. It even started up without having to do a special prayer. Peyton patted Precious on the head while he held onto the side of the door, muttering, "Aren't all vehicles supposed to have seatbelts?"

David showed up just as Bubba was backing out. Bubba stopped the truck, and David climbed in. It was a tight fit with three grown men and a Bassett hound on a bench seat, but Precious sprawled over David and Peyton's laps and stuck her head out the window.

"It dint come with seatbelts when it was made in 1954," Bubba said as he backed up. "Did you see anyone down by the cellphone tower?"

"There was a hunk of metal on the road," Peyton said. "No one was about. Did you hear that other boom?"

"There's the smoke," David said, pointing. The sun was on its last legs, but the billowing cloud was clear in the skies as it went upward. "I deduce that something is amiss. Possibly something has been blown up by means nefarious."

"The cellphone tower looked kind of blown up," Peyton said. "No one ever said Texas would be so exciting. Did you know your scar is coming off?" he asked David.

"Did you know your wings are smudged?" David said promptly.

"Urg," Peyton muttered and produced a compact with a mirror. "Good God, I look like a besmirched drag queen on the morning after."

"Peyton, why are you here?" Bubba asked.

"Your mother and Willodean's mother decided on the bridesmaids' dresses. I just wanted to run it past you," he replied, dabbing at his eyes with a silk handkerchief he had produced from nothingness. "And I won't mention that Miz Demetrice and Miz Celestine...now you've got me calling them with the southern honorific...were discussing whether they could shoot the nose hairs off a denuded cicada at fifty feet. They were drinking glasses of wine like they were Kool-Aid, and Miz Demetrice was talking about a very special gun she'd been saving for a rainy day." He waved his hands briefly, and the handkerchief dropped to his lap. "Not that there's any rain about."

"Yeah, well, Ma has a liking for all things NRA," Bubba said.

"She probably meant the Bergmann 1986 pistol she recently acquired," David said. "It has a complete lack of any mechanical system of ejection. One hopes that the fired shell bounces off the next bullet. Sometimes it's a complete balls up and jams the mechanism."

"Ma showed it to you?"

"Typical breakfast conversation," David said. "Look, there's the cellphone tower!"

Bubba pulled to a stop, turned the ignition off, and all of them got out. Precious scampered down the side of the Chevy in a controlled fall as she scrambled for purchase. She wasn't going to miss anything if she could help it. Food might be involved.

Bubba walked off the road and toward the base of the tower. It had fallen from a high point on the top of the cliffs. He looked at the tangled mess of metal and scorch marks. He almost wished his mother was present. She had an unofficial degree and a very special interest in munitions, and would have much to say on the matter. He glanced up the hill.

It was only a guess that the cellphone tower hadn't been meant to fall on the road. It could have easily fallen in the other direction. But there was no doubt in Bubba's mind that it had been meant to be destroyed, or at the very least disabled. Of course, blowing it up would likely do that. Someone had deliberately weakened the supports so that it would tumble in a certain direction when whatever had been done to it had been done.

Bubba clambered his way back to the road, and Peyton had made his way around the downed tower. The wedding planner was extracting a case from the trunk of the rented Charger. "I've got to fix this mess," he said as he propped it on the car and unclipped the fasteners. Inside was a makeup kit with a lighted mirror. Even David was seemingly impressed.

"Can you do disguises?" David asked.

"I can do Tammy Faye Bakker," Peyton said. "I can do Snooki. Even Lady Gaga isn't beyond my reach."

David nodded with apparent admiration.

"Let's go see what the smoke is from," Bubba said, working his way across the wreckage. He had a very good idea of what it was, and it made his stomach clench up. On one hand he was glad that he was on this side of the Sturgis River, but on the other hand, if he was correct, then it was going to be a long night. Likely Miz Demetrice and Willodean would be sending in the Army in the morning once they figured out where he was.

Bubba frowned. He hadn't told anyone, had he? No, on the way out the Snoddy Mansion's door he had said he was on his way to the insane asylum and to et some pickles. Given the way that he had tossed the statement over his shoulder, it was likely that both Miz Demetrice and Celestine would have thought he was joking.

The biggest problem wasn't that no one knew where he was at, but that someone had blown up both a cellphone tower, and a...

"The explosion caused an avalanche," David said from behind him. They stopped in the road as they stared at the narrow bridge and the ravine's cliffs that had disintegrated into a mass of rocks and debris. It had missed most of the bridge, but it blocked everything else. The roiling heap covered the road and most of the sides of the road. The other side was the Sturgis River, and the river was washing the muck away.

"No one's driving back that way," Peyton said. He

held his cellphone in his hand. "I don't have a signal. I suppose it's because of the tower that I almost ran over. What was this? An earthquake that caused a gas line to explode? That's the reason I don't live in California, you know."

"It wasn't an earthquake," Bubba said. Some of the trees on top of the ridge were still smoking. "Ain't no gas mains come out this way."

Peyton crossed his arms over his chest. "Well great googly woogly, then what? I cannot imagine what would cause this."

"I reckon someone doesn't want anyone to leave," Bubba said. It was said matter-of-factly as if Bubba was discussing the mild weather they were having. He frowned and thought about something insidious. "Peyton, how did you know where I was?"

"You said you were going to the insane asylum, and that Lloyd Goshorn told me this was the only one about. Then I used my GPS. Voila, I'm here, and here is all atwitter."

David's mouth opened and then shut.

"Surely there's another road," Peyton said.

"There's not another road," Bubba said, "and don't call me Shirley." There was one road into the hospital's property. It was at the top of a mesa, and the only way someone might get back out at that point was a dirt bike and a lot of luck. The river cut off one side. The deep canyon cut off the other side. There were cliffs on the northern side. The southern side had just been taken out. Bubba supposed there were a few trails, but he didn't feel like looking for them on the verge of the sun going down.

Peyton looked at the great lump of dirt and trees and then glanced back toward where his car was parked. "I just missed being in that," he said. "And there's no cell phone coverage or any way out?"

"The hospital's got landlines," Bubba said. "But ifin I was someone who went to the trouble of blowing up such, I would have thought of that, too. Bet there's a big junction box about." He glanced up at the telephone poles. His eyes followed them as they followed the road, down to the edge of the river and crossed it to one side of the narrow bridge, where they then encountered the same tremendous pile of debris. "I reckon that probably took care of it, too."

"What about people with 3G or 4G?" David asked.

"They need a cellphone tower," Peyton answered.

"This explains the searches about explosive devices," Bubba said. Those were the searches that had really bothered David.

"I daresay it does," David agreed, but his voice was dull. "Perhaps we should look at my Xoom again and get an idea of what else is planned for this fun-filled weekend."

"What searches?" Peyton asked.

Bubba sighed and looked at Peyton. "I suspect that some murderous soul is trying to kill folks out here and then blame it on David here. Part of that evidence is a history of searches on his Motorola Xoom. But you done forgot we don't have the Internet, and I ain't sure if you can see the history without being able to log on."

Peyton considered David with careful eyes. "How do

you know he didn't do this?" Peyton clearly meant David.

"I've known David for a bit of time, and besides, he was with me during both the blasts."

"He could have had a...timer or a device in his pocket with a button," Peyton said. His hands fluttered in the air. "Goodness, we could be in the company of a murderer."

"Pegram County seems to attract them lately," Bubba said with no little amount of bitter irony.

Chapter Nine

Bubba and the Ten Little Loonies Plus a Wedding Planner

Saturday, April 6th

There wasn't much to be done, so Bubba, Peyton, David, and Precious got back in the truck and drove back to the hospital. While he was parking the truck between the same Mercedes and Rabbit, Bubba noticed that the orange Pinto was in residence. Blake had, in fact, stumbled past them.

Great. They had a social worker, too. Bubba would have preferred a law enforcement official with a gun and possibly a shovel, but beggars couldn't be choosers.

"Who's in charge now, David?" Bubba asked.

"Dr. Adair," David said. "He's the head psychiatrist. I would have said the hospital administrator, but he's in South Padre right now sitting on a beach drinking a tequila sunrise."

"I wish I was in South Padre," Peyton said. "I could use a tan. You don't have a tanning bed around, do you? I would think psychiatric patients would benefit from a good tanning bed, even if they get skin cancer later on."

"It's called the sun," Bubba said. "It'll be out tomorrow." He turned off the engine, and everyone climbed out. Oddly all the lights in the hospital were still on. "There's a generator here," he said to himself more than anyone else.

"Five," David said. "This is Texas, Bubba. One never knows when a tornado will strike. Occasionally a hurricane wanders up this way, or the remnants of one. It is a hospital, after all."

"All right," Bubba said in his best authoritative voice. "We need to talk to Dr. Adair. We need to find out if the phones work. Barring that, we need to find out if anyone is getting a signal by any random act of God."

"We should probably do a head count," David said. "Just to ensure who's about."

They should probably lock everyone in the dayroom simply because it would be more difficult to do anything to anyone else if they were all together at the same time. But then what would they do if people had to go to the bathroom? What if one person got paired with a killer, and only one person came back? Then they would have to pee in groups of three or more. Just in case.

Bubba grimaced. It was starting to sound like an Agatha Christie screenplay.

"Buuuubba!" someone called, and Bubba turned to see a man in a sheet walking toward them. He was in his early forties and balding. He smiled beatifically at them. "It is gooood that you're heeeere."

"Jesus Christ," Bubba said.

"There's no need to swear at the man," Peyton said. "This is a place with people with mental problems, you know."

"No, this is Jesus," Bubba said to Peyton. David and Jesus bumped fists, tapped the top with one, repeated with the other, and did a finger wiggle as the hands flew away. There was an apparently secret, mentally ill handshake. Bubba wasn't sure if he should be glad or jealous he didn't know it.

"Jesus, this is Peyton. He plans weddings. He's planning our wedding. I mean, mine and Willodean's wedding. You do know, you and I aren't getting married, Jesus, don't you?" Bubba glanced around. They went in the side door as the patients obviously knew that they could bypass Cybil the Chipper when they so desired.

"Praise yoooou," Jesus said to Peyton. "Weeee encourage all on our Eeeearthly plane." He smiled again. "Nice eyeliner."

"Jesus Christ," Peyton said with a perfectly straight face, or as straight as he could manage to get it. "Sherlock Holmes. Nikola Tesla. Is anyone else famous here?"

"There's a movie star here," David said. "I think she's in her room right now. She likes to eat food that's shipped in. Lots of beta-carotene and protein stuff." He looked over his shoulder, evidently to ensure no one was listening. "She's got a little weed problem."

"So whaaaat was the smoooke from?" Jesus asked. "The movie staaaar was iiiin her roooom so iiiit wasn't heeeer stoking up a doooobie."

"Since you're Jesus Christ, shouldn't you already know?" Peyton asked.

"Suuuurely I knoooow, but do yoooou know?"

"Big boom," Bubba said because he didn't want to listen to the meandering direction of the conversation. "How many people are here?"

David thought about it. "There's Jesus, Thelda, Abel, Dr. Adair, Nurse Rachet-er-I mean, Nurse Ratchley. Let's see. Cybil's about. Blake, also. There's Tandy and

Leeza, too."

"Then there's you, David."

"Dooon't forget Siiiinclair," Jesus said helpfully.

"No, Sinclair left to spend the weekend with his kids," David corrected. "That's ten, plus Bubba and Peyton."

Bubba blinked. Ten. Then he added himself and Peyton, who weren't supposed to be there. Then he took them away. Ten. That couldn't be correct. He'd wandered in and Peyton had followed him, presumably to ask about some wedding detail but more likely to get away from Miz Demetrice who had both a gun and alcohol. Who knew what Celestine had? A bazooka sprang to mind except he didn't know where his future mother-in-law might be hiding a weapon of that caliber.

He shook his head.

They ended up in the dayroom, and Bubba was surprised to see how empty it was. People had drifted away while he was busy thinking about other things. They must have gotten out before the cellphone tower had come down. There had been an earlier mad rush (no pun intended) that Bubba had noticed peripherally.

Mebe.

Bubba scanned the room. There was Jesus Christ who stopped to chat with Thelda, who had added a fifth sweater. David hovered in the background studying everything diligently. Cybil was helping the lady in the silk robe with a crossword puzzle. The lady in the robe was probably Leeza or Tandy. Blake Landry the social worker was sitting with the man in the t-shirt and jeans. That was probably Abel. A man in a long white jacket wandered in and looked at everyone. The nurse Bubba had seen earlier was at his side. Those were probably Dr. Adair and Nurse Ratchley. Finally in walked a woman in jeans and a t-shirt that said "The only thing we have to fear is fear itself." Below that in smaller letters was "And spiders, giant, radioactive, alien spiders."

Bubba looked closely at her. He had seen her before and finally it dawned on him that it was Tandy North, the star of *The Deadly Dead*, a pot-smoking fiend if ever he'd seen one. She nodded at him and lit up a Marlboro, clearly a pot substitute for the moment. So the lady in the robe was Leeza.

Dr. Adair said, "No smoking in here, Ms. North."

Tandy rolled her eyes and went for the door.

Peyton made a squealing sound. Startled, Bubba looked around. He would have sworn the wedding planner had been poked in the tush with an electrified cattle prod. "That's Tandy North!" Peyton said in a high singsong voice. "She was in *Bubble People*. Squee. I might tinkle."

Tandy glanced back and saw Bubba. "Dude," she said. Her eyes lowered to Precious. "And dude's dog."

"Tandy," Bubba said, almost expecting her to tell him to mind his mark. "You still got all those cellphones?"

Tandy shrugged. From her front jeans pockets she pulled out a Blackberry, an iPhone, and an Android. Then she dug in a back pocket and found a Samsung Galaxy. She carefully managed them while looking expectantly at Bubba.

"You getting a signal on any of those?"

Tandy puffed while she checked each phone. The cigarette moved expertly to one side of her mouth and she said, "Nope. Nada. Zilcharino." She replaced all the phones in their proper locations while she smoked.

"What's all this?" Dr. Adair asked as he walked up. A tall man with gray hair, he was in his sixties and well-preserved with an orangish tan. He eyed Bubba like Bubba was a particularly noxious bug. "You're not a patient here. You need to leave. Visiting hours are over."

"He can't leave," David said.

"Of course he can leave. He simply goes the same way he came," Dr. Adair pronounced.

"No, he cannot," Peyton interjected. "There's a cellphone tower across the road and also someone blew up the cliff by the bridge."

"And you're not a patient either," Dr. Adair said to Peyton. "Although you probably should be."

"And what kind of attitude is that from a psychiatrist?" Peyton complained. "I'm *metrosexual*. Does no one in Texas understand the meaning of that?"

"Do you often enjoy wearing women's clothing?" Dr. Adair asked meaningfully.

"Sometimes I wear my girlfriend's thongs," Peyton said. "She gets them from Victoria's Secret. It's fun. It tickles a little. I highly recommend it."

Dr. Adair winced. Bubba winced after he thought about where the string part of the thong went. Then he wondered if Willodean ever had bought a thong from Victoria's Secret. Of course, if she did, then...

Bubba shook his head violently. "I suspect

someone's up to no good. Do the phone lines work?"

Nurse Ratchley shook her head. She was in her thirties and had blonde hair with blue eyes. "When we saw the smoke, I tried to call," she said. "There was just dead air. No buzzing for the line or anything."

"Have you tried emailing the police?" Tandy asked. "Or maybe the fire department?"

"The Internet is connected to the phone lines here," Dr. Adair said. A worried expression began to form on his face. "What makes you say someone's up to something?"

"My name's Bubba, Bubba Snoddy," Bubba said.

"Bubba Snoddy," Dr. Adair repeated. A certain look of understanding came over his face. "Oh. Yes, I've heard of you. Maybe we'll have an interesting conversation about that later. Do you often have feelings of persecution?"

"There's only the one road in to the hospital," Bubba said. "And it ain't feelings ifin someone's actually persecuting you."

Dr. Adair glanced over his shoulder. "That's right. We had a problem a few years ago when the Sturgis River went above the flood stage. No one could drive across the bridge, but it subsided within two days, and the engineers checked out the structure of the bridge before we used it again. You say there's a cellphone tower down?"

"Someone blew it up," Bubba said. The doctor didn't look convinced so Bubba added, "Ka-boom."

"That's correct, Dr. Watson," David said. "And based on the smell of explosives in the air, someone also blew up the cliffs beside the road causing a massive rockslide. The road is blocked, and no one will be driving in or out for some time. It's probable we won't be missed for a few days." He waited for a long moment and said, "Dah-dah-daaaah."

"David?" Jesus said.

David's shoulders straightened. He yanked the fake scar from his cheek and then removed the fake nose. Bubba winced as some of David's actual skin went along with it. "I am truly Sherlock Holmes, master investigator. I shall determine the outcome of this mysterious scenario."

"Note to self," Dr. Adair said, "check Mr. Beathard's medications."

Precious bumped against Bubba's leg.

Dr. Adair said, "Is that a therapy dog? Because it shouldn't be in here otherwise."

"Where do you expect us to go?" Bubba asked. "Ain't like there's a hotel next door. Trapped here with some fella or gal who decided to blow stuff up." He thought about it. "Although that's something else that happens a lot in Pegram County for some reason." He sighed. "It dint used to be like this. It was a rightly peaceful county."

Tandy took the Marlboro out of her mouth and blew a smoke ring. Then she blew a smaller one through the larger one. "Are you saying someone trapped us here on purpose?" she asked with more aplomb than Bubba would have thought a movie star would have at the moment.

"Madam," David said with his imperious British

accent back in place, "the evil perpetrator has already struck twice."

"No one's been murdered," Dr. Adair protested.

"What about Mrs. Ferryjig and Hurley Tanner?" Bubba asked.

Dr. Adair paused to glare at Bubba. "A heart attack and a suicide. Both regrettable but hardly homicidal. I looked at both of their bodies. I can say categorically that no foul play was involved."

"What about the bruises on Hurley's arms and the evidence of him being restrained?" David asked. "There is substantiation to suggest that his suicide was never just suicide." He dug into a pocket and withdrew a badly wrinkled deerstalker cap. He straightened it out and put it carefully on his head. The calabash pipe came out of another pocket, and he inserted the end into his mouth.

"No smoking in here," Dr. Adair asserted with a meaningful glance at Tandy who blew another smoke ring in response. He sighed deeply. "I will go and see about the phones. There must be one working in here somewhere." He walked out of the dayroom without looking back.

Nurse Ratchley watched him go. "Like the woman with a BS in nursing wouldn't have thought of that," she muttered. "David, how would you know that Mr. Tanner had bruises on his arms?"

"I looked at his mortal remnants of course, and call me Sherlock. Mr. Holmes would do, but seeing as you've already seen my arse, formality would be wasted."

Leeza and Jesus both tittered.

Nurse Ratchley said, "He had a tetanus shot!"

"It's true. I stepped on a particular virulent and vile nail," David explained. "All this blasted construction about."

Bubba thought of something. "Only twelve of us. What about the cooks?"

"They left in the hospital's helicopter," Tandy said. "Right after dinner. They're going to catch a plane to South Padre from Dallas. Didn't you see it take off?"

"How did you get in touch with the helicopter?" Bubba asked.

"It was all arranged earlier. After they dropped those people off, the helicopter is going in for routine engine maintenance, so it isn't coming back for a week," Nurse Ratchley said. "I *knew* I was going to be sincerely sorry I got picked to stay this time."

"Got picked," Bubba said. He was sincerely sorry, too. He looked around. There was likely a statue of ten little Indians about. Someone was due to make an anonymous announcement of why they had all been chosen, except possibly Bubba and Peyton who were collateral damage. Then people were going to start disappearing one by one. He watched AMC too much. "How did you get picked?"

"We drew straws," the nurse replied.

"I believe I see where you're going with this, Watson," David said. "Your conjecture is that Nurse Ratchley, as well as the rest of us, were somehow chosen."

"We need to take a look at that Xoom again," Bubba said.

Blake the social worker stepped closer. "I think this is enough of this line. There's no need to be quite so encouraging. There's no evidence of murder nor is there any evidence that murders will be committed here. Everyone needs to go back to doing whatever they were doing and relax."

Bubba huffed. David handed him his Xoom and said, "I need to go to the little detective's room. All this excitement makes the world go round...and round. Then some more."

Tandy puffed on her cig as she went outside. Abel and Peyton followed her while Leeza went back to her crossword puzzle. Jesus and Thelda got into a conversation involving Biblical verses and Shakespearean insults. Cybil and Blake walked out while Cybil said, "I swear, I can't make up the stuff that goes on around here. Bless their little hearts."

Nurse Ratchley gave everyone remaining a long look. She finally looked at Bubba. "We have some rooms. We can put you up for the night with no problem no matter what the doc has to say. Then tomorrow we can get the bobcat from the shed and put that cellphone tower on the side of the road. Someone here's got to know how to operate it."

"The bobcat isn't going to make a dent in the avalanche," Bubba said.

"Maybe not, but it's a start." The nurse nodded. "One of us could walk out to the nearest place. It's several miles but doable."

Bubba couldn't quite understand why no one except David was really taking the whole murder business seriously. It was reminiscent of how things worked whenever he found a dead body. They didn't believe it until it was too late, and the murderer was looming over them. Then they would be all like, "Oh…"

Not even Brownie Snoddy armed with a homemade Taser and jury-rigged booby trap could save them.

Precious nudged his leg again because she had been forgotten. Bubba knelt to scratch her behind the jowls. "No one counted you, girl, did they?" he murmured. "Silly of them not to count the best looking lady in the whole hospital, right?"

Precious leaned into the scratches until she apparently remembered that she hadn't played hard to get for hours. She leaned away and put her prodigious nose into the air. *I'm not that easy, mister.*

"Who's the best dog a fella ever had?" Bubba crooned.

Not me. I will pee on your fishing poles, all three of them.

"Who wants to go outside to the truck with me to get a few Milk-Bones out of a bag in the glove box?"

Not me. Wait. Milk-Bones? Maybe. No, absolutely not. Precious turned her nose further away. It twitched once. Then it twitched again. *Milk-Bones? Real Milk-Bones? Not the cheap kind that Miz Adelia bought by mistake? No generic Milk-Bones for this dog!*

Precious forgot that she was supposed to be put out and bayed energetically. Bubba led the way, happy that someone could be pleased for the moment.

•

Bubba came back in the front way and was buzzed

inside by Cybil. Precious followed at his heels, content with the knowledge that she had consumed three Milk-Bones when she normally could only mooch two at a sitting.

Cybil nodded at Bubba before she hurried off, muttering something about having to do all the paperwork in the hospital herself, adding, "Useless Ulrics."

No one was in the dayroom. No one was in the hallway. Bubba turned around and opened the Xoom. He turned the device over and found the button. It took him a moment to realize he was supposed to press and hold. The screen came on with a little green lighted figure.

An abrupt soul-clenching shriek made his fingers slip. The scream hadn't ended by the time the Xoom hit the tiled floor and broke into about thirty pieces. "Crap," Bubba said. "I mean, carp."

Then he realized the shriek had stopped and that someone was likely in some kind of trouble.

Bubba ran. It took him thirty seconds to find Cybil holding her hands over her mouth and biting her index finger to keep from screaming again. He followed her horrified eyes into the office to see Blake, what was his last name?, sitting at a large mahogany desk. His chair matched the desk. Pictures of pastoral scenes lined the walls. However, Blake wasn't looking at his desk or the pretty pictures. He was staring at the ceiling with sightless eyes, and his tongue slightly protruded from his mouth. That was caused by the fact that someone had strangled him with a jury-rigged garrote made with a length of computer wire and a steel ruler. The garrote had been left around his neck.

Several other people appeared behind Cybil, including David. They peered inside the office and made noises ranging from gasps to appalled moans.

Bubba couldn't help but notice two things. One was that everyone was accounted for. There were eleven people there and one dead body. Two was that he hadn't discovered this dead body, a fact for which he was profoundly grateful.

Chapter Ten

Bubba and Some Investigating Goin' On

Saturday, April 6th

Dr. Adair was the one who first regained his equanimity. He stepped around Bubba and went to Blake's very still form with a composure that most people would have envied. He carefully put the index and middle fingers of his right hand on the pulse point of Blake's left wrist. Without saying anything else, he stepped back, rubbed his chin with the same hand he'd checked the social worker's pulse with, and grabbed a sweater from a brass coat tree. He spread it out with both hands and covered the dead man's body.

Finally he looked at the crowd with his eyes coming to rest on Bubba. "You said that someone was up to something bad."

"What I said was that I thought someone was up to no good," Bubba corrected. "This—" he pointed at the covered body— "ain't good. You might even say it's no good." He made himself look around at everything but the concealed corpse. Blake had an infinity for knickknacks. There were dozens and in collections, too. He had globes, statues, and doodads. There were a lot of tiny oil derricks as if he had been haunting local tourist stands too much. There were Georgia peaches in all forms. There was a miniature Eiffel Tower. Bubba couldn't put it all together in his head. There was no rhyme or reason.

David interjected, "I deduce that Blake Landry has likely been murdered. Strangled to death. Perhaps we should examine the ligature in detail."

"No one's looking at the ligature or anything else," Dr. Adair said. "That's for the police to do." He grimaced. "Once we get them in here."

"I walked down to the bridge," Tandy said. "They're right, you know. The cellphone tower's across the road in large chunkies. There's also a big rockslide just beside the bridge. No one's going anywhere unless they walk out of here."

Dr. Adair gently shooed everyone away from the office. He shut the door behind him. "Let's talk in the cafeteria. I think Leeza made cupcakes."

"Who can eat at a time like this?" Abel asked plaintively.

Jesus Christ said, "Iiii can eeeeat. Blessings oooon him whoooo maketh theeee cupcakes. Or her."

Thelda said, "Thou clouted swag-bellied joitheads!"

Nurse Ratchley said, "I don't think any of this is a good idea. You all don't pay me enough for this." She glanced around nervously. "I didn't think Bubba was right. I thought he was just messing with us. But this, this is murder. You don't accidentally fall into a garrote, and it self-strangles you. If there's just the lot of us, then that means…"

Bubba said, "I think we should go into the cafeteria, all of us, all at the same time."

Peyton looked around. "Am I getting this straight? There's a murderer in this hospital and since it's just the twelve of us, then…"

"Eleven," Bubba said plainly. "Eleven of us now."

"And it's dark outside now," David said. "No one's going anywhere. The moors are a deadly place at night, even if the hound of the Baskervilles is among us and seemingly calmed."

Precious whined lamentingly. It was a shame there wasn't a moor about.

"I reckon we can stand in the hallway and be talking about this situation," Bubba said, "or we can talk it out in the cafeteria with the bright lights on and all. And there's cupcakes."

"Chocolate zucchini carrot cupcakes," Leeza said, clutching her robe closely to her body. "I love to bake when I'm stressed, and you'll never know there's veggies in the recipe. I swear! Cupcakes will make you better." Her voice began to escalate in pitch. "Cupcakes can cure ANYTHING!"

"Come on people," Dr. Adair said, "let's do just that. I'll make coffee from Chef Thomas's special stash, and we can all just work this out."

"I get dibs on the cupcakes!" Jesus yelled and bolted toward the cafeteria. Everyone else followed.

●

"There were twelve cupcakes," Leeza whined. "I made twelve." She pointed at the silver cupcake tree sitting in the middle of the table. "Now there's only eleven."

"It's okay," Nurse Ratchley said gently, "cupcakes do not equal love, Leeza."

"But there were twelve," Leeza persisted. "Now there are eleven. There are eleven of us. What if someone wants two cupcakes? What if someone doesn't want a cupcake, and there's one left over?"

Precious yipped hopefully. Bubba muttered, "You cain't have chocolate. I have Milk-Bones."

Everyone had made it to the cafeteria and sat around the table closest to the buffets. They watched through the cafeteria windows while Dr. Adair made coffee, and in the case of Tandy, Darjeeling tea. "Two sugars," she called. "In fact, just dump it in until the spoon stands up straight."

Nurse Ratchley went to help the doctor.

"They're not going to drug that, are they?" Peyton whispered to Bubba. He had his compact out and was examining his makeup with interest. He touched the corner of his eye with the tip of his little finger. "I wonder if anyone here is planning on getting married in the near future."

"I don't reckon," Bubba said. He was thinking fiercely. What everyone was dancing around was that they were well and truly trapped with a murderer. The doctor didn't want to address anything about Mrs. Ferryjig or Hurley Tanner, and he probably wanted to ignore a rapidly cooling social worker, too.

He glanced out the window and saw that there was a light fog forming. A cold front had come through, and the air had rapidly cooled. The whitish fog clung to the ground and moved sluggishly. All they needed for the atmosphere to be complete was for Precious to start baying. Or perhaps someone could start telling a ghostly story about a haunted insane asylum.

"Iiii don't thiiiink I'm huuuungry now," Jesus

remarked in a regretful manner. "All thiiiis death cuuuurbs the Soooon of God's aaaappetite."

"I couldn't eat anything," Abel added. Bubba wondered why the man was at Dogley. He didn't know much about anyone except David. Thelda was a Shakespearean mystery complete with five competing sweaters and an affinity for poker. Jesus Christ had his holy persona, which he kept to and basically didn't waver from. (Bubba didn't think he even knew Jesus's real name, but he did know that Jesus liked to go commando under the sheet he habitually wore.) Cybil the Chipper-Hearted was simply a young woman who manned the receptionist desk at Dogley. She also helped with the thrift shop. Tandy was a chain-smoking, pothead movie star who had starred in two movies that Bubba knew about. One of them had been *The Deadly Dead*, in which Bubba had played a redneck zombie, which hadn't been much of a stretch for him. All Bubba knew about Leeza was that she wore a robe, made cupcakes, and didn't care to flirt with David. Then there was Peyton. Peyton was the wedding planner who liked his facial makeup and said he had a girlfriend named Ginger in New York City. That left Dr. Adair, supposedly a psychiatrist, and Nurse Ratchley, supposedly a nurse. Why they were supposedly was something that Bubba couldn't figure out.

When murder was rampant, everything seemed like it should be supposedly.

Everyone was *supposedly*. It really came down to the fact that if they were the only ones left in the Dogley Institute for Mental Well-Being, then one of them was a murderer. Supposedly.

Bubba had to suppress an urge to back into a corner until he could see where everyone else was located.

Dr. Adair carried in a tray with coffee cups galore. Nurse Ratchley followed with another tray. The pair passed out cups. The one cup with the tag of a teabag hanging from it went to Tandy.

"I don't think we need to get too upset," Dr. Adair said as he finished and offered the last cup to Nurse Ratchley. He didn't get any coffee for himself.

Ratchley put out a silver creamer and a matching sugar bowl before she collected her cup. Dr. Adair went on, "I will go over the hospital myself and ensure that no one else is about. Tomorrow we will undoubtedly be noticed missing, and the police will make their way to us."

"Thou craven, hell-hated harpy," Thelda proclaimed.

"Now, now, Thelda," Dr. Adair admonished, "that's no way to talk to me. I'm simply trying to help."

"What ifin the po-lice don't come tomorrow?" Bubba asked. He reached down to scratch Precious as she lay across his feet.

"What makes you say that?" Dr. Adair asked.

"That's a dang big avalanche out there," Bubba stated. "Ain't that easy to get through it. Shore they could send a helicopter in too, but they won't unless they know someone needs some urgent care. Ain't like Pegram County has a fleet of helicopters. They borrow one from Smith County. They're goin' to know about the downed phone line and prolly suspect the cellphone tower too, but they ain't goin' to worry until it's too

123

late."

"You don't call being murdered urgent?" Abel asked.

"I do, but how they goin' to know that?" Bubba tapped the table. "First they got to figure out we're out here. Anyone know about who's expecting them?"

"I'm divorced, and no one's expecting me," Dr. Adair said with deceptive composure. Bubba could tell by the twitching muscle in the doctor's forehead that he wasn't really composed.

Ratchley said, "I'm working the weekend. My husband will expect me to call, but I don't think he'll worry about it until tomorrow or even the day after. When I don't show up on Monday, he'll come looking."

David said, "No one's looking for me this weekend."

"Your brains are as dry as the remainder biscuit from a voyage," Thelda remarked in a matter-of-fact manner. Bubba took that to mean she wasn't expected either. However, for all he knew she could be the guest of honor at an inaugural ball.

"Not me either," Abel said.

"My mother will think I spent the night with my boyfriend," Cybil said. She was remarkably subdued. "The cellphone will just roll over to voicemail. My boyfriend will think I'm at Mom's. They won't think anything until tomorrow or Monday. Probably tomorrow evening. They'll call up here and figure out the lines are down. Then they'll wait a little longer."

Tandy squeezed her teabag with her fingers and put it on the table. "I'm down for twenty more days. No one will expect me until then. I'm not even supposed to have all my cellphones."

Peyton said, "Ginger will be calling, but she doesn't know where I'm at per se. Miz Demetrice and Miz Celestine know that I was running an errand. I suppose they'll miss Bubba before they miss me." He brightened. "Maybe Ginger will throw a fit at the police station in the city once she realizes I'm not returning messages or texts. That would be great for publicity."

"Willodean will worry to-*night*," Bubba said. "She'll know when I don't come home. She'll put out the word tomorrow. She might even do it late tonight. But the problem is that I dint tell no one where I was going. Well, I did tell them, but I don't think they will think I was serious. They ain't going to know where to start looking." He thought about it. "Peyton heard me. Peyton, did Ma and Miz Celestine hear me?"

"I think they were talking about guns," Peyton said.

"What does that mean?" Leeza asked. "That it could be tomorrow at the best case scenario? Or that it could be Monday at worst?"

Dr. Adair sighed and paced in front of the table. "There are no deliveries on Sunday. A few people might have visitors like Abel, Leeza, David, Thelda, and Tandy."

Bubba looked at them, and each of them shook their heads in turn. No one was expecting any visitors who might report to the police that the road was completely blocked off.

"Monday will be different," Dr. Adair said. "I'm sure they'll figure it out and then when they're at the avalanche we can yell across for them to drop off some detectives and such. Tuesday is when the rest of the staff is due to come back, and the construction crew is due to start on the northern wing. I'm not sure about them because they said probably Tuesday, Wednesday at the latest."

Bubba didn't think it would work out the way that Dr. Adair was figuring.

"So we all stay together," Ratchley said. "That way, no one gets hurt, right?"

"I've got a better suggestion," Tandy said. She pulled a package of Marlboros from somewhere. (Bubba thought her pockets must be bottomless with all of the phones and the pack of cigs in them.) She extracted a single smoke and lit it with a Bic disposable lighter while she put the pack back into a pocket with the other hand. Then the lighter vanished into another pocket. "We go to our rooms and lock the doors," she said, speaking around the cigarette. "All the rooms have bathrooms, so no problem. We've got water and toilets and beds and relative security. When the cavalry arrives, then we come out. Problem solved. Well, mostly solved."

"Who's got the keys?" Bubba asked.

Dr. Adair winced. "I've got a copy. So does Nurse Ratchley. So did Blake Landry. So do some of the doctors who are in South Padre, along with the hospital administrator."

"Mebe ifin we sleep in groups," Bubba said. "Nurse Ratchley, Tandy, Leeza, Cybil, and Thelda, for example."

"What happens when we have to go wee-wee?" Leeza asked. "We could be locked in a room with a diabolical killer."

"I want to sleep with Bubba," Peyton said and then grimaced. "I mean in the same room as Bubba. I trust Bubba."

Bubba wanted to say some nasty words. It certainly hadn't been his intention to come out to Dogley and get embroiled in a mystery worthy of Pegram County's venerated infamy. People had tried to kill Bubba before, and he had come out ahead. The problem wasn't that he was going to get killed by someone, but that Willodean was going to kill him once she found out. Even if he had already been killed. She might bring him back from the dead in order to kill him. "I'll walk out," Bubba said. "I don't need nothing but a flashlight with some extra batteries. I should make it in a few hours to a phone. Folks with digging machines will be here by morning."

David nodded. "We will need help sooner rather than later. Look, the blasted fog comes rolling in." He indicated the windows.

"I've never seen fog like that," Cybil said. "It reminds me of the night of the Foggy Mountain murders. Old man Hovious stayed up on the top of the mountain with his wife and his six children. One night a terrible fog moved in, and no one ever left the mountain alive. No one knows what happened."

"Old man Hovious had a stroke. Then when his wife was hurrying to call for the ambulance, she tripped on the stairs in the fog and broke her neck. There weren't any children." Bubba sighed. There was the ghost story, but it wasn't about a haunted insane asylum like he'd expected.

"What if Bubba is the murderer?" Abel asked. "I

don't think any of us can go anywhere. If one is the murderer, they could double back and do us in, one by one. Or worse they could escape." He considered. "Or would that be better?"

Dr. Adair glowered. "It's a good point. Best to stay here, Bubba."

"I ain't a murderer," Bubba said. "I only came up because David asked for he'p. When a friend asks for he'p, then you give a friend he'p. I ain't got no cause to murder no one up here."

"Sherlock," David corrected. "If we are trapped in this place, then we must ferret out the true perpetrator. Each of us must give an accounting of their actions during the time we last saw each other until the time Blake's corpse was discovered."

"I'm not saying anything," Peyton said. "I know my rights, and besides, I have nothing to do with this hospital. I'm a wedding planner, for God's sake. I didn't plan that poor man to death. Someone strangled him. Bubba, tell them."

"Someone strangled that poor man," Bubba said obediently.

"That I'm a wedding planner," Peyton said with obvious irritation.

"And yes, he's a wedding planner."

"I smoked on the patio," Tandy said. "I went to the bathroom. I listened to my iPod for a while. I looked at two scripts, which were both crap by the way. You star in one zombie movie and then everyone wants you to be in a zombie movie. Then I walked down to see the cellphone tower and the avalanche."

"Iiii was iiiin deep praaaayer," Jesus said. "The soooon of the hooooly one iiiis very buuuusy."

Thelda said, "Thou slobbering crook-pated foot-lickers." Bubba interpreted that as the fact that she had been busy doing whatever it was that she liked to do and not murdering Blake Landry, but he could have been wrong. For all he knew, her Shakespearean insult could have been a full confession to any and all murders committed in the immediate vicinity.

Dr. Adair said, "I went to my office. I did paperwork. Three partial evaluations. The electricity's still on."

"You mean the gennies are on," Bubba said. "We're goin' to have to find them and make sure they have enough gas for the night."

"I was in the kitchen getting a Pepsi," Nurse Ratchley said. "And a Twinkie. Also a bearclaw. I might have also eaten three chocolate chip cookies. There could have been a bag of chocolate-covered pretzels."

"The cupcake," Leeza breathed.

"No, I didn't eat your cupcake, Leeza," the nurse said. "Everything else maybe, but not the cupcake."

"Then where else were you?" David asked.

"I went to throw up because I ate too much," the nurse admitted.

"I went to my room, then to the kitchen," Leeza said. "I didn't see Ratchley, so I must have missed her. The cupcakes were all still there so I suppose she's telling the truth. I was looking through recipe books. It makes me feel better. And where do you get off telling me that food isn't love when you eat when you're stressed, Ratchley?"

Ratchley shrugged.

Abel said, "I went to my room. I slept for a while."

"I was at the receptionist's desk," Cybil said, still with a subdued voice. "I caught up on some paperwork. I didn't see anyone except Bubba and that was right before I found Blake."

"I went out to get Milk-Bones for my dog," Bubba said. "Precious will back me up. Right, Precious?" Precious woofed softly from under the table.

Everyone turned to look at Peyton. Peyton winced. "I went and redid my makeup. I checked my cellphone at every corner of the property. You never know when you might get a bar or two."

"That's one, two, three— " Bubba counted aloud as he pointed— "ten. Who are we missing?"

Thelda pointed at David.

"Surely, you cannot suspect the greatest detective of our time," David protested. "I was detecting with every enacting visceral aspect of my abilities. There were clues galore."

"So, you're saying, ain't no one saw you neither," Bubba said.

"That's about right."

Bubba would have sighed, but he suddenly decided that sighing didn't amount to a hill of beans.

Chapter Eleven

Bubba and More Interestin' O-ccurrences

Saturday, April 6th – Sunday, April 7th

"David," Bubba said to the would-be Sherlock Holmes when the rushed conversation began to lull. Most of the others didn't know what else to say or what else to do. They drank coffee or tea and apparently thought dark thoughts. "What do you remember about those searches on your Xoom?"

"How to make someone look like they committed suicide, how to make someone look like they had a fake heart attack, how to make your own explosive device, which really makes me nervous even in Pegram County." David chuckled uncertainly. "Do you remember when your mother had the improvised munitions book?"

"I remember she took all kinds of cleaning supplies out of the kitchen cupboards and everyone was right anxious," Bubba said. "It seems to me that she mentioned something about blowing up Pa with stuff that was bought from the corner drug store. I think she collected the gunpowder for the muzzleloaders and made it into something them folks in Afghanistan would think was right special. She used nails and broken mirrors. She might have spit into it, too."

"Why don't you just look at the Xoom again?" David asked.

"Dropped it," Bubba said with a little flush rushing

across his cheeks. "Someone screamed, and my fumble fingers let right go. Sorry. I'll replace it."

David's eyebrows went up. "If we happen to live through this, then we'll talk about replacing it, Watson."

Bubba wondered if Watson had the same mother as Bubba. That would make for interesting reading. He hadn't looked at an Arthur Conan Doyle novel for almost fifteen years. "Shore you don't recollect some of them searches, David?"

"Sherlock," David corrected. He took the calabash pipe out and then a tobacco pouch. He precisely loaded the bowl with tobacco and tamped it down with a silver bifolding tool. Then he replaced the tool in the pouch and withdrew a match. He scraped the match on the table and lit the pipe, puffing on it carefully. Then he choked and gagged noisily.

When David had recovered, Bubba said, "Mebe you shouldn't really smoke that."

"There are studies to suggest it isn't really healthy," David admitted with a hoarse voice. He looked at the pipe for a moment and tapped it against the table. "I'll just go dump this into an ashtray outside."

Bubba watched David trudge toward the door. He opened it and went outside into the fog.

Bubba looked around and saw no one else missing. Everyone had their hands wrapped around their cups or their heads bent, visibly lost in thought. Precious lay on top of his feet, snoozing and snoring lightly. He looked at his cup and wished he had a little more coffee, but he didn't want to feel like a racecar on the verge of the light changing. In fact, he felt a little sleepy. His eyelids were heavy. A little shuteye would be a welcome...

•

Bubba woke up with a snort. There was something wet dribbling down his face, and he wiped it away with the back of his hand. He would have used a shirtsleeve, but he was still wearing the "Bun in the Oven" t-shirt with its short sleeves. He looked around and saw he had been using the cafeteria table for a headrest. There was a little pool of drool right below where his mouth had been located.

The silver cupcake tree sat directly in front of him in the middle of the table, and he tiredly observed it. There were only nine cupcakes there. Bubba blinked. He counted again just to make sure. Someone had obviously regained their appetite.

His head came up, and he looked around. In various states of repose, sat or laid nine people including himself. Dr. Adair sat in a folding chair with his feet propped on a table. Ratchley had her head resting on folded arms. Abel laid on one of the tables on the side. It didn't look like a particularly comfortable bed, but it beat the floor. Cybil was snoozing on two chairs pushed together. Tandy sat on the floor against the wall and clutched a pack of cigarettes as if it would save her life. Her eyes were closed and they twitched, revealing she was deep in REM sleep. Peyton had found a corner to prop himself in, and his chin rested on his chest. David had retrieved his Inverness coat from somewhere, and it was wrapped around him as he lay prone across the floor near the entrance to the kitchen. He used his arms as a pillow and the deerstalker cap had fallen across his eyes. Finally, Jesus was sprawled face down on another table. He didn't look comfortable.

For a moment, there was the thought that Jesus was way too still to be alive. *Resurrection wouldn't be in his immediate future,* Bubba thought unkindly and immediately chastised himself. Then Jesus's arm jerked and moved slightly, revealing that not only was he not dead, but that he was not comfy. Jesus grunted and shifted to his side. The sheet he used as clothing shifted also, revealing that he still liked to go commando.

Looking away swiftly before his eyes went blind, Bubba thought about how something seemed to be missing.

Bubba checked under the table and sighed when he saw Precious with all four paws heavenward. She snorted in unintentional mimicry of her master, and her brown eyes opened to look at him. As she didn't immediately perceive any danger and Milk-Bones were not raining from the skies, she closed them again.

Bubba started to put his head back down on the table. *Wait,* something told him, *something is as warped as a dog's hind leg.* His head came back up, and the errant thought gave him a little pick-me-up.

Dr. Adair. Ratchley. Abel, Cybil, Tandy, Peyton, David, and Jesus. That was eight.

Bubba crossed his eyes in concentration. *Eight plus me and the dog. That's nine and the dog. Should be eleven because Blake is under a sweater in his office. Who's missing?*

Leeza and Thelda were absent. He slowly panned the room. They weren't about. Initially, Bubba wasn't really concerned. After all, folks needed to use the bathroom upon occasion. He needed to use the bathroom right now.

Bubba slowly got to his feet. Precious took note of that despite having closed eyes and did a clumsy roll to her feet. She shook her head and ears flapped everywhere. She blinked sleepily and then yawned.

The kitchen, Bubba thought. He looked in the kitchen and found everything there but a woman in a silk robe and a woman in five sweaters. Then he checked in the cafeteria again and found eight people still in snooze mode. No one else had vanished since he walked into the kitchen. There were still nine cupcakes, which was just short of miraculous since Precious had been known to climb on tables to consume defenseless food. (Miz Adelia had even used her smart phone to film the pooch moving a chair with her hind end in order to get where she could use it as a step stool to get to a box of pizza on the kitchen counter.)

Precious followed him without complaint, only bumping against him once when he passed the exterior door. He unobtrusively let her outside where she found a bush that needed moisturizing and returned to his side as if she was well aware of the urgency.

Trying to be quiet, Bubba meandered down the hallway and found a set of bathroom doors. While he didn't know for certain if these were the closest restrooms, he thought they were close enough. He checked the men's room, did his business, and then checked the ladies' room. The ladies' room had a basket of freshly cut flowers on the counter and an air freshener that the men's room did not. The ladies' room didn't have anyone inside it. There wasn't anyone to even sniff the flowers.

Bubba let himself out, glad that no one had seen him in the ladies' room. Willodean would have giggled her tushy off if she had seen him. He glowered with remembrance. Somewhere Willodean was worrying about him, and he couldn't do anything about it. He glanced at his watch and saw that it was half-past two a.m.

Everything was mysteriously quiet, and Bubba was disconcerted. While he didn't know Leeza and wouldn't wish a stranger harm, he sort of liked Thelda and her Shakespearean invectives. Plus Miz Demetrice knew and liked Thelda enough that the woman was invited to the weekly Pokerama parties. The truth was that Bubba didn't want anything to happen to either one. (Hopefully Leeza wouldn't prove to be the unmasked murderer and hopefully Thelda hadn't put herself into harm's way.)

In the lobby, Bubba found a roster of patients on Cybil's desk complete with room numbers. He proceeded to check both rooms of the missing women. Their doors were locked, and no one answered. He didn't see anyone or anything besides himself and Precious.

The blanketed emptiness of the hospital, and the deep shadows that haunted the hallways gave him the heebie-jeebies something fierce. Sure he was used to ghosts. His mother often talked about all the ghosts that haunted the Snoddy Estate. There was the Civil War lady in the upstairs powder room of the Snoddy Mansion. A black slave haunted the back ten acres. Supposedly, a midnight coachman came rumbling around in an ebony carriage when a Snoddy was about to die. No one had seen that one since Bubba's father, Elgin Snoddy, had died of a heart attack.

There had been a fake haunting when Bubba's former girlfriend had attempted to frame him for the murder of his former fiancée, but that had been a realtor with a sheet and a recording of screams and chains, so it didn't really count.

Bubba himself had seen some odd things on the estate grounds upon occasion, but he wasn't necessarily a superstitious man. Through tried and true methods he had discovered that if something was amiss, it could generally be attributed to the acts of man. Or woman, if the case may be.

Bubba started to search in earnest. He went through the hospital from top to bottom. He went back to the cafeteria and appropriated the keys from Dr. Adair's belt. Dr. Adair didn't budge as the keys lightly jangled. He opened doors with the keys and then relocked them. He searched the entire southern wing. He stopped at the doors to the northern wing because they were blocked with warning tape as well as nailed shut with three 2x4s. He even tugged on the 2x4s to make sure they were well connected and they were.

By the time he made his way back to the cafeteria, the rest of the group was stirring in fits and starts.

Dr. Adair rubbed his eyes. "Where'd you go, Bubba?"

"Looking for Leeza and Thelda," Bubba said. He

tossed Dr. Adair's keys to him. The doctor caught them with a confused expression on his face.

"They're gone," David said. He stood up and put on the Inverness coat. He finished his adjustments by tilting the deerstalker hat just so.

"Nice detecting, Sherlock," Tandy said. Her fingers trembled as she shook out a Marlboro. "You know, this is my last pack of cigs, and when I go cold turkey, the world might end. The murderer should be afraid of me."

"He could have done it," Abel said, pointing at Bubba. "We were all asleep, and he dragged them out without us hearing. They're probably in little pieces in a shallow grave behind the hospital."

"That seems unlikely, silly bean," Cybil said. "He doesn't have a shovel." She yawned sleepily. "Besides it's not like we were doped up."

Dr. Adair winced. Everyone looked at him.

Peyton examined his cup by holding it so that he could see the dregs inside. "Did you drug us, Doctor? What kind of doctor are you? What kind of lawsuit insurance do you have?"

"I'm a licensed psychiatrist," Dr. Adair protested, "and everyone was getting hysterical. It was just a little medication to calm the nerves."

"That's what they said before they took them to the ovens at Auschwitz," Abel accused. "I don't know how I ever came to be at this place. My family talked me into it. I should have never listened to them. I could be perfectly depressed at home with a bottle of Jack Daniels and a little coke chaser."

"Why were you asleep then, Doc?" Bubba asked.

"I had a little of the milk before," he admitted. "I'm not sure why I fell asleep."

"I have to go to the little grade-b movie actress's room," Tandy announced. "Any nonmurdering individual wish to accompany me?"

"I could pee," Cybil said.

"Me, too," said Ratchley. "Three's a good number."

Bubba watched the three lumber out the cafeteria door. "More coffee? Without special additives?"

"I'll help you make it," Peyton said.

David said, "I'll just be a third disinterested party."

Bubba managed to make the coffee without the kitchen or any part thereof being blown up. He brought the pot out into the cafeteria and people helped themselves. By that time the three women returned.

"You say you were looking for Thelda and Leeza," the doctor said.

"I dint find them," Bubba said. "They ain't anywhere that I looked, and I looked into everything I could including the bathrooms."

"They weren't in the closest bathroom," Tandy said as if Bubba hadn't just said that.

Dr. Adair paced the floors anxiously. Bubba could practically read his mind. The man was wondering about the legal ramifications of not only having a patient murdered, but losing two more. It wasn't going to look good on his resume.

"Maybe they went for help," Abel said. He shook his head. "I should have never come here. I mean, it's not like my family really cares or anything. They just didn't want the bad publicity. Wait until the publicity gets out about this."

Dr. Adair moaned.

Bubba took David aside. Peyton followed, and they crowded into a corner with a ficus plant. Precious tried to nose her way into the group and succeeded by nipping one of David's ankles.

"David, er-Sherlock, we have to know what all these people have in common," Bubba said. "Mrs. Ferryjig, Hurley Tanner, and Blake whatshisknickers."

"Blake Landry," David said. "They were all associated with the hospital. They were all in the mental health system. Mrs. F. and Hurley were both independently wealthy, but I don't think Blake was. The man drives an old Pinto, for goodness sakes."

"Could the Blake guy be collateral damage?" Peyton asked. "Maybe he was in the wrong place at the wrong time?"

"It's possible he knew something that someone else didn't want him to blab about," David suggested.

"Why trap us all here?" Bubba asked.

"Easy pickings," David said. "One place. Nowhere to go. Most of us can't hike out in the dark."

"The killer wants to kill someone here and now, ifin he or she ain't done it already," Bubba said, thinking of Thelda and Leeza. "Thelda ain't independently wealthy, is she?"

David nodded. "Dogley is an expensive place. Her children just wanted her to be safe and have the help she needs. Plus no one really enjoys the Shakespearean insults that much."

"I enjoy them," Peyton said. "You can say, 'Yo dickhead,' or 'You odiferious fen-sucked strumpet.' I rather liked that it wasn't a typical insult." He looked at Bubba and David staring at him. "What? I talked to Thelda earlier. Kind of."

"What about Leeza?" Bubba asked.

"Bubble gum money," David said. "Seriously her family makes bubble gum. It's the kind that has something crunchy in the middle. She said she has a swimming pool in the shape of a wrapped piece of bubble gum. She showed me a photograph. They're very proud of their bubble gum-shaped pool."

"So everyone dead or missing at Dogley, with the exception of Blake, is wealthy," Bubba mused. "What about diagnoses?"

"All different," David said. "They didn't always go to the same group therapies. They didn't have the same doctors. Some of them overlap. They didn't have the same nurses. I looked into all of this when I first investigated Mrs. Ferryjig and Hurley."

Bubba frowned. "Dint you say something about bein' the last one with them two?"

"I played cards with Mrs. F. and dominoes with Hurley." David's face became pinched. "I had a word with Blake earlier. He wanted to ask how I was feeling, so we chatted for a few minutes. I had the impression he wasn't impressed with the illustriousness that is the greatest detective of our times." The British accent abruptly returned. "Pip pip," he added for what Bubba assumed was authenticity's sake. Bubba didn't think a Brit would necessarily agree with the authentic part, but as he wasn't British, he couldn't really say for sure.

"Did you have anything to do with Leeza and Thelda?" Peyton asked.

"We sat together after Bubba fell asleep," David admitted. "It's not the best thing I could admit. I didn't do it. You believe me, don't you, Watson?"

"Of course, the greatest detective of our times couldn't be reduced to base murder," Peyton said before Bubba could say anything. Then he glanced meaningfully at Dr. Adair and whispered out of the side of his mouth, "but I've never trusted shrinks."

"Thelda and I have been friends for the entirety of my stay at Dogley," David said, "and I could never hurt a hair on her English Renaissance-abusive head."

Bubba didn't think David could hurt a fly, but evidence was mounting up and in a way that pointed at the formerly piratious superhero psychiatrist. "Did you play games with Leeza or Thelda?"

"Not tonight, but of course. Leeza preferred canasta, and Thelda was always good for Yahtzee. Oh, the insults she could toss out when she didn't get five dies of a kind."

"And Blake?"

"Gin rummy," David answered woodenly.

"Anyone else here?"

David nodded.

"Who?"

"Jesus, Abel, Ratchley, Cybil, Tandy, and sometimes Dr. Adair and I would play Cribbage while we worked on mental health issues."

"Mebe I should have asked who you don't play

games with," Bubba said.

"You and Peyton here." David brightened. "But I'm always open for something new. I have a deck of cards, you know."

"Forgive me, Sherlock," Peyton said, "if I decide to pass on a rousing game of snooker with you."

"We don't have a snooker table," David said.

Bubba cogitated. "David, I think you might have been right."

"About what?"

"Someone's trying to set you up," Bubba said. "It don't look good neither."

"What's that mean?" Peyton asked.

"It means ifin we don't figure this out, then David's goin' to be as sorry as a mud-covered fella who stole a widow woman's dog in a tornado."

Chapter Twelve

Bubba and a Mounting Conundrum

Sunday, April 7th

"I reckon we need to hunt them two down," Bubba said and offered one of Thelda's sweaters to Precious. He'd retrieved it from Thelda's room. She had quite a collection. Bubba stopped counting after twenty-three, and not one was the same color.

Precious sniffed delicately and then tossed her head about.

"Find Thelda, girl," Bubba said to Precious. "Hunt. There's a Milk-Bone in it for you."

Precious sniffed again and then began to shift her head around. She positioned it about six inches off the floor and began to shift it back and forth, systematically skimming the area for a scent. After a moment she stiffened and bayed.

"Hunt," Bubba repeated. There was a reason that as a pup Precious had been given to him and that was because Precious was one of the worst hunting hounds on record, but she had previously found Willodean for him, so he was hopeful. Furthermore, Thelda hadn't been known to be cruel to the animal. In fact, Thelda made a point of scratching behind Precious's ears when she thought no one was watching her.

Precious threw her head back and bayed again. The sound was loud and echoed in the room. Dr. Adair stepped back with an alarmed expression. The canine brought her head down and charged out the cafeteria doors with Bubba, David, Peyton, and Cybil in close pursuit. She went down a hallway, passed the bathroom with a distinctly unladylike snort, and trotted down another hallway, ending up at...

"This is Thelda's room," David said. Bubba knew that. He'd been there twice already, and although he knew that the woman wasn't there, he looked inside to see if she had returned in the meantime. Nothing was inside the room except an inordinate amount of sweaters and a complete collection of Shakespeare's unabridged works.

Bubba said, "Hunt, girl." Off Precious went again. She returned down the hallway, turned left, and hurtled down another hall. The lights were few and far between in the hallway, but Bubba could see this was an area where most of the rooms were offices of some sort or another. The dog stopped at a door that said "Library" on the outside. She pawed the door and looked at Bubba expectantly. He looked. Thelda was not inside with the racks of books and magazines.

Bubba tried again. "Hunt, girl."

Precious sniffed and snorted again. She tossed her head back and forth, and she trotted down a hallway at the fastest speed a canine of her distinct proportions could go. Finally, they ended up at the cafeteria again with Dr. Adair saying, "Did you find anything?"

Bubba sighed. "Good girl," he said to Precious. He passed her a Milk-Bone, and she inhaled it with the alacrity of a vacuum cleaner. He knelt by her while she chewed the part she hadn't already swallowed and stroked her back. "Ain't goin' to help," he said to the people watching them. "Thelda lives here. Her scent is everywhere. Mebe ifin she was outside, but not in here. Precious will just track wherever the scent is strongest. Go in circles all night long ifin we keep doing this."

"Her room, the cafeteria, and perhaps the library," David said. "I should have deduced it earlier. Those are Thelda's favorite places. Likely the hound would lead us to the dayroom, as well."

"And Leeza has been all over the place, too," Cybil said. She shook her head.

Bubba gave Precious a last scratch and stood up. He looked over the people in the room. Eight people. Eight suspects. One murder. Two possible murders. Two missing women. It was making out for a long night.

"I need some more coffee," he said abruptly and went into the kitchen to brew some more. It might not taste great, but it would have caffeine in it, and it would help him keep awake until someone came through the front door in a law enforcement capacity. Peyton followed him and wrung his hands nervously. Bubba couldn't help but notice that the wedding planner's makeup had recently been reapplied with little extra curlicues on the ends of the wings above his eyes.

"What do you think of all of this, Peyton?" Bubba asked as he measured coffee.

"I think Texas is a lot more thought-provoking than I had hitherto given it credit," Peyton said with a little laugh. "All these rich people in a rural Texan asylum. I wouldn't have thought Pegram County such a hot spot. Bubble gum money. A Hollywood actress. That Abel fellow is the CEO of a Fortune 500 company, did you know?"

"I did not know," Bubba said. "How did you know?"

Peyton rolled his eyes. "I am a wedding planner, dear ignorant redneck," he said imperiously. "I work in the city. New York City. We do weddings for all the best, i.e., richest families. One simply has to know who has the right amount of money to pay for the most extravagant affairs. The daughter of the president of Ultracon, Inc. had a wedding that cost three point five million dollars. I didn't really approve of the peacocks in the wedding party. Those birds look far more attractive than they act in real life, let me tell you. And if you think Canadian Geese poop a lot, then you haven't been around a peacock."

"I reckon I ain't." Bubba gave up on measuring the coffee and just tossed all of it in. The stronger the coffee, the better off he would be. If he had to spoon it into his mouth, then that was just a cost of doing business in a mental institute with a murderer about. "Wait, I think Ma once said she sicced peacocks on my father. She said they were just like piranhas." He shuddered briefly.

"They say Abel is in a big fight for power with his brother," Peyton said. "Neither one has daughters of a marriageable age, so I didn't really pay too much attention. They have sons, but both are married already and not likely to divorce. Usually we try to cozy up to the parents of the daughters, since the tradition is for them to pay for the wedding. Traditions, of course, vary, but you do never know where business is coming

147

from."

"Sounds like an iffy business," Bubba remarked. He found a carafe and filled it with water from the sink. Then he wondered if he should use filtered water from the oversized refrigerator. He shook his head. It didn't really matter.

"On the contrary," Peyton said, "it's a great business. I get to know all the people. I get the satisfaction of accomplishing a wonderful yet exhausting deed. Sometimes I take the hectic right out of the wedding for the participants. Your Willodean, for example, couldn't be happier that she's not doing all of the legwork."

"Me neither," Bubba said, "but you done got all these questions. Do I want grayity grey gray, do I want three types of almonds on dry white toast?"

Peyton's hand fluttered in front of his chest. "I just want you to have the best wedding possible." His voice almost broke, and Bubba glanced at him in alarm.

"You dint reckon on getting all wrapped up in this," Bubba said, referring to the hospital and all of the recent idiosyncrasies.

"No, I did not," Peyton said. "I figure if I stick close to you, I will not only survive, but will have a great story to tell Ginger. Publicity would be good. I can see the headlines. 'Wedding Planner Plans a Fabulous Wedding and Unmasks a Murderer, Too.'" His face wrinkled. "There's got to be an upside to this."

Bubba poured the water in the right spot, figured out how to turn the coffee machine on, and pushed the button. He almost smiled when the machine began to percolate without blowing up or something equally insidious. Then he turned back to Peyton. "You know about Abel. What do you know about some of the rest?"

Peyton shrugged. "The rich ones I can discuss. It's all about who can afford the best weddings in my business. Leeza is into the bubble gum business. Really they've branched out in candy, too. You know about Tandy, right? Her net worth is about twenty million. She made a bundle on *Bubble People*. She took a cut of the profits instead of a salary, and it paid off. Of course, *The Deadly Dead* did pretty well, too. Oh, my God, you're the redneck zombie in there, aren't you? That's just so kitschy!" Peyton paused to smile, then went on blithely, "I don't know if she took a cut on that one. She doesn't really seem the type to get married, so I didn't really pay attention to her bottom line after that. Thelda, the one with the sweaters, comes from family money. They like to make sure she's all taken care of. Jesus is a mystery. I mean, I don't even know his real name." Peyton paused, clearly to think about it. "Your David the Sherlockian is a member of old money, thus his tenure in these vaulted halls of mental inscrutability."

Bubba happened to know that David used to be a mailman, but maybe it made sense that he came from money, the same money that paid for his continued residence at the Dogley Institute for Mental Well-Being. It wasn't likely that Dogley had a scholarship program.

"You know anything about Dr. Adair or Nurse Ratchley?"

"Nothing springs to mind, but then my mind tends to focus on wedding-related issues." Peyton looked at the coffee machine. One of his fingers delicately touched the side of his nose. "Is it supposed to smoke like that?"

Bubba said a bad word and went to get the fire extinguisher.

●

David paced back and forth in front of the cafeteria windows. He nervously puffed on the empty calabash pipe. His deerstalker cap listed badly to one side. The Inverness coat was critically rumpled. The black circles under his eyes gave notice that he was tired.

"David," Bubba said, "er-I mean, Sherlock."

"What news, Watson?"

"The coffee is finally ready," Bubba said and handed David a steaming cup. "No special additives."

"I'm worried, Watson," David said, putting the pipe into a pocket and taking the cup in both hands.

"Do you think Thelda and Leeza went for help?" Bubba asked. "I shore don't like the idea of two ladies stumbling around in the darkness, going down near the river. Ain't rained much lately, but the water level's bin up."

David sighed. "I can't say for certain, Watson. I wouldn't have said that Thelda or Leeza were either of the I-will-hike-out-for-help types. We must work quickly." He glanced around furtively at the remainder of the people in the room. Most of them were ignoring everything and everyone. "We're ducks with targets on our feathered backs here. 'Twill only be a moment before the hunter brings his shotgun to bear on us."

"I bin thinking, Sherlock," Bubba said. "Ifin we cain't figure out who is doing it, then mebe we kin figure out why they're doin' it."

"Ah," David said with understanding, "explain the motive, and it will lead to the perpetrator. I concur, dear Watson. Proceed with your methodology."

Bubba glanced over his shoulder to see who was paying attention to them. "We should go look at Blake's body," he whispered.

"I agree," David said. "Should we take the wedding planner?"

"He might puke," Bubba warned. "I doubt he's used to dead bodies." He thought he might puke himself, and not because he wasn't used to dead bodies, but because his stomach was saying strong words to him.

"You haven't dealt with a third-generation motor matriarch with ties to the mafia on one side and some to the landed gentry on the other," Peyton interjected, having appeared from nowhere. "I think I can handle a dead body."

"The three of us might leave without incident," David said. "We could pretend to go and look for poor Thelda and Leeza." He frowned. "We *should* look for them."

"I did look for them. Ain't in this hospital."

"Then we should look outside," David proclaimed loudly.

Everyone looked at them.

"Come on, Peyton," Bubba said noisily. "We're goin' to look for them womenfolk again."

"Is that a good idea?" Dr. Adair asked.

"Better than sitting here, you daft cow," David said. Apparently, he didn't have a high opinion of the doctor.

"Hey," Dr. Adair protested.

"Let's go," Peyton said, clearly used to the art of interrupting a conflict before it escalated, and there wasn't even a wedding about.

Precious scrambled to catch up to Bubba. They went out the door and into the fog. Several of the others pressed their faces against the glass and watched them.

"Go out into the woods, then parallel the hospital for a bit, and back into the front door," Bubba said.

"Isn't it locked?"

David rattled a set of keys. "I appropriated these from Nurse Ratchley, eh what?"

"I don't think Brits really say some of the things you say, and if they do, they don't say them in that context," Peyton commented.

"You obviously don't know your onions, you bloody opinionated wanker," David said.

"He looked that up on the Internet," Peyton said.

Bubba shrugged. "Pip pip."

They waded into the fog.

Peyton giggled. "I can't help myself." He paused. "This fog is as thick as pea soup." He waved his hands in the air. "I've *always* wanted to say that."

"It *is* as thick as pea soup," David admitted, albeit sounding like he was reluctant to agree with Peyton.

"I don't reckon I ever et pea soup," Bubba said. "Bean soup. Clam chowder. Miz Adelia makes a right proper baked potato soup. Stew. All kinds of stew. No pea soup. I assume it is thick."

"Have we made it to the tree line yet?" Peyton asked.

"I ain't sure." And Bubba wasn't sure. The fog was

so thick he could barely see to the end of his arm. Peyton and David were vague dark shapes that could vanish in the blink of an eye.

"I can't see the hospital anymore," David said.

"We're not lost are we?" Peyton asked. "I saw this movie where there was a scythe murderer in a heavy fog. He always struck from behind." He looked over his shoulder in a nervous fashion. "I can't see anything except you two."

Precious yipped.

"And of course, you too, darling one."

"How does one murder a scythe?" David asked.

"I meant the murderer used a scythe to kill with," Peyton said. "Like cutting wheat." He paused. "I wouldn't think it would be as easy, however. I mean to cut someone's head off, not cutting wheat. Cutting wheat probably is easy. Oh bother, I should just shut my mouth."

"It's this way," Bubba said. On the inside he added, *I think. I hope.*

"If this was a real movie, we would trip over a dead body now," Peyton said. "Then I would scream like a little girl and run. I'd trip because I was wearing high heels, and pffft, that would be the end of me."

"It's my investigatory opinion that you watch too many movies," David opined. "Are you really wearing heels? I thought you were wearing loafers."

"I have some in my closet," Peyton said. "Hey, is that a light?"

They all stopped moving.

Bubba squinted. It looked like a light moving in the

dense fog. "Who's there?" he called.

The light vanished straightaway. Bubba had an idea that couldn't be good.

Peyton stepped forward and immediately tripped over something in his path. Then he screamed like a little girl before he could get up and run and trip again. Bubba couldn't tell if it was because of his loafers or not. After Peyton fell, he tossed about with his hands and squealed, "EEEEEEEE!"

David crouched next to Peyton and reached out tentatively with one hand. He touched the shape with one hand, retreated, and then touched it again. He poked it. Then he poked it harder. "It's a...it's a...it's a...garbage bag with lawn clippings in it."

Peyton scrambled away anyway. "It was horribly lumpy!"

Bubba frowned. He'd seen gardeners earlier. Was it possible they were still around, trapped like the rest of them? Was it possible that there were other people around they hadn't run into yet? Maybe the murderer wasn't even one of the people trapped in the hospital? A light didn't go out like that unless someone was trying to hide.

"Come on," Bubba urged, the thought of a person swinging a sharpened scythe in the forefront of his mind. "We should prolly get out of the fog."

"I nearly died," Peyton whined. David helped him get up.

"Look on the bright side," Bubba said.

"What bright side?" Peyton asked.

"Ain't no scythe."

"Are you sure it was just a bag of yard trash?"

"David?"

"Sherlock."

"Sherlock?"

"Grass and leaves. Nary a bloody limb to be found."

"Oh, thank God," Peyton said with devout gratefulness.

•

It took them about fifteen more minutes before they found the front of the hospital. It was another ten before they found a door. Precious had to stop to bay into the fog.

"Listen," David said, "it's the hound! The hound is after her prey. She will go for the throat and leave no evidence of her passing save for mysterious paw prints in the bog."

"Ain't no bog around here," Bubba said, "and that's Precious, not the hound of the Baskervilles. Dint you watch any other Sherlock Holmes movies?"

"Movies?" David asked with evident confusion.

"Shouldn't you be more worried about Professor Moriarty?"

"Moriarty!" David blasted. "What foulness do you know about the dreaded professor? Has Inspector Lastrade been about? Tell me!"

"Calm down, David," Bubba said. "I need them keys. Here's the door. Ain't no professor about that I know about."

David eyed Peyton carefully. "Inspector, is it you in disguise? Demmed if it isn't. I'll be gobsmacked and knackered at the same time." David took a step closer

155

to Peyton who winced. "Man, you're wearing makeup. You have curlicues above your eyes."

"I'm not Inspector Lastrade, and this isn't Baker Street," Peyton said. "Yes, I watched Sherlock Holmes, but it was the Robert Downy Jr. version."

"Then you shall be a Baker Street Irregular," David proclaimed and handed the keys to Bubba. "*Very irregular,*" he added under his breath.

Bubba glanced at Peyton and murmured, "He's just nervous."

Peyton looked at David who was staring into the fog and muttering, "The hound, the hound."

"Is he dangerous?" Peyton asked.

"Not unless you diss Sir Arthur Conan Doyle," Bubba said.

"Never," Peyton swore. "I'm a little nervous myself."

Bubba sighed as he found the key that opened the front door. He threw it open and yanked Peyton in after him. Then one of his large hands reached out and clasped the collar of the Inverness coat and drew David in. "Precious!" Bubba bellowed. A moment later, the Basset hound leapt through the door and skidded to a halt on the marble floor. Bubba shut the door with a resounding sigh as if the mere act would keep all the evil out.

They trudged through the hospital not bothering to be particularly quiet. When they reached Blake Landry's office, they discovered that the door had been left ajar. Bubba couldn't help the grimace running across his face as he pushed it open.

"That figures," Bubba said, looking inside. The light

from the hallway showed everything. David peeked around Bubba's body and said, "I see, or rather, I do not see."

"What?" Peyton asked. He looked. "Hey, didn't we leave it right there?"

"Unless it got up and walked away," Bubba said. "Ain't no more dead body there."

"I seem to recall that you lost a dead body before," David said.

"I dint lose it," Bubba denied. "Someone else done carried it off. They found it...later."

"But there wasn't any one who could have carried this one off," Peyton said. "No one was alone except Bubba." He slowly looked at Bubba. "Did you carry the body off?"

"I did not," Bubba protested. "It was here the last time I was here."

"Elementary, my dear Watson," David said, clearly proud of himself because he finally got to say those words.

Chapter Thirteen

Bubba and the Solitary Attempt

Sunday, April 7th

"What do you mean it's gone?" Tandy asked, puffing furiously on a cigarette.

"The corpse is amiss," David announced as if he were saying there was a thirty percent chance of rain later on in the day. The calabash pipe had returned to his mouth where he chewed on the end, almost as furiously as Tandy puffed. He removed it briefly while he added, "Vanished. Disappeared. Departed. Misplaced. Lost. Absent. Mislaid."

"That sort of implies that we put him somewhere and then forgot where it was," Tandy said. "I specifically recall him being in his office with a garrote around his neck." She demonstrated with her index finger and thumb of her right hand wrapped around her throat. Crossing her eyes and sticking her tongue out, the cigarette briefly dangled out of the side of her mouth before she abandoned the parody in favor of smoking the cigarette again.

Bubba looked at the eight people who variously stood and sat around him. Dr. Adair drank from a cup of coffee and stared at the floor. Abel chewed on the end of a pencil and pulled on the ends of his hair with the hand not holding the pencil. Ratchley played with the cords on her scrubs, appearing dismayed. Jesus prayed. Cybil frowned and looked more like a chipmunk than ever before with her puffy cheeks. She was even developing black-rimmed eyes to match the look. David seemed like he was pretending to be the brave and stalwart detective, Sherlock Holmes. Peyton brushed his streaked hair from his face, careful not to muss his makeup. Tandy continued to puff like a maniacal steam engine on crack.

Still nine. No one else had mysteriously vanished, or worse, been mysteriously murdered. Bubba looked at the table with the cupcake stand. He counted. Nine cupcakes. No one else had eaten one. Nine cupcakes. Nine people, plus one dog. It made Bubba think about things he didn't want to think about. "Why would someone want to hurt Blake?" he asked.

"Maybe he knew something," Cybil suggested. "I don't think he was rich like the others. So I think it's a safe bet saying it wasn't for his money."

"So you think the others might have been killed for their money," Bubba said.

"Well, that's a stretch," Tandy said, sarcasm evident in her voice. "If it was one person who died, then a finger could be pointed at the person who stood to gain the most. Like it's the husband or the butler."

"There isn't a butler handy here," David interjected.

"Feeeear not," Jesus proclaimed, "Iiii will prooootect you. Iiiif you haaaave faith."

Dr. Adair jumped to his feet and said, "Obviously, a body can't vanish into thin air. You must have looked in the wrong office." He marched toward the door and Tandy and Ratchley trailed after him. Bubba sighed and went after them. After another moment, Peyton and

159

David followed.

Three minutes later, Dr. Adair stared at the office that was sadly, or not so sadly depending on one's perspective, devoid of human remains.

Bubba couldn't help himself. "See." Unfortunately for Bubba it seemed a little too much like déjà vu.

"You must have moved it," Dr. Adair accused.

Precious barked once and then growled at Dr. Adair.

"You know we don't allow animals in the hospital except service animals," Dr. Adair said nervously. "She doesn't look like any service animal I've ever seen."

"What, you want me to tie her up outside?" Bubba said. "I stay, the dog stays. Ain't no if, and, or but to it." He sighed. "Precious, hush."

Precious shut her mouth with a last lingering glare at the doctor. Evidently, the canine didn't care for psychiatrists any more than David did.

"Peyton, do you know anything about Ingrid Ferryjig?" Bubba asked.

Peyton touched the tip of his nose. "Old Hollywood money," he said. "She had three children, all of which are entering prime marriage age, albeit a little on the young side. The daughter is most eligible but isn't engaged or anything yet. The two sons are in college. One has a girlfriend, but it doesn't look serious. They're on my C-list." He looked at Bubba and Bubba's confusion must have shown. "People on the C-list," Peyton explained, "have marriage potential but nothing that should be followed up on yet. It's always good to have lists, you know."

"Ferryjig," Tandy said. "Wasn't her grandfather that

director, Jason Meister?"

"Yes," Peyton said. "He had four wonderful weddings. Very frou-frou, but the fifth one was in Las Vegas." He shrugged. "Ironically, that was the one that lasted the longest, until his death in 1980."

"Do you know why anyone might want to kill Mrs. Ferryjig?" Bubba asked.

"She had a heart attack," Dr. Adair wailed. "No one murdered her. I speak from a professional level when I say some of you might need some additional help."

"From all reports, she was a nice lady. She was old money and married into money, too. The Ferryjigs were the forerunners of Internet commerce. Lots of nice weddings there, too. Nothing I did unfortunately."

"Enemies?" Bubba persisted.

Peyton shook his head. "I expect people with money always have relations who want their money. However, no particular person springs to mind. Jason Meister left trust funds for all his grandchildren, which wasn't as big a number as one might have expected."

Bubba cogitated.

"Did someone say that Mrs. Ferryjig was murdered?" Tandy asked. "I don't think you can fake a heart attack."

"You *can't* fake a heart attack," Dr. Adair said vehemently.

"What about Hurley Tanner?" Bubba asked.

"Suicide," Dr. Adair said. "It's sad, terrible even, and a tragic event the hospital deeply regrets, but we can't be held responsible for narcotics brought in from an outside source. We're not a prison here."

"What do you know about Hurley, Peyton?" Bubba

asked.

"Oilman with expansions into various other fuel-related enterprises," Peyton said. "One daughter of marriageable age. She and her boyfriend haven't made the next step yet. Mr. Tanner's alcoholism has been an ongoing problem for the company, and stocks have slid a bit. He was probably going to step down from the company once he finished rehab. That would have been a good time for a wedding. Recovery is a celebration of life, just like weddings. Especially in Atlanta, which is where the Tanner family is based. They have killer Southern weddings there. Absolutely to die for." He grimaced. "I've got to stop saying that."

"Are weddings all you think about?" Ratchley asked Peyton.

"Why, yes," Peyton answered honestly, "yes, they are. Are you married?"

"Yes, I'm married," Ratchley snapped. Her face suddenly mellowed. "But I always wanted another wedding."

"We'll talk," Peyton promised.

Tandy lit up a fresh cigarette. "I have two left, peeps. Just warning ya." She inhaled deeply and exhaled smoke into the air with a gusty sigh. "Why are you asking about reasons for someone to have killed these people, Bubba? I mean, obviously what I said was true. If a person is murdered, there's usually a reason why. It can be money, revenge, insanity, just because the guy had a blue tie on, stuff like that."

The doctor overtly glanced down at his tie. It wasn't blue.

"But you're lumping all these people together. No one is going to wait until they're all together to murder them off for a reason like money. No one person is going to get all the money." Tandy puffed again. "Plus Blake was a social worker. No offense to social workers, but he probably only made forty grand a year. Who murders for that? I mean, did he have group life insurance?" She didn't wait for an answer. "Think about it. Even if Ferryjig was done in in a way that made it look like a heart attack and Tanner was murdered instead of committing suicide, who would benefit?"

"We're in an asylum," Cybil said. "There doesn't have to be a reason the average sane person would understand, silly Sophie."

Bubba glanced back at Cybil. Abel was standing behind her. He mentally counted again. There was the doctor, the nurse, Peyton, David, Tandy, and himself. Then there was Cybil and Abel. And a dog, of course. That was meant one person was all alone. "Where's Jesus?"

"Heaven?" Tandy said. "Oh, you mean *Jesus*. He was in the cafeteria with the rest of us." She craned her neck. "And he's not here, which is a bad thing. God, did I give up pot at the worse time ever."

Cybil glanced over her shoulder. "Jesus was right behind us."

Abel looked around in an apprehensive way. "He can't be far. What were you saying about Mrs. Ferryjig and Mr. Tanner?"

"Bubba thinks it's the same person doing it," Tandy

said. She puffed again and didn't bother taking the cigarette out of her mouth. "I gather that's what you're trying to say, isn't it, Bubba?"

"'When you have eliminated the impossible, whatever remains, however improbable, must be the truth,'" David quoted, obviously using his best British accent.

"What's been eliminated?" Abel asked.

"We could say that the dead didn't do this," Tandy suggested. "They're dead, and this isn't a zombie movie." She grimaced. "I probably shouldn't say that."

Bubba pushed past everyone and rushed back toward the cafeteria. The clicking of toe nails told him that Precious was in close pursuit. The clicking was followed by footsteps. "Jesus!" he yelled.

He burst through the doors and stopped, staring. No one was there. There wasn't a man in a hockey mask with a machete or man with steel-tipped fingers and a burned face, and there wasn't a man with a screaming mask wearing a black cloak. There wasn't even a chainsaw present.

It was almost anticlimactic. Everyone else piled in behind him as he made his way into the kitchen. He found no one in there either.

Bubba returned to the cafeteria with a glum expression. He glanced around, and his gaze settled on one of the tables. He didn't really like what he was looking at because he frowned deeply.

The seven remaining people and one pooch stared at Bubba expectantly.

"The answer to the question that you dint really ask,

Tandy," Bubba said finally, "is that someone was planning it for a reason I don't reckon I understand. Might be because that person is crazy, nuttier than a five-pound fruitcake at a Christmas dinner, and it might be because someone's got a plan I don't get, but it's happening all the same."

"You don't know that," Tandy said.

"Someone thought ahead," Bubba said. "They searched on the Internet, planted evidence, and when they thought the hospital was goin' to be the most empty, they blew up the cell phone tower and caused an avalanche to take out the only road in or out. Don't sound that crazy to me that someone is doing all them things so methodically. Sounds like premeditation to me. Except he or she dint count on a couple extra folks crashing their party."

"You mean you and the wedding guy," Tandy said.

"Wedding *planner*," Peyton corrected. "And I've never crashed a party."

Bubba nodded. "Look," he said and pointed at the cupcake stand on the middle table. Only eight cupcakes remained.

●

Bubba dragged all of them from one end of the hospital to the other. Then he dragged them outside into the dense fog. Eight people trudged around the perimeter of the hospital only stopping when he ran into the solid chain-link fence the construction company had erected to keep people out of the wing that was to be renovated.

Bubba stared into the fence and said, "Doc, ain't no

one supposed to be in that wing, right?"

"It was cleared and then the doors were sealed. The administrator had them nailed shut to prevent anyone from going in from the hospital side once the renovations started. There's an asbestos issue. The abatement will take at least two weeks. They've already put up plastic sheeting on the inside of the wing." Dr. Adair looked around and shivered. It wasn't cold, but it wasn't particularly warm either.

Bubba weighed in his mind whether to break into the wing or not, just to be sure. He couldn't find an entrance by which someone could be carrying in bodies. He chewed on his lower lip and thought, *I could et something. Not cupcakes. Mebe eggs. Eggs with peanut butter on top. Wonder what Willodean is doin' right now.*

"Jesus wouldn't go anywhere with a stranger," David said into Bubba's ear. "He was planning on visiting his family next week. They're doing a charitable vacation in Bolivia. Feeding the poor, building a clinic, and there was something about immunizations for the people who didn't have access to medicine. He wouldn't just disappear."

Bubba knew Jesus. He'd known Jesus for a while now. He wasn't a bad sort for a man who thought he was the savior. It was true that he didn't favor underwear and that he'd once stolen a case of hemorrhoid cream, but that had only been a nonverbal cry for assistance. Jesus was also loyal to his fellow mental patients. Perhaps he was trying to get help for Thelda and Leeza. Perhaps he'd eaten the cupcake and then gotten lost in the fog.

"We should go back inside," Tandy said. "I think the schizophrenic in room 34 keeps a carton of Luckies in her nightstand."

"We should stay together until help comes," Abel said.

Ratchley said, "I'm afraid to go the bathroom by myself. I have the bladder the size of a walnut." Everyone looked at her. "What? Too much information?"

"I'm afraid that this fog is going to eat me," Cybil said. "I think I read too much Stephen King when I was younger."

Bubba wanted to growl with frustration. Eight people left. No ideas on what was happening. The sun wasn't going to come up for another three hours. Who knew when someone would figure out that the hospital had been cut off?

He led them back to the front door and waited while Dr. Adair opened it. Bubba made a decision. "David, keep an eye on Precious, will you?"

"Sherlock," David corrected automatically. "I will watch the hound of the Baskervilles, but if she begins to salivate salaciously, I will not hold myself accountable."

"She's had her rabies shots," Bubba said, "and the only way she'll salivate is if you hold a steak above her head and don't give it to her."

"I don't have a steak," David said.

Bubba pulled a baggie of Milk-Bones out of his pocket and passed it to David. Precious's head directed itself to the baggie and followed it like a laser beam locked on target.

"What are you going to do?" Tandy asked.

"Goin' for help," Bubba said. "I'm goin' to hike on out and hit the nearest house with a working phone. I reckon it's about five miles to the northeast. I swim the river and head for the Wormwood place."

"I should go with you," Peyton said.

"You'll ruin your loafers, Peyton," Bubba warned.

"And you're on your own, my dear pedantic redneck," Peyton added cheerily. "I shall attach myself to Sherlock Holmes and weather out the remainder of the foggy night. I'll pee in a bottle in the corner if I have to."

Dr. Adair frowned. "The hospital can't be responsible for what happens once you step off the grounds."

"Why not cross the bridge and clamber over the rocks and such?" Tandy asked.

"Ifin there's another fella running around, isn't that where he would expect a soul to go?" Bubba asked. "So I won't go there. It'll give me a better chance. I reckon I can be to the Wormwood's place in two hours or less. In three hours the po-lice will be at the avalanche area. They'll send some folks over to take care of things. Ya'll stay together. Take bathroom breaks together and such. Keep the dog handy." Precious whined. "We'll be laughing about it come suppertime."

Abel giggled halfheartedly. "What if there's two of them?"

"What do you mean?" Tandy asked.

"I've been thinking about it," Abel said. "This was all planned. Very well planned. But stuff happens. No one can predict everything. They couldn't predict Bubba would be here, but they probably had an idea that things wouldn't go exactly the way they wanted. That doesn't sound like one person to me. It sounds like two."

"Keep together," Bubba said. "Lock the door after me, doc."

"I do not approve," the doctor said, but he opened the door for Bubba.

Bubba hesitated and held out a hand toward Tandy. "Borrow one of them phones, Miz North?"

Tandy handed him the Samsung Galaxy. "That gets the best reception. Maybe after you've crossed the river, you can find a bar or two."

Bubba stuck it into his pocket and started to turn away.

Cybil said, "Wait." She turned to David and said, "Empty out that baggie with the Milk-Bones." While she waited, she pulled a Mini Maglite out of her pocket and handed it to Bubba.

Precious's ears flipped as she heard key vital words. David shrugged and obliged. Then Cybil plucked the baggie out of his hand and handed it to Bubba. "Put the phone in there. If you swim across the river, you'll need to keep it dry. Maybe you can call for help way before you get to the Wormwood's place."

Bubba removed the Samsung and put it into the baggie. He sealed the bag and tested it to make sure. "There. All tighty and dry." He put it into his pocket and took a last look at the other seven people and one dog. "Stay, Precious," he said and went into the fog.

•

The only thing that reassured Bubba was that a killer, or killers, couldn't have known about the odd nighttime fog that covered the area like a thick blanket. On the other hand, the Sturgis River was right there, and fogs in an area adjacent to the river were common, especially in the spring.

Still, Bubba thought, *it ain't like someone has a row of fog machines all ready to make a fog so thick a slasher movie director would be happy.* He waded through the murk toward the road and almost brained himself on a light pole. The gennys inside might be powering the inside lights, but it didn't include the street lights in the parking lot. He would have pulled out the Mini Maglite that Cybil had provided, but he didn't want to be a big walking, flash-lit target. He'd save the flashlight until he was well away from the hospital and possible murderers.

Bubba made it all the way to the end of the parking lot, passing the Mercedes Benz and the Volkswagen Rabbit with Ol' Green between them, before someone clocked him in the back of the head with what felt like a 4x4 post dipped it cement. His last thought was that Doc Goodjoint had been correct about him needing a football helmet.

Chapter Fourteen

Bubba and the Treacherous Escape

Sunday, April 7th

There was something tickling Bubba's nose. He would have picked up a hand and scratched it, but he couldn't move his hands. In fact, he couldn't move anything below the neck and above the waist. *Paralyzed?*

Nope.

Bubba slowly looked around and could see gloomy walls and a solitary window up high as if he was in a storeroom or such. The trickle of light was almost as vague as the room. He glanced down at himself and realized he was encased in an old-fashioned straitjacket. Leather straps crossed in front and one through the legs. All the buckles were secured; the arms wrapped around his front as if he was hugging himself. The cloth went around to the back where he assumed more buckles were securely attached.

In addition, his head hurt, and he could feel something trickling down the back of his neck. *Someone had hit him*, he comprehended. *Again!* At least it hadn't been with a set of manacles. No one could hit like Willodean could hit. It was a fact that he should have been grateful for at the moment.

Running through a mental checklist, he went over the parts of his body. His knees seemed sore, and his feet were a little cold. He looked down and saw that the

171

knees of his jeans were torn, and his boots were missing. It took him another minute to understand that someone had dragged him from Point A to this place, Point B.

Bubba glowered. His nose still tickled. A piece of cobweb hanging from his hair and fluttering in his face was the responsible culprit.

He wasn't glowering about the cobweb, however. He was glowering about the fact that someone had dragged off all two hundred forty pounds of him. That made him think that Abel's belief might be correct. There were two of them. It was possible there were three of them. One was still with the other seven people, keeping an eye on them until they could get their hands on whoever was the prize and ready to melt into the woodwork when the authorities arrived. One or two were outside in the fog, waiting to pick off those silly or stupid enough to wander off alone. After all, they'd seen someone with a light in the fog before, and Bubba hadn't put it together.

More importantly they hadn't killed Bubba. They had knocked him out and incapacitated him. Somewhere an angel was watching over him, giggling helplessly but still watching over him.

Bubba rolled onto his side and looked around for something to help him get out of the straitjacket. He didn't even know how anyone got out of the danged things. He'd once seen a movie where Mel Gibson's character dislocated his shoulder to do it, but Bubba didn't think he could dislocate even his finger, so that was out. He'd a knife in his pocket but had given it to

Cybil when he'd first entered the hospital, so that was out, as well.

He looked at his feet and found that the same someone who'd bundled him up also had tied his feet together with thick jute twine. It shouldn't have done much, but it was wrapped around his ankles about a hundred times and tied in a nice neat knot.

Bubba was momentarily at a loss. He didn't have anything at hand. He didn't have a knife. The flashlight was still in his pocket, but he couldn't feel the boxy shape of the Samsung, so he could only assume that someone had taken that. He would have shrugged if he had been able, but the straitjacket wasn't about to let him shrug. It wasn't like the cell phone would have helped him get out of the restrictive garment.

Why not just slit his throat out in the fog? Bubba frowned in concentration. The frown pulled on the muscles of his head and reminded him that someone had smashed him there. One person was a murderer. The other person was not a murderer. Bubba hadn't seen their face, so voila, he was spared.

Perhaps there were other people who had been spared. Jesus, Thelda, and Leeza, for example. None of it really made sense. Why kill a social worker and spare a local redneck?

Bubba began to struggle. He kicked, rolled, and bumped. His head throbbed in concert with his exertions. Most of what he accomplished was to sweat like a pig and that reminded him that he was still hungry. What he really wanted was something bizarre. Deep-fried pineapple with a side drink of pickle juice.

The sweet/salty combo would perk him right up. What was wrong with him?

His foot pulled free of the twine, and he panted appreciatively. A fella was supposed to rescue himself. Then he would rescue all the other damsels in distress, or in this case, the loonies in liability. Of course, he had to remember that some of them weren't really loonies. He wasn't positive about Peyton, but a certain amount of insanity had to go hand in hand with being a wedding planner.

Bubba raised his right foot and admired the sock. That was one of his favorite pair of socks. Willodean had given him those socks. They were comfortable and didn't bind up when he put on his best pair of boots. He didn't know what he was going to do with it. He eyed the straitjacket and thought about it. If he could just get a little bit of leeway, then he could wiggle one arm over his head. If he pressed his back and neck into the floor he could feel the top buckle pressing into the flesh there. It wasn't a complicated affair; they were simple buckles that merely needed to be unlatched.

Bubba began to struggle anew. He jerked his arms back and forth, stretching the material and the leather straps. He heard the crackle of old leather as it pulled. It wasn't a brand new piece of equipment; it had probably been sitting around the hospital for a decade. Did the original hospital need a straitjacket or two even though it had started off as a regular hospital? That wasn't unlikely. It was probably a piece of just-to-be-on-the-safe-side gear. Emergency rations, generators, extra bandages and sutures, gallons of water, and...a couple of straitjackets for those who might need to be battened down because they were inclined to stick a knife in all the purple elephants they were seeing.

Stopping to catch his breath, Bubba thought that he could make a million bucks by making a new type of exercise video. Straitjacketercizing. Talk about the calories someone would burn. The DVD comes with its own straitjacket. Try two for extra weight loss.

The thing was that Bubba didn't want some law enforcement type like Sheriff John walking in on him while he was still encased in canvas and leather straps, laying on the floor like a beached whale. Sheriff John would be laughing until the following Christmas. That would be the good part because if the man figured out that he could take a few photos with his cell phone and post them to the social media of his choice, Bubba would be hearing about it for the next decade.

Bubba struggled harder. His head was a drum solo in a heavy metal group's favorite song. The last thing he needed was another concussion. At the rate he was going, Willodean was going to refuse to marry him. Their baby would be born without a real last name. She would go on to marry a Kardashian and do a reality show. Then Bubba would be stuck forever in a straitjacket. He might even be buried in it. His child would forever wonder what happened to his or her daddy. Miz Demetrice would be ashamed to admit that her only son had died in a straitjacket even though she had purportedly once done the same to her infamous dead spouse. Bubba wouldn't even be there to say in a snarky fashion, "It was a heart attack, Ma."

Bubba suspected his head had been hit harder than he had previously thought. Sweat dripped into his eyes and burned like napalm on a distant jungle. The sock from the freed foot flew off and hit the wall with a low thump. He was able to use the shoulder of the straitjacket to wipe his eyes, but it didn't absorb like Charmin TP.

Taking another break, Bubba looked around while he panted. The room was empty. There was some trash in a corner and what looked like mouse turds near his head, but there wasn't anything he could use to help him get out. He decided to climb to his feet and see if that would help him attain a little slack in the jacket. If he could just get one of his arms over his head, then he might be able to unbuckle the top and work his way down. That was provided he could make his big sausage-sized fingers work the buckles.

Bubba flopped over onto his front and used his head (screaming internally with protest and with a request for a large ice bag while he was at it) and his knees to lever himself upward. With a great deal of awkwardness he was able to get onto his knees, and then with his freed leg, he climbed up. He first checked the single door. After all, if he could walk out, who cared if he was not freed from the straitjacket? He could simply walk back to the hospital and politely ask David to take the bleeping thing off.

While Bubba was on the subject of bleeping things, he added a few more swearwords just to make himself feel better. Then he did some combinations in order to create an air of bonhomie. It didn't make his head throb less, but it helped his inner turmoil.

David needed him. So did Thelda and Jesus and a few of the others. Obviously, the unnamed murderer(s) did not need him, but that was neither here nor there. His mother needed him. Willodean and the baby needed him. He wouldn't let the beauteous sheriff's deputy marry any of the Kardashians, no matter how much money they made or didn't make.

Bubba threw his shoulders upward. He threw one down. He jerked it to the side as hard as he could. He was rewarded with what he perceived as a touch of slack. He smiled grimly as he continued to lurch and judder. If someone had entered at that moment, it was highly debatable as to what they might think.

The thought made Bubba aware that just because he was still alive didn't mean the murderer(s) wouldn't come back to finish him off. He didn't want to be here waiting on them just because he hadn't tried hard enough. He took a deep breath and struggled harder. He forced his right arm up, and it stuck in place across his face. Momentarily smothered, he nearly panicked. Then he was able to move it just enough to allow himself to breathe. He decided that whoever had invented straitjackets had been a diabolical fiend worthy of existence in the seventh level of hell, reserved for people who left empty toilet paper rolls in the bathroom for the next unsuspecting soul to discover after it was too late to move to another stall.

Bubba jerked again. He heard something pop and realized his shoulder had done something weird. His shoulder said a few appropriate swear words. He

177

clenched and flexed the muscles there. Then his arm was over his head. He pulled to one side, and fabric-covered fingers touched the top buckle. It took a little effort, but he popped the buckle open and smiled to himself with success. The second buckle was a little more difficult. He couldn't reach the third buckle, so he brought his arm back down in front of him. There was a lot more slack now, and he was able to pull the cloth down his arms so that he could yank his left arm into the body of the straitjacket. With the arm free to roam, he unbuckled the strap between his legs.

Bubba resisted a triumphant yell. With a lot more judicious wiggling that would have made a go-go dancer popular with the customers, he writhed and twisted the straitjacket over his head and dropped it to the floor. He glared at it as if it was full of the power to restrain him anew. He was seriously thinking about dancing over it with size-12 feet. Instead, he kicked it away and went for the door.

It was still locked as he had expected. Bubba wasn't about to be deterred. He thumped it once with his shoulder and then listened. He didn't hear anything on the other side. He thumped it again and listened again. After ten more seconds, he simply plowed through it, tired of the whole thing.

The door cracked and fell to the floor, shattering some tiles along the way. The screws that attached to the wood had failed when he had put enough pressure on them. Bubba cautiously stepped through the broken tile and threaded his way down a blackened hallway. It looked like part of the hospital but a disused one. There was a path of footprints leading through thick dust that he followed before pausing.

Bubba sighed and went back for the sock he'd left behind. After all, he didn't have a clue when he would get back to it, and his bare tootsies were getting cold. Of course, it didn't really need to be said that it was a gift from Willodean.

•

Based on the view from the first window he encountered, it was still dark outside. So Bubba surmised that it was somewhere between 4 a.m. and 7 a.m. There wasn't even the hint of sunrise to come. He was going to guess that it was about 5 a.m. He would have looked at his watch, but it had vanished. He didn't think someone would steal it because it was a cheap Timex, but he did think it might have come off when he was being dragged around, which was what had likely happened to his footwear. Plus, not only were there drag marks on his knees, but his wrists and forearms were somewhat scuffed. (Someone had gotten a work out this morning; he was a big corn-fed bubba, after all. Also gumbo, pot roast, and peach cobbler fed.)

Additionally, he judged that he was in another building altogether. Bubba hadn't realized that the Dogley Institute for Mental Well-Being had more than the one building. He had only visited the one and only because he'd needed the help of the psychiatrist persona of David Beathard. In his place, he'd found The Purple Singapore Sling, who had been of more help than Bubba would have imagined. (The PSS's ability to see inside people's souls had made them nervous and chatty, which was a bona fide plus in Bubba's book.) In any case, Bubba hadn't been checking the layout and structure of the mental institute.

Solely based on the issue of transporting something his weight, Bubba also surmised that he couldn't be far from the actual hospital, unless someone had used a convenient Radio Flyer wagon to transport his bulk over a longer distance. (In no scenario he could imagine were Radio Flyer wagons standard equipment in a mental institution.) The road was likely still closed off, so he had to be in the immediate vicinity. Also, he might be able to sneak around in the darkness and find out a few things before it was discovered that he had escaped from his straitjacket prison. He might as well take advantage.

He went out a door, slowly opening it so that it didn't creak. Then he shut it carefully behind him, making certain that it remained open a crack just on the off chance that he might need a place to hide.

Bubba attempted to think back to his basic training days in the Army. There had been two night courses where sneaking had been instructed upon. Low crawling and high crawling had been fine arts to be perfected in the sand pits, over and over and over again. The state of Bubba's knees did not preclude itself to relearning the low crawl, so he inched through the shadows all the while thinking of a drill sergeant who had once screamed at him for breaking a branch with his foot.

Bubba tilted his head and listened. The hospital property sat on a mesa of old growth forest. There should have been crickets and other night life making it difficult to hear one's self think. The mournful hoot of an owl wouldn't have been out of place. There were the distant strains of "Happy" by Pharrell Williams. Somebody was happy. It wasn't Bubba.

Then someone yelled faintly, "Everyone drinks every time Pharrell sings 'HAPPY'!" It didn't seem like that someone was being threatened by a murderer, or that they had disappearing bodies or were even vaguely disturbed by being cut off from the civilized world.

Bubba shook his head and immediately regretted doing so because of the piercing headache that resulted. He made an estimation of where the hospital was located. The fog was beginning to dissipate, and he could see through the trees to some murky yellow lights. He looked up and could see the North Star. He was on the east side of the hospital, the one farthest away from the entrance and the one least likely to be seen. The building was something like an office space or some kind of separate quarters for the staff.

The eloquent strains of "Happy" were coming from behind Bubba in a northerly direction where there might have been a few more buildings. He didn't know, and he didn't feel like stumbling around the darkness to see who was singing about their emotional state and drinking to the word denoting joyfulness. He didn't want a drink; he wanted an aspirin, preferably two or three. Possibly an X-ray machine would be helpful. Willodean stroking the errant lock of hair out of his face would be beneficial and extremely appealing.

Bubba steeled his shoulders. David and the others

needed him. They were being threatened. He inched through the darkness and stepped on a patch of goatheads. He bit his lip to keep from crying out while he did the sticky-thorns-in-my-foot dance. It didn't matter a bit to the goatheads that he had replaced Willodean's gift on his foot. Sitting on his butt well away from the patch of wayward thorny weeds, he plucked a half dozen out of his foot.

After he limped toward the yellow lights and made his way through a wretched patch of poison sumac, he came to the large yard where the patients had been playing with foam darts.

The doors to the hospital burst open and Nurse Ratchley, ran out shrieking, "WE'RE ALL GOING TO DIE!" Then she proceeded to run in a tight circle repeating the same until Tandy stepped up beside her and slapped her across the face. The movie actress seemed to take entirely too much enjoyment out of the act.

"Get a hold of yourself, woman!" Tandy yelled.

"But there's only SEVEN cupcakes left!" Ratchley clutched her face and dragged in gasping breaths of air. "SEVEN! Bubba's gone! Gone! GONE!"

Precious leapt out of the open door and was followed by Dr. Adair, Cybil, Peyton, and David. The dog's prodigious nose immediately pointed in Bubba's direction. She threw back her head and bayed in triumph, which was followed by a charge across the lawn. Bubba braced himself for impact as the canine threw herself at him. It didn't help because she still knocked him into the ground.

Precious was still attempting to lick his face clean to the bone when the others circled around him. David said, "I say, Watson, whatever have you been doing? Bad form, old man."

Bubba sighed and looked up at the people staring down at him. "Where's Abel?" he asked.

Chapter Fifteen

Bubba and Supplementary Shenanigans

Sunday, April 7th

Abel was missing. So were Bubba's boots.

"What about Abel?" Bubba asked. The entire group had dragged him inside and sat him down at a cafeteria table. Unfortunately, he could see all too well how many cupcakes remained.

"I can't talk about his diagnosis," Dr. Adair said, looking at the bump on the back of Bubba's head. "That's privileged information. I am under a mandate not to discuss this with people like you." He sighed. "Maybe a concussion. You'll need an X-ray. Don't go to sleep anytime soon." He came around and looked into Bubba's eyes. "Your pupils look all right. You lost consciousness?"

Bubba nodded.

"We'll get you some over-the-counter painkillers and hope the police show up on our doorstep today," the doctor said.

"I told you already," Peyton said, "CEO of Vetcorp. They had a fabulous profit last year. He has two sons, both already married; I didn't plan their weddings, which is their loss if you ask me. Of course it was years ago, before Pure Love Weddings, LLC was ever established. " He made a noise not unlike a mini-raspberry full of contempt and added quietly, "They should have waited."

"There was something about his brother," Bubba said. If he hadn't been looking in the doctor's direction, Bubba wouldn't have seen it. The doctor flinched slightly. He had a terrible poker face. Miz Demetrice would love having the psychiatrist at one of her Thursday evening games.

"Power struggle is what comes to mind," Peyton said. "I wish my phone worked. I could just Google it. I think the brother wants to take over the company, but Abel holds the majority share at the moment. There was a hint that the brother could oust Abel based on the alcoholism, but seriously, who cares about that? It's not like he drove drunk and hit a crowd of pre-schoolers. No, he peed on the ice sculpture at one of their fancy fundraisers while having a rabid discourse on the pros and cons of the Tea Party. Didn't you see it? It was on YouTube, and every other channel, too."

"What kind of ice sculpture?" Tandy asked.

"Swan maybe," Peyton said. "It could have been a goose. It was some big water fowl type of bird. Ice sculptors never get it exactly right. Do you know how many people want ice sculptures at their weddings? I mean, there's a significant wedding business in the summer, and ice melts in the heat. It melts quickly." He fanned himself as if he was melting.

"Are we going to die?" Ratchley asked plaintively.

"You senseless Suzy," Cybil said. "Not while we're all together."

"So the brother might want to do Abel in," Bubba stated, half to himself.

"But what about all the other people who got

murdered and went missing?" David asked. "Watson, you're off your corker. You haven't been using my seven percent solution have you? Have you been relying too much on the Baker Street Irregulars? Perhaps there's a brain disease going on."

Bubba knew he was grasping at straws.

"They all went off and committed suicide," Dr. Adair suddenly proclaimed. "It's a rare case of mass hysteria. I'll write it up for *The American Journal of Psychiatry* and maybe *The New England Journal of Medicine*, too. I need another paper published." He patted his rumpled jacket as if he was looking for something to write with.

Bubba shook his head. He stood up and went into the kitchen. David, Precious, and Peyton followed him. "Ya'll seen an ice bag around? Mebe remnants of an ice sculpture?"

"There's frozen corn in that freezer," Peyton said, pointing. He shrugged at David's look. "What? I was looking for something sweet to eat. They have to feed you people some kind of treat, right? Not a Popsicle in sight, for goodness sakes. You know that gives me an idea. We could freeze fake worms and plastic bait in Popsicles." He clapped his hands together. "A redneck slash fishing themed wedding. We can put straw and fake cow patties on the floor. Buckets of peanuts on the tables. What fun!"

"That would prolly make Willodean spew," Bubba said, opening the squat floor freezer, not adding, "and me, too," although he wanted to say it. He located a two-pound bag of frozen corn and applied it to the back of his head. "Did I mention that someone knocked me out?"

"What? Again, Watson?" David said. "One day that's not going to turn out for you so well."

"That *is* a nasty lump on the back of your head," Peyton said. "The wedding photographer can work around it. We should probably avoid profile shots."

Bubba saw a clipboard with a menu on it. Taco night was supposed to be followed by Cold Cut Sunday and Order-a-Pizza Monday. (Clearly the kitchen staff wasn't planning to come back for a few days.) A plain Bic pen was connected to the clipboard with a string and lots of scotch tape. He snagged the board with his free hand and put it where he could retrieve it in a few minutes.

Peyton sighed. "Fake cow patties is probably not the best idea. I need to store that away for future reference. Somewhere there is a groom who is wild about fishing and hunting and who will die for a themed wedding. No pun intended. I've *got* to stop saying that."

"You could have a camouflage cake," David suggested. "A little pair of boy and girl hunters on the top. Or two boy hunters for that matter. Or two girl hunters. I'm open-minded."

"Oh, and when the bride and groom walk out of the venue, the groomsmen could have their fishing poles out and crossed for the couple to walk underneath," Peyton said excitedly. "The bridal gown can be decorated with iridescent fishing lures."

"You do know we're in trouble here," Bubba said dryly. "Not wedding trouble, but are-we-going-to-live-through-the-night-trouble."

Peyton rolled his eyes. "You deal with stress your

way, and I'll deal with it my way, which is by planning weddings I have yet to be contracted upon. Oooh, chocolate-covered grasshoppers. They're delicious if they're roasted before they're covered with the chocolate. And it has to be a dark chocolate, not milk chocolate."

"That sounds disgusting," David said.

"What do you know?" Peyton asked dismissively. "Your imaginary character's country eats kippers and Shepherd's pie."

"I'm partial to mincemeat pies," David said loftily.

Even food that Bubba had never had before was beginning to sound good. He even thought about eating one of the cupcakes, but they didn't seem like something that would be a good idea to touch. (Eat a cupcake; someone dies or vanishes. Lesson: Don't eat a cupcake.)

Bubba found a loaf of bread and made himself a sandwich with bologna from one of the walk-in refrigerators. He slathered mayonnaise on it and even found a slice of American cheese. It wasn't fried onions with blackberry jelly, but it would do. *Wait, fried onions with blackberry jelly? Yuck. Well, mebe with rainbow sprinkles and a few red hots on top.*

While cutting the sandwich in half with a chef's knife, Bubba tried to convince Peyton and David to partake of the bologna goodness, but both men refused while they continued to argue the merits and deficiencies of British food. Precious, however, ate three slices of bologna without pausing to taste them. Then she licked her chops delicately.

Bubba thought best with a full stomach. His stomach wouldn't be really full, but he would definitely feel better. Holding the frozen corn package to his head, he swallowed the sandwich with a minimum of chewing. Evidently, Precious was rubbing off on him.

He burped and murmured, "Excuse me." He located a bottle of Coca Cola in the refrigerator. It wasn't an RC Cola, but it would do.

When Bubba was done with the Coke, he burped again and sighed. "Okay, then. Let's get this thing done."

David and Peyton paused in their argument to glance at Bubba. Bubba retrieved the clipboard and said, "There was Mrs. Ferryjig, who they said had a heart attack." He wrote the name down. "It seems unlikely that a gal could be murdered in a way that would look like an actual heart attack, but I reckon we need to include her seeing as how that search was included on your Xoom, David." He paused and chewed the top of the pen. It didn't taste bad for a pen. "There was Hurley Tanner, who supposedly committed suicide but had bruises on his arms and remnants of duct tape." He wrote that down. "Then Blake Landry, social worker, who was strangled. No question about that one." Bubba jotted some more. "Those were the ones who were dead, well and truly dead, correct?"

David and Peyton both nodded. Precious found a corner to lay in and digest in peace.

"Then Leeza and Thelda vanished." Bubba wrote some more. "No evidence of them being dead yet."

David developed a stone expression on his face.

"Followed by Jesus and Abel," Bubba said. "That's it for now. Did I miss anyone?"

"And the sun isn't even close to being up yet," Peyton added helpfully.

"We should look at the missing people's rooms," Bubba said. "We need clues."

Peyton shrugged.

"Here, here, Watson," David said. "Do I need a new disguise? I do a wonderful rector's wife. I can quote from three passages of the Bible. I make a smashing high tea with biscuits."

"I can do his makeup," Peyton threw in.

"No makeup," Bubba said. He put the clipboard back where he'd found it because writing things down didn't seem to help in solving anything.

Bubba beckoned to Precious, and the three of them plus one tired canine went back into the cafeteria. Bubba looked at Dr. Adair, Ratchley, Cybil, and Tandy. "We're going to look at people's rooms for clues."

"That's not even remotely legal," Dr. Adair protested.

Bubba cast the doctor a stern look. Bubba wanted the look to say "I know you're keeping something to yourself. It's something about Abel's brother. I know it on account of the look you made when I said something about it. You know it. You know that I know that you know. We all know that something, something, something," but all he could come up with saying was, "Don't matter much now. Stick together."

"You know," Peyton interjected, "no one has been sticking together."

"I had to pee," Ratchley protested. "I don't want to

die with a full bladder. I drank five cups of coffee and two lemonade smoothies. I also ate an orange, a Pop Tart, and two bagels with cream cheese. Then after I peed, I threw up. I'm having a very bad day."

"Not just her, but him—" Peyton pointed to the doctor "— and her" to Cybil, "— and her," at Tandy."

"You went off by yourself, too," Dr. Adair accused.

"I wanted to check the bars on my phone," Peyton explained. "Just in case I could get through to Ginger. Besides the murderer doesn't want me. I'm just here to plan a wedding. No one ever wants to kill the wedding planner."

No one could argue about that, although Bubba recalled a fleeting moment of wanting to strangle a wedding planner.

"Besides, I can't be the murderer," Peyton went on. "I didn't know any of you except Bubba before yesterday. It's not a crime to not have an alibi. Or is that an interesting Texas quirk I didn't know about?"

"So no one has any alibis," Bubba said. "Could be any of us."

"You've been alone more than anyone," Dr. Adair said quickly.

"But you were gone when Bubba was getting knocked out," Peyton pointed out.

"I thought I heard something," Dr. Adair said. "It was strange. I thought I heard music. It sounded like 'Gangnam Style' by Psy." He momentarily mimicked the dance and then caught himself with an embarrassed grimace.

"I thought I done heard something like that earlier,"

Bubba admitted. "Is there more buildings than the one to the west?"

"There's a lodge back there," Ratchley said. "We usually use it for the VIPs." She glanced at Tandy. "It had a water leak last month, though, and needs some work." The nurse shook her head. "They said it was really torn up and dangerous."

Bubba paced back and forth for a minute. Things were starting to percolate in his head, which was still banging like a bad drum. "Does anyone have some aspirin?"

"Are you kidding?" Ratchley asked. "This is a hospital."

"From something what ain't bin opened," Bubba amended.

"There's a pharmacy on the second floor," Dr. Adair said. "Come on. Does anyone else need their meds?"

Tandy, David, and Cybil raised their hands.

"Cybil," Dr. Adair protested.

"I could use something to calm me down," Cybil explained. "If ever there was a situation that that was necessary, this is it."

"Okay, let's all go," Bubba said.

"I'm going to need some of those NicoDerm patches," Tandy said, "or I can just start ripping out people's throats."

Dr. Adair led the way. He didn't think they could fit in the tiny elevator, so they went up the large staircase located in the oversized foyer. He said, "Meds were prepared for the patients before the pharmacists left, so they'll be on a cart in the locked facility with everything labeled in baggies. They'll have some aspirin for you Bubba, and we can get Ms. North her nicotine patch."

"Maybe five or six," Tandy said.

A few minutes later they were standing at the pharmacy's heavy steel door. Bubba had looked in here before, sticking his head up to the walk-up window and carefully peering into the corners looking for Thelda or Leeza. He'd opened the door with Dr. Adair's keys and stuck his head inside, but the place had been as deserted as most of the remainder of the hospital.

"Those carts are preloaded," Dr. Adair said, "and brought in by truck. They're locked so that employees don't have a temptation to help themselves to meds. Particularly the more narcotic ones." He jingled his keys. "Only the staff doctor on call and head nurse have access."

"That cabinet has all the non-narcotic samples in it," Cybil said. She pointed. "Ibuprofen, acetaminophen, et cetera." She tapped the end of her nose. "I think Leeza had a script for a light anti-anxiety drug which would be very helpful at the moment."

"I am *not* giving you Leeza's meds," Dr. Adair said. "And how would you know where all the drugs are going?"

"Disagreeable doodad," Cybil muttered. Then she added, "You think there are any secrets in a hospital? Really? Seriously?"

"Just open the door," Bubba said, holding the dripping bag of rapidly unfreezing corn to his head. "I've got a splitting headache what ain't helping me think better."

The doctor opened the door and spent about five minutes getting the correct medications out of a cart labeled Sunday, April 7th. Then he opened another cabinet and asked, "Aspirin, ibuprofen, or acetaminophen, Bubba? There's naproxen, too."

"Pass 'em all over to me. I'll take the aspirin first." Bubba adjusted the corn.

Ratchley passed out small paper cups filled with water.

Dr. Adair passed Cybil a cup of pills. "There. A very mild sedative," he said. "That'll take the edge off."

Then he handed two small packets to Tandy. "NicoDerm CQ patch," Dr. Adair said to her. "You simply—"

"This isn't my first tobacco withdrawal rodeo," Tandy snapped and snatched the packets from his fingers. She sighed and added, "Sorry. Quitting pot and tobacco in the same week is just not the easiest thing to do."

Bubba swallowed the pills from one of the small packets he'd been given. He took a cup from Ratchley and chased it down with water. "That's got to be better soon."

While Bubba waited for Dr. Adair to make notes on the paperwork that came with the cart, he thought about murder.

"I am the murderer," he murmured.

"What was that, Watson?" David asked. "You can't be the murderer, old chap. You didn't even know some of these people."

"I'm trying to put myself in the murderer's shoes,"

Bubba said. "That's what works in the TV shows."

Bubba went into the hallway and waited while everyone but the doctor followed. The doctor locked up the cart, put the paperwork away, and then locked the door of the pharmacy. He also wrote on a chart hanging on the wall.

"I'm the murderer," Bubba muttered again. "What do I want?"

"What does any murderer want?" Tandy asked. "It's like I said." She ripped one packet in half, removed the backing from the patch, and slapped it on her upper arm. Then she pressed all around the edges so as to maximize the effect. Then she repeated it with another patch on the opposite arm. "Revenge. Money. Because you're nuts. You do realize we're in a mental institution, although I'm not exactly nuts, except when I don't have a cig." She giggled. "Like now."

"If I'm nuts, don't I just kill in any old way?" Bubba asked. "I get out the nearest convenient weapon and start whaling away. Mebe a knife around here."

"Or a garrote made out of a telephone cord, pointless Perry," Cybil added helpfully.

"It was computer wire and a metal ruler," Dr. Adair pointed out.

"Whatever," Peyton said. "If you're nuts, I would imagine you wouldn't be picky. It could be a banana plant—" he waved at a nearby potted plant— "or a pen through the ear— " he waved at the pen in Dr. Adair's hand— "or anything that could be used in a deadly fashion." He smiled. "At one wedding I did, one of the bridesmaids went after another one with a stiletto heel.

195

Very messy. They shredded the wedding bouquet they were fighting over."

"But if you're crazy," Bubba said, "you don't really plan ahead, right?"

"I dislike the terms, nuts and crazy," Dr. Adair said virtuously. "It doesn't help the mindset of the patients."

"The point Watson is attempting to make," David said, "is that whomever is killing here is not mentally deficient. On the contrary, the perpetrator has all the canniest wits about him or her and is ready to use them at a moment's notice. Indeed, this person, or persons, is a mad genius."

Ratchley said, "That doesn't make me feel better."

"I want to look at Mr. Tanner's room," Bubba said.

"Why not Mrs. Ferryjig's room?" Peyton asked. "Wasn't she the first?"

"Because you cain't make a murder look like a heart attack," Bubba said. "I reckon poor Mrs. Ferryjig had a heart attack, then someone took advantage of that. That someone went to David's Xoom and did a search on how to make a murder look like a heart attack."

"That's ironic since all those people on the movie set were trying to make a heart attack look like a murder," Tandy said. "Poor Kristoph didn't have a clue so many people thought other people hated him." Kristoph had been a movie director for *The Deadly Dead*, which had been recently filmed at and around Pegramville. Kristoph had also had the bad fortune to kick off in Bubba's house, which had been the questionable beginning of events that rapidly went south, so south that it made hell look good. It didn't make Bubba particularly happy because no one wanted someone to die in their newly constructed house. Regardless of Bubba's wants, all the publicity, good and bad alike, had sped the film through its process, and it had been released in record time, with Kristoph's widow at the helm.

"I loved that movie," Cybil said. "They were going to fly away to an island and live happily ever after." She glanced at Precious, who was waiting patiently for someone to give her food or do something to entertain her or for a doggy bed to appear before her. "The zombie Basset hound didn't really work for me."

"It wasn't my idea," Bubba said, then he lowered his voice for Precious, "She dint mean it, Precious woobie. You were the best dang zombie Basset hound ever."

Ratchley said, "So someone thought they would point a finger at David about Mrs. Ferryjig's heart attack. Then what?"

"More searches about how to make murder look like suicide," Bubba said.

"Hurley Tanner," David said.

"Okay, but isn't that a little hard to do?" Peyton asked.

"Not if he's drugged first," Bubba said. He glanced meaningfully at the doctor.

"I didn't drug Hurley," Dr. Adair protested.

"His wife and daughter came to visit him," Bubba said. "Maybe they did."

"But then why is the rest of this happening?" Cybil asked. "That doesn't make any sense."

"Let's take a look at Hurley's room," Bubba said

gently. "Is it still got his stuff in it?"

"It's all there," Ratchley said. "The hospital was waiting on the coroner's report on Mr. Tanner's death just to make sure all the i's were dotted and the t's were crossed."

"Lead the way, doc," Bubba said, and Dr. Adair winced again.

Chapter Sixteen

Bubba and Mysterious Motives

Sunday, April 7th

Bubba had, in fact, looked at Hurley Tanner's room before that moment. But he hadn't been looking for clues; he had been looking for Leeza and Thelda. Leeza and Thelda were still not in the room.

Now the door was open because Dr. Adair had opened it with his keys. Bubba stood just inside the room. Dr. Adair stood beside him. David crouched on the floor, holding an enormous magnifying glass in one hand. The magnifying glass's frame was decorated with dragonflies and butterflies. Bubba guessed that it was the largest one David could find, and it had originated in the toy section of the nearest Walmart. As a result it appeared rather curious in Sherlock Holmes's hand. Furthermore, Bubba had to wonder where David had been keeping the oversized instrument, but not too much.

The others peered around the edges of the doors, intent on what Bubba was looking for.

"Of course, they cleaned up," Dr. Adair said. "The sheets and bed were stripped. The towels were taken away. The police took the pill bottles and tumbler. The family requested that they be allowed to pack the remainder once they arrived to claim the body."

"Was he in bed when he died?" Bubba asked.

"Yes. He apparently drank a glass of water with the

pills and then laid down to, er, complete his task." Apparently the psychiatrist found it distasteful to say the s-word.

"He was secured to the bed with duct tape," David corrected. He slid past them and indicated several locations on the hospital bed's frame. "Remnants of tape here, here, and here." He used the magnifying glass to point.

Bubba knelt next to the bed. "Looks like something sticky was there all right. And it was in the four spots someone might use to make someone be still for a bit."

Tandy rubbed her arms where the nicotine patches were located. "If he was tied down, how did they get the pills in him?"

"Shoved them into his mouth and held it shut," David said. "A reflective ultraviolet photograph revealed perimortem bruising on his jawline." He held up a hand and spread out his fingers. "Four very suspicious finger end-sized bruises on the right side and one thumb end-sized bruise on the left side of his face."

"You took a camera into where the body was stored?" Dr. Adair asked, appalled. "Is our security that lax? Was the door open?"

"Of course not," David replied in a matter-of-fact tone. "I had keys that I borrowed from one of the doctors."

"Mental note to self," Dr. Adair muttered, "change all the locks. Beef up security. Check with our attorneys. We need a whole new key inventory. Perhaps we should upgrade to key cards."

"Reflective ultraviolet photography is a technique

used by police to document bruising on children," David explained with his pseudo-British accent back in place. "It's a time-consuming method but highly valuable in the area of revealing bruises that might not have had time to appear once death occurred." He took the dragonfly-embellished magnifying glass and observed a section of the bed mattress. "The bruising on his biceps were a tad older and showed before he died."

Bubba realized that everyone was staring at the former PSS. Bubba didn't know anything about reflective ultraviolet photography, but David was pretty clever. He probably had read up on as many police investigatory procedures as he could. However, it didn't really fit into the era that Sherlock Holmes fit into, so David's persona had adapted for the present. (Not unlike the dragonfly-ornamented magnifying glass.) "Do you know anything about that type of photography, doc?"

"I've read some papers on it," Dr. Adair said weakly. "We occasionally get called upon to testify in court cases and such. It's a natural side effect of dealing with our area of expertise. We're not, however, really forensic specialists at Dogley."

"Sometimes it can find fingerprints, too," David said mysteriously. "Fingerprints on a corpse, for example. Fingerprints not made by the corpse upon himself, you see."

Bubba almost bit the side of his lip as he considered what David was saying. "Uh, David, you saying that you took a bunch of special photographs of Hurley Tanner?"

"Without permission of the decedent's family," Dr.

Adair said. "I demand you give all the photographs and negatives to the hospital."

"What was it that you wanted to look at, Dr. Watson?" David asked in lieu of responding to Dr. Adair.

Bubba stood up and slowly turned around looking at the room. It wasn't a complicated affair. He would have thought that a CEO would be entitled to a fancier room, but maybe that was part of the process of recovery. There were some framed photographs on the nightstand. There was a book by Isaac Asimov. *Foundation* was the name. Bubba didn't really care much for science fiction, but he knew the book all the same. A single man works to save humanity from itself.

Bubba thought about irony and put a cork in his thinking. David had just announced to a group of people that he probably had evidence against one of them. He might as well have stuck a target on his forehead and closed his eyes and waited for someone to start shooting. "You told me, David, that Hurley was a second generation oil man. He had family money, right?"

"Lots and lots of family money," David agreed. "A great bloody pile of it."

"His wife and daughter visited him. You said you played a game with him."

"Dominoes," David confirmed. "He seemed happy. His twenty-one days were almost up. He was doing well in his program. He'd agreed to an Antabuse program for continuing abstinence after his release."

"Antabuse?"

"It's a drug that inhibits the metabolism of alcohol,"

Dr. Adair explained. "Alcoholics can participate in a ninety-day program to continue their abstinence. If you are taking Antabuse and you imbibe, you become very ill. It establishes both a psychological and physiological mechanism in alcoholics."

"But instead, he took a bunch of barbiturates," Bubba said. "Pills that dint come from the hospital."

"Hurley dint, I mean, didn't commit suicide, Watson," David declared. "Clearly, the barbiturates were forced upon him after he was immobilized with duct tape."

Bubba slowly turned around the room. At this point he didn't doubt David, but he wasn't happy with David's big mouth. He looked at everything he could. There were slippers under a chair, two more Asimov books on the corner desk, a desk calendar, a bag of lollipops, and a soft navy blue robe hanging on a hook behind the door. He looked at the closet and opened it up. The closet was constructed for short stays. One side allowed for clothing to be hung up. The other side possessed a built-in dresser. Bubba pulled out a few of the drawers. He saw socks and underwear. The socks were Champion. The underwear was Fruit of the Loom. For a rich man, Hurley hadn't taken on airs. Bubba had more than a few Fruit of the Looms himself.

"I'm distinctly uncomfortable with the direction of this search," Dr. Adair said, eying the tartan plaid boxers neatly folded in the drawer.

"What difference does it make?" Ratchley asked. "If someone is going to kill all of us, then we can look in everyone's drawers."

"I bet someone has some more smokes around

here," Tandy said. "For example, I haven't had a chance to look at the schizophrenic's room for those Luckies. Those Luckies are screaming for me to discover them."

Bubba was missing something obvious. He had a reason that had led him to this man's room. It wasn't one that most people would have said had substance to it, but it was a reason that made sense. He shut the drawers and closed the closet.

"I'm the murderer," he said again.

David shrugged and twirled the magnifying glass. "Well, old chap," he said to Bubba, "let's go with that."

"I want to kill someone," Bubba said.

"I'd like to kill a few people," Peyton admitted from the door.

"I'd like to kill the person or persons who are keeping us here," Cybil said. "That murdering Maude." She hesitated and then added, "Or murdering Maudes."

"It's not just because I feel like killing," Bubba went on. "It's because I have a reason. What's my reason?"

"If we knew the answer to that," Tandy said, "then we wouldn't be here. Who wants to explore Room 34 for cigs? It'll be just like a nicotine treasure hunt, except I'll be the winner."

Bubba turned around again. "I have something against Hurley Tanner."

"Is it because using oil is bad for the Earth?" Ratchley asked. "It is finite, you know."

"Did he do something to you personally?" Peyton asked. "Maybe he hit someone with his car while he was drunk. Is that why he was here, doc?"

"No, there weren't any DUIs involved," Dr. Adair

said. "It was only an unfortunate episode while he was intoxicated."

"Hurley and a few friends did a pub crawl in Atlanta," David said. "They were trying to hit as many bars as they could in one night. I suppose one can only estimate the sheer amount of establishments with alcohol in the large metro area of Atlanta. After the fifth bar, he and his friends found a police car parked outside the bar. Hurley decided he desperately wanted a nightstick, probably because he was that inebriated and could not recall that he could easily purchase a thousand nightsticks if he so desired. They tried to break into the car, which didn't work very well. The five of them picked up a mailbox and threw it through the windshield of the police cruiser, which was extremely bad for both the mailbox and the cruiser. Then just as the police officers returned, the others ran off while Hurley threw up. The Atlanta Police Department was very unhappy."

"Did he get the nightstick?" Tandy asked.

"No, he didn't get the nightstick," David said. "He ended up paying for the mailbox and the police cruiser. I believe he was somewhat ashamed of himself. He ended up donating funds for five cruisers to the township, and that was after he'd made a plea bargain with the prosecutor. Hurley was turning himself around. He was serious about making this time stick. His brother made a statement about it. Hurley didn't do pills. He didn't do illegal drugs. He did bourbon. Lots of bourbon. Kentucky bourbon. Scotch bourbon. There was even mention of a Japanese bourbon. Someone should have remembered that when they staged the suicide. If they had used bourbon with the pills instead of water, I mightn't have had an initial doubt."

David had lost the British accent, which was fine with Bubba. Bubba glanced at David and saw the sad look on his friend's face. He reached out and patted David's Inverness coat-clad shoulder.

"Ah, Watson," David said quietly, "whatever would I do without you? It won't be the same after you marry the beauteous sheriff's deputy."

"I don't remember Dr. Watson marrying a beauteous sheriff's deputy," Tandy said, "or an ugly one for that matter."

"Willodean ain't ugly," Bubba protested.

"And she can kick some serious ass," Tandy agreed. "I've never seen someone throw a person over their head like that in real life." It was true. Willodean had thrown a would-be killer over her head.

"Ain't she wonderful?" Bubba sighed. "But that's neither here nor there. We've got to figure this thing out." He straightened his shoulders, adjusted the rapidly melting bag of corn on his head, and looked around the room again. It was picking at the edge of his consciousness; something was yelling at him to notice it.

The desk calendar. Bubba approached the little desk. It was only there for patients to do a little bit of writing and catching up on whatnot. There wasn't even a laptop, although there was a switch plate on the wall that included Ethernet adapters. "Dint Hurley have a computer?"

"They're not allowed in the initial drying out

period," David said.

"Did you look at this calendar, David?" Bubba asked.

"It's Sherlock, Watson, and I gave it a peremptory glance."

Bubba thumbed to the current date. It was blank. He paged back a few. There wasn't an entry that said "Due to be murdered by X today," but there was a notation about his wife and daughter's visit. A smiley face was drawn next to it.

Bubba frowned. Not a frowny face, but a smiley face. He paged over a week into the future and found where Hurley Tanner had noted his expected date of release. Certainly, to Bubba's expectations, he had already gone through the roughest part of the recovery program.

"Hurley was leaving next week," Bubba said.

"That's correct," Dr. Adair confirmed.

"Don't seem like a fella who's about to commit suicide."

"Perhaps he was focusing on what it would be like without support on the outside walls of this hospital," Dr. Adair said. "It can be devastating without that kind of support."

"Not sending happy vibes my way, doc," Tandy said.

"Your strength is innate, Ms. North," Dr. Adair said smoothly. "Once you've decided on your course, I believe you have a high chance of keeping clean. However, as a physician you should know that I don't approve of smoking tobacco."

"That's noted," Tandy said. She tapped the patches on both her shoulders. "I think these are wearing off."

Cybil cleared her throat. "You know, Hurley told me

he was excited to get back into the world. He said he was looking forward to seeing it without the alcohol goggles he'd been wearing for the last ten years. That his daughter was getting married. He wanted to walk her down the aisle without tripping and stinking of stale bourbon."

"Married," Peyton exclaimed. "No one told me. I need to get a card to the Widow Tanner. Oh, dear, I wish these people would simply announce impending nuptials in the correct venues, and I wouldn't have to go to these troubles."

"You said something about the daughter having a boyfriend," Bubba said to Peyton.

"Lots of people have boyfriends," Peyton said. "Sometimes it takes them a bit of time to come to the conclusion that they need a fabulous wedding to go along with it." He snapped his fingers three times when he said fabulous, drawing out the word in long syllables, "fab-u-lous."

"I'm going to elope to Las Vegas," Cybil said. "I need a civil servant or maybe a preacher dressed like Elvis to perform the ceremony. As soon as I can convince my boyfriend, the waffling Wally."

Peyton gasped violently, as if the very notion upset him. "Heathen," he hissed. "You'll always regret not having a *real* wedding."

"Some more reasons why Hurley dint commit suicide," Bubba said. "I think there's more than enough evidence to bring the Pegram County Sheriff's Department back into it." Bubba didn't really want to mention that Steve Simms had been the investigator on the suicide, and consequently it was likely his lack of interest that had this one falling through the cracks. Of course, it wasn't all Steve's fault since the doctors at the hospital wanted to rush it through and then pretend it was just a minor hiccough in the universe of sobriety. If one of the doctors had said "But..." it was just as likely that Steve would have backed up and taken another look. Even Doc Goodjoint had rubberstamped it.

However, someone wanted people to know about it. Someone had done the searches on David's Xoom in preparation for pointing the finger at him. Someone had cut the hospital off from civilization for a few days at an inopportune time. Someone waited until David was alone before people vanished. Someone was probably waiting right then and there. Someone had more reason than ever to wish David wasn't so inquisitive.

"Are we done in here?" Dr. Adair asked.

Bubba nodded. "Until we catch someone or I think of something else to look at."

They slowly filed out of the room. Bubba adjusted the dripping bag of corn and then gave up with a long sigh. He threw it in the nearest garbage can.

Tandy was attempting to get Dr. Adair to go to Room 34, saying, "I only want one pack. One. I'll buy her a case. Besides, she's a schizophrenic; she'll think one of her other selves took it."

"You can't combine the NicoDerm patches with actual smoking," Dr. Adair told her. "You'll overdose on nicotine."

"And that would be worse how?" Tandy asked.

Bubba dropped back and gestured at David and Peyton to come closer. They both did, leaning their heads in to hear what Bubba might have to say to them. "It's all about Hurley Tanner," Bubba said quietly.

"Watson," David said quietly, "why are you so fixated on Hurley Tanner?"

"Ifin you're out to kill someone," Bubba said just as quietly, "then you want to make sure it gets done, am I right? You don't want to take any long cuts or detours."

Peyton nodded. David shrugged.

"I mean, a person wants another person dead. He don't want to get caught before he gets the job done, or get caught at all."

"Okay," Peyton said. "What does that have to do with Hurley?"

"Mrs. Ferryjig was coincidental," Bubba said, "but Hurley was the target. The social worker and the others were cover-ups. So..."

"The motive behind Hurley's death is the real reason, Watson," David said, and as if he couldn't help himself, he added, "How very elementary."

"I'm not sure I understand," Peyton complained.

"The killer don't want to go to prison," Bubba explained. "So if he or she kills the person they want to kill, then people are going to point fingers at him or her as the one with the most motive. Specifically, they decided to kill off a bunch of people who weren't really connected except to direct the police to the one person they thought might have done it. I'm goin' to get another headache from all this thinkin'."

Peyton glanced at David. "That's why someone did

those searches on your tablet?"

"Yes and because I did associate with all of the people, dead and missing alike."

"But why Hurley? Why not Thelda or Abel?"

"This is all one big crap shoot," Bubba said. He waved his hands around. "This person, he don't know how long it'll be before the po-lice show up. They could have come within a few hours, or they could have come in three days. He don't know when or where, so his chance, his golden opportunity, was to do it quickly. In fact, he did it first. He dint kill Mrs. Ferryjig, but he took advantage of it."

"You're saying he and him," Peyton said.

"I don't know for sure," Bubba said. "It shore don't sound like something a woman would do, but then the Christmas Killer was a woman."

"So the real murder, I mean the one that he really wanted to commit, was accomplished before all of this smokescreen?"

"That's right," Bubba said. "That's where all the clues are, on account of the rest is just lagniappe to this fella."

Peyton frowned. "But it could have been anyone who wanted Hurley Tanner dead. I mean, his wife and daughter probably had the most to gain, in a monetary manner. They're not here. They're not patients or hanging out with us, so that kind of eliminates them." He paused and then added, "What if murdering Hurley and framing David are just the appetizers? What? It needed to be said."

"They might not be here ifin they had someone

helpin' them," Bubba said grimly. "David," he added, looking the former PSS in the face, "where are them photographs you took?"

Chapter Seventeen

Bubba and the Question of Whodunit?

Sunday, April 7th

"Well," David said slowly. He stopped and waited for Dr. Adair, Tandy, Cybil, and Ratchley to pull ahead of them. Bubba was about to bump into the would-be master detective before he caught himself in time. Peyton steered left, and Precious pranced ahead to sniff a water cooler on the off chance it suddenly began to produce steak bones by the bucketful.

"That type of photography requires a very specialized camera," David said, resuming walking slowly. "And film. And it needs to be developed in a precise manner. You can't just take it to the corner photo place."

"You don't really have any photographs of fingerprints," Bubba stated, "much less ones you kin give to the po-lice."

"No."

"You never did."

"I could," David protested. "I could have them a week from Thursday. That's when the order for the camera and film comes in from eBay. But there's this terrible business about decomposition of the corpse and such, which will make the fingerprints not photographable, not to mention that by that time the remains will have been returned to Atlanta. Accessibility would be a problem in actually taking the photographs." He paused and took a deep breath. "I was merely attempting a calculated ruse, of course, Dr. Watson."

"You're making yourself bait?" Peyton asked. "How very clever for an individual from an asylum."

"Don't be hatin'," David said and then immediately added, "I wonder where *that* came from?"

"Just because they're here don't mean they're stupid," Bubba snapped.

"Why, Bubba," David said with obvious surprise, "that's the nicest thing you've ever said to me." Bubba didn't miss the fact that David had addressed him by his proper name instead of Dr. Watson.

"So ain't no photos," Bubba said just to be certain.

"No. But I surmise that the villain within our group will break away to find them, so we can follow that person," David said and smiled triumphantly. "You see, someone had to hold Hurley's jaw open to force pills down it, and people aren't genuinely aware of the forensic ability to retrieve human fingerprints from flesh. Of course, if one buries one's victim or throws him into a body of water, that point becomes moot. Future reference for future crime-solving scenarios."

"So that's our plan?" Peyton asked. "We wait for someone, one of those four ahead, to go off on their own?"

"We follow the first one," Bubba said.

"But what if the first one just has to go to the bathroom?" Peyton asked. "I mean, that nurse is drinking and eating everything in sight. She has to pee every five minutes."

"It's a calculated gamble," David proclaimed. "We must take it. It's like Americans voting for the President of the United States. It doesn't really count, yet they do it anyway. Fie on the Electoral College."

"Oh-kay," Peyton said with clear skepticism.

"We should have a plan," Bubba said. "Ifin one of them peoples goes off by his or herself, and then another one tries, two of us follows the first one. The other one attempts to distract the second person leaving ifin they can do so safely."

"How does one distract someone who might be a murderer?" Peyton questioned.

"I recommend an expanding steel baton," David said, his voice dripping with excited probability. He produced the item, flicked his wrist, and revealed a baton that was like a child's toy light saber, except made from steel. Then he swished it three times, demonstrating its lethality.

Peyton's eyes went large.

David expertly compressed the item. "Hitting the nose, scrotum, shins are all areas of vulnerability. With a woman, of course, hitting the groin does not produce the same effect."

Bubba and Peyton both automatically covered up the area with a hand.

"Perhaps the bread basket would be an acceptable alternative," David suggested. "If an individual is busy throwing up, they will rapidly lose interest in murdering you." He handed the baton to Peyton.

"Is there anything else you recommend?" Peyton asked.

"There's a nice leather sap I favor," David said and extracted it out of the Inverness coat's pockets, swinging the ten-inch tool in the air with aplomb aplenty. "It's weighted on the end with iron ball bearings. I tried it on a watermelon, may it rest in pieces."

"Is that all?" Peyton asked quietly, holding the baton as if it was electrified.

David replaced the leather sap and next pulled out a set of brass knuckles. The brass was bright and polished. The engraved smiley face on the bottom of the knuckles was innocuously sinister. "Aim for the jaw," he advised, "when using this."

Peyton wiggled his fingers apprehensively. "Really? You have brass knuckles, a sap, and a baton in a hospital?"

"There's a murderer or two afoot," David explained. "It's best to be prepared, old snort."

"It makes sense ifin you take in his plan to isolate a killer," Bubba said. It did make sense. David might be acting foolhardy, but he had the equipment to back him up. At least he didn't have a stun gun, homemade or otherwise.

David offered the brass knuckles to Bubba. Bubba shook his head. "Don't need none of that," he said. He experimentally punched his fist into the palm of his other hand.

David glanced at the people at the other end of the hallway. They disappeared around a corner. "We should go," he said. "Death waits for no man."

"Or dog," Bubba added before he whistled sharply

for Precious.

•

Tandy looked out the window. She had located Room 34 and persuaded Dr. Adair to unlock the door for her, where, with great glee, she had appropriated three packs of Lucky Strikes from the schizophrenic's nightstand. Presently, she stood next to the window and smoked while watching the exterior. "It's starting to get light outside," she said.

"Good," Ratchley said, "I could use something else to eat. Eggs and bacon. Some toast. Do we have kippers? I wonder if sardines would taste like kippers if you fried them. I think there's a case of Vienna sausage, too. I'm pretty sure I could eat a few of those. You know, if we're going to die, then I want a full stomach."

Bubba sat by the double exit doors and thought about what David had said and what Peyton had said. Bubba was gambling with all of his not-so-calculated responses. He could go and look at Blake Landry's office again, searching for clues or for his body, but Bubba knew that he wouldn't find anything that would make sense to him. Someone who had planned all of this so meticulously wouldn't leave that kind of clue for an average Texas redneck (Rednecki Texasicus) to find.

Bubba could also go look in Leeza's, Thelda's, and Abel's rooms for clues. He didn't know exactly what he would or wouldn't find, but again he suspected it wouldn't be that easy. He could even look in Ingrid Ferryjig's room, but Dr. Adair said it had been completely cleaned out the day after her death. There was nothing there for Bubba to see.

Bubba was sure of one thing. Hurley Tanner was *the* target. The emphasis was on *the.* (Not thuh, but thee.) The rest of the murders/disappearances were just CYA. In fact, Bubba could picture Sheriff John biting at the lure he'd been provided. David was a shiny, iridescent spinner waiting for a big fish to chomp. Sheriff John wasn't stupid, however, and he would listen to Bubba and Bubba's theories, but the evidence was somewhat damning. The Xoom would be reconstructed and the memory examined. David didn't have a good alibi for anything. Never mind that someone would have marks on his or her hands from the garrote, and maybe they would have to explain…

Wait.

Bubba glanced around the room. Everyone's hands were seemingly unmarked by the computer wire that had been used. There were two explanations for that. One was that the killer had worn gloves or that…

Swinging his head around, Bubba looked at Dr. Adair.

It had been a decade or more since Bubba had seen *And Then There Were None* on TCM. Sure there were remakes galore, but the first one had been the best. Bubba had even gone through an Agatha Christie phase, reading all the books, and getting movies from Netflix. He'd liked the original film version of that one the best. The plot wasn't hard to understand. It was a locked-door mystery. Ten people come to an island. They find out someone arranged it. Then people start dying of various causes and in relationship to the Ten Little Indians rhyme. Bubba couldn't remember all the details of the rhyme except that one by one, Indians disappeared or died, and hey presto, one was left, who hung himself.

It was kind of like being deliberately trapped in an insane asylum on a mesa in rural Texas. *Kind of.*

Stupid games folks play, Bubba thought. He eyed everyone again, slowly panning the room. He'd seen a man and a woman kill because 1) they thought there was gold treasure, and 2) framing Bubba might mean that the property would be sold to them so they could sell it to Walmart. There was a revenge killing or two, or was it three? He'd lost count. Then there was two killings because someone had wanted money. The last death hadn't been a murder at all. He was wholeheartedly getting tired of it. He was supposed to be getting married, enjoying Willodean's pregnancy with her, and anticipating the birth of his first child, not all this dram-*a.*

Willodean. Bubba pursed his lips. It was likely the poor dear hadn't gotten a wink of sleep the previous night worrying about him. He hoped she was taking her blood pressure medicine and trying to rest a little. Likely, she was probably cleaning her weapon in expectation of having to kill someone over his disappearance. *Cain't do nothing about that now 'cepting stay alive and figure out who's doing what.*

Who?

David paced back and forth in front of the windows, holding the calabash pipe again. Peyton sat primly at a cafeteria table, grimly examining his fingernails. Dr. Adair was leaning over a table, holding his head in his hands, looking immensely worn. Cybil lay on the floor with her eyes shut. Tandy was still at the window, puffing and watching the gray in the east turn to gold. Ratchley was contemplating the kitchen while one hand tapped nervously on the cafeteria table. Finally, Precious lay near Bubba's feet, snoring gently as behooved a lady of her esteemed position. She followed that up with a fart, and she rolled over so her feet all pointed heavenward. A moment later the snoring resumed.

Six little Indians left. And a Bubba. And a wedding planner. And a dog.

Bubba couldn't help the feeling that he should be out looking for Abel, Leeza, and especially Jesus and Thelda. But it was a double-edged sword. If he went looking, then something could happen to the people left behind. There was, of course, no guarantee that one of the remaining people in the cafeteria was a murderer. There was definitely someone else out there, or more than one, waiting and lurking. But on the other hand, what if one of the remainder was a murderer?

Bubba could cross off David because David had asked for help, and he knew David. He could probably cross off Peyton because he had nothing to do with all of this. However, what if Peyton was part of some elaborate plan that involved Bubba's wedding, braised almonds, and grayish grey graying greyful tuxedos?

Bubba shook his head. Peyton wasn't a murderer. He was a metrosexual wedding planner.

Then there was Tandy. She was a movie actress who liked to do the doob. She'd seemed rational when he'd interacted with her before, except of course for tobacco withdrawal. The logic was that an actress who was doing reasonably well in the Hollywood business wouldn't be a logical candidate for a mass murderer. Bubba could probably blow holes in his theory, but he went with it for the moment.

There was Cybil. Cybil was usually chipper and upbeat when she wasn't being actively stalked by a murderer. However, Bubba didn't really know a lot about her. She was a receptionist at the Dogley Institute, sometimes she worked at their thrift shop, she had a boyfriend, and she was allergic to sand. Or was it the beach?

Who was allergic to sand? That was suspicious all by itself. Wouldn't a murderer say she was allergic to sand to get out of a trip when she needed to murder people instead?

Bubba had difficulty imagining the petite redheaded receptionist on the serious end of a garrote, leaning backward with all of her body weight as Blake Landry slowly strangled to death.

Bubba looked at Dr. Adair. He really didn't know anything about the psychiatrist. He didn't live in Pegramville because Bubba would have remembered that. That probably meant he lived in a bigger city and commuted, which wasn't unusual for people with specialties. Pegramville might be in need of a psychiatrist, or three, but they didn't want to pay for one, or three. Consequently, there wasn't a psychiatrist in town. (There was a licensed marriage and family counselor, but he didn't work at Dogley.)

The doctor had said he was divorced and that no one was expecting him. There wasn't anything suspicious about that. Working at the Dogley Institute didn't seem like a bad gig to Bubba, and the man was a medical doctor, so his salary couldn't be too awful. It was even possible that he liked living in rural Texas where the cost of living was almost too good to be true. (Unless you were unemployed, and then the cost of living was not too good to be true.)

There was a similar story with Nurse Ratchley. Bubba didn't know her. She'd said she was married, that her husband was expecting her to work the weekend, and that if he didn't hear from her on Monday or Tuesday he would come looking. That implied a lot of things. One was that she didn't live in Pegramville or Pegram County because there was always a nursing shortage in the area. The hospital probably had special rounds for the psychiatric nurses just to make things work. After all, with their exalted clientele they could pay a nurse to come in and work for 32 hours and pay her for 40. (In one of her more friendly moments, Dee Dee Lacour, the short, irritable African American nurse who worked for Dr. Goodjoint, had explained to Bubba why nursing could be a lucrative business. The conversation had occurred right after filming for *The Deadly Dead* concluded, and the director's wife had been generous with several cases of Dom Perignon, which explained Dee Dee's loquaciousness.) A nurse might want to murder her patients, but Ratchley seemed more interested in eating everything in sight.

Consequently, that meant that everyone was a

suspect. Even Bubba was a suspect. All the recent wedding stress suddenly caused a vein in his brain to explode, transforming him into a multiple personality, which caused him to come to the Dogley Institute to murder people not connected to him in any way.

Bubba sighed. *Right.* The best plan was to hold on until the police showed up, and let them take over. Except if it was Willodean, and she could just sit on the sidelines eating pickles with cream cheese until she realized what Bubba had done and rushed over to bash him over the skull for intimating that she couldn't handle her job. *Of course she can handle her job*, he justified, *but she's pregnant, not that I like her job much when she's not pregnant neither. But I ain't stupid enough to demand she stop being a sheriff's deputy. Not this corn-fed bubba, no sirree.*

Bubba shook his head. Precious snort-snored and rolled onto her side. Clearly, she was missing her comfortable doggie bed in Bubba's room. The movement reminded him he was on a clock, even if it was a kind of death clock.

If Bubba had to narrow it down to immediate suspects, it would be Dr. Adair and Ratchley. Ratchley got up while he watched and went for the kitchen. Through the pass-through windows, he could see her open a refrigerator door and pull something out. She exclaimed, "There's Jell-O cups!" and pulled three more out, holding them in the air as if she had discovered something truly worthwhile. (Perhaps Jell-O cups *were* valuable to Ratchley.)

Does a vicious cold-blooded killer cry with joy over the

extracting of gelatin desserts?

Bubba looked at Dr. Adair. The psychiatrist didn't seem like a viable candidate either. He looked like a tired hospital employee with a rumpled shirt. He had discarded his tie and jacket hours before. His orangish tan appeared a little jaundiced in the fluorescent lights of the cafeteria. He appeared pooped and upset. What psychiatrist wouldn't be upset that a murderer was running around his ward killing off his patients and/or also making his patients disappear?

Bubba glowered. All this thinking was bad for a fella's health. It made his head hurt even worse than it already did. *Leave it for the po-lice*, he advised himself. *That's the best thing I kin do.*

The problem with that was that Bubba couldn't leave it for the police. Not just couldn't, but wouldn't. The very idea went against everything in his nature. People were in danger, not excluding himself, and he couldn't just stand there and let the train wreck go on.

Bubba slowly climbed to his feet and prepared himself to find another cup of coffee. His stomach said some nasty words to him, lurched irregularly, warned him that all was not well within his digestive system, never mind his head, and then growled loudly. He had a sudden urge for the pickled turnips that his Aunt Caressa used to make in the summer. She swore they cured canker sores and ingrown toenails, but they tasted awful. Pickled turnips with a little bit of honey on top sounded pretty good at the moment. However, he was fairly certain that there were no pickled turnips in the hospital's kitchen.

Of course, that was when something blew up outside and knocked Bubba tushie over teakettle.

Chapter Eighteen

Bubba Loses Some More Loonies

Sunday, April 7th

From his position of lying flat on the floor, Bubba looked up at the fluorescent lights and realized they were very dirty. One was blinking frenetically like it was sending messages in Morse code. He also realized that he had been in this position before. Perhaps it hadn't been in this exact place, but it definitely had been the same position. Being knocked tushie over teakettle wasn't an unknown occurrence in Bubba's life, and he knew that fact was wrongity-wrong-wrong.

He lifted his head and looked around. Most of the seven people and one dog in the room had changed their positions and were presently on the floor. The only exception was Dr. Adair. He'd managed to keep his seat at the cafeteria table, and as Bubba's eyes settled on him, the doctor rose up to his feet and asked, "What the holy hell was that?"

"My deductions lead me to believe that it was another detonation of an explosive device," David said authoritatively. He slowly crawled to his feet. Then he bent over to help Tandy get to her feet. She was covered with glass and the pseudo-master sleuth carefully brushed her off. Tandy said sadly, "I lost my cig." She suddenly brightened. "There it is." Then she bent and picked up the semi-broken butt, expertly putting it back between her lips.

Bubba glanced from one figure to the next. Cybil sat on her butt looking flabbergasted. Ratchley lay on her back, saying, "We're gonna die, I just know it." Peyton had been knocked into a wall and sat with his legs spread wide. He rubbed his shoulder and muttered something Bubba couldn't hear. Finally, Precious, who had already been on her back, lurched to her feet in her usual incomparably graceless technique. Her head swung back and forth clearly searching out the humongous, noisy booger who had just threatened them.

Bubba finally came to himself and scrambled to his feet. He could see the pink light on the horizon outside, but he wasn't immediately certain if it were the leading edge of the sun or something else. A billow of black smoke appeared and blocked out the meager light. It came from the direction of the parking lot. If a fire had started, the whole hospital could burn down, so he put his head down and barreled out the nearest door.

"Wait, Bubba!" Peyton cried out, but Bubba ignored him.

Bubba followed his nose, and Precious kept right on his heels. Dimly, Bubba perceived that several people were following him, but he wasn't thinking about them. When he came around the corner of the hospital, he didn't need the dim morning light to see one car burning fiercely in the lot. Whatever explosive had been used had caused it to blow upward and flip upside-down. It sat on its roof, blazing merrily away. Its four rubber wheels spun lazily, as if they might take themselves away from the threat of the fire below them.

It took him another second to realize it was the eightysomething Mercedes Benz he'd parked next to earlier.

Bubba took another second to check to see where Ol' Green was sitting. It was safe and sound, even the scorch marks on it from the last bomb to which it had been exposed were still present. (He was never going to get that dent out from when he had landed on it from that other explosion, but fortunately he had managed to find another vintage windshield from where the front wrought iron gates had gone through the original.) (Were those some new scorch marks on the driver's side door from the most recent explosion? Why, yes indeedy.)

It took Bubba a third second to realize that the Mercedes had landed on another car, but he couldn't tell which one it had been. He was guessing it was the Volkswagen Rabbit of indeterminate age. It took Bubba another second to process that information. His brain seemed to be working in extreme slo-mo.

I parked between the Mercedes and the Rabbit, Bubba thought. *The Mercedes blew up and over Ol' Green onto the Rabbit. I need to find me some wood to knock on. And mebe I need to thank someone.* He looked heavenward. "Thank you, God. I shorely love that truck. Also, God, ifin you kin let Willodean know I'm okay, I would appreciate it."

Peyton appeared beside him. "Oh my great pugnacious pearl putters," he said and handed Bubba a portable fire extinguisher. "I figured you would know how to use this better than I."

Bubba happened to know exactly how to handle a fire extinguisher. (This wasn't his first fire rodeo. It wasn't even his second fire rodeo.) In preparation of future fiery events, he'd watched a video on them and installed three in his house, even though the manual only recommended one upstairs and one down. He'd also put several in the Snoddy Mansion and schooled both Miz Demetrice and Miz Adelia on their proper usage.

He broke the plastic seal on the top of the lever. Then he pulled the pin in the lever mechanism. Holding the extinguisher in one hand, he aimed the hose with the other one. He sprayed in a sweeping motion, aiming for the base of the fire, which in this case was the engine of the Mercedes Benz.

Ain't no one goin' to restore that one, Bubba thought regretfully. He thought it was a 500SEL, which had never been available in the United States, so someone probably had purchased it in Germany and shipped it back to the US. He shook his head to get obscure car facts out of his head. *V8 engine. Optional air bag. Self-leveling hydro-pneumatic suspension. Too bad.*

He shook his head again. He really was tired, and his head was aching terribly. The pills hadn't done much of anything for him.

Someone stepped up beside him and aimed another fire extinguisher. Tandy kept a cigarette in the side of her mouth while she sprayed the chemical at the Mercedes and what might be the remains of the Rabbit. Clearly, a woman who smoked as much as she did was well used to putting out fires. She filled in the gaps he missed in the fire. By the time they ran out of flame retardant, which wasn't all that long, most of the fire was quenched.

"I can go find another one," Peyton offered.

"No, best not to go anywhere by yourself," Bubba said.

"That was my Rabbit," Ratchley said, appearing from behind them. Obviously, she recognized her diminished vehicle when Bubba couldn't. "My car *died.* I loved that car. It belonged to my father. He loved that car, too. He's going to be very pissed at me."

"For what?" Tandy asked. "You didn't blow up your own car, right?"

"No one blew up the Rabbit," Bubba corrected. "Someone blew up the Mercedes, and it came down on top of the Rabbit."

"I think that's a point that won't sink in with my father," Ratchley said with obvious despair. "I should just kill myself before he finds out." She brightened. "But maybe the murderer will take care of that before my father finds out."

Bubba looked back to see if Ratchley was serious and found her peeling open a package of Hostess Sno Balls. She shoved an entire Sno Ball into her mouth. It didn't look like she paused to chew, and he wasn't sure if she was really swallowing or it was just forced down into her gullet by a means that even Albert Einstein wouldn't understand. (Bubba was reminded of the time Precious was begging for one of the boiled eggs Miz Demetrice had brought to a picnic. She'd tossed it to the dog, and the canine had swallowed it out of midair.

Unfortunately, the egg lodged in her esophagus. It had taken a couple of hard slaps to Precious's back to dislodge the egg. Precious never, ever caught another boiled egg from the air again. Lesson learned.)

"Where did you get those?" Peyton asked, pointing to the pink coconut-covered treat.

"I have an emergency stash," Ratchley said, but it didn't actually sound like that because she had already put the second Sno Ball into her mouth. "You have no idea how nerve-racking it is to work in a mental institution. I'm looking for another job if I manage to live through the weekend. Maybe something in a cubicle where I never actually have to talk to another person face-to-face."

"You're going to barf again," Tandy said, lighting up another Lucky Strike by using the last flames on the Mercedes Benz's engine.

Ratchley pulled out a short can of Pringles Pizzalicious flavored chips. Bubba wasn't sure where she'd been hiding it in the scrubs she was wearing. She tossed the plastic cap, pulled the seal off and threw it and then dumped most of the can into her mouth. Crumbs went everywhere.

Peyton said, "You need to calm down and tell me where your stash is, so we can hide it from you. Look, we're all here, no one is going to hurt you, and...oh, fiddlesticks."

"What?" Bubba asked.

"We're *not* all here," Peyton said pointedly.

Bubba looked around. They weren't all there. That was bad. "Come on," he said, putting the empty fire extinguisher on the ground. "Back to the cafeteria. We need to make sure everyone's okay and still there."

Bubba rushed back, only slowing down to ensure that Peyton, Ratchley, and Tandy were following him. Precious plunged ahead, not exactly certain where she was going but in pursuit of something, nonetheless.

The cafeteria was empty. There was no Dr. Adair. There was no Cybil. Most importantly there was no David.

Bubba's eyes immediately went to the cupcake stand. He counted. *One, two, three, four, five cupcakes.* Five *cupcakes.* He looked at Peyton, Ratchley, and Tandy. He was so tired that he would have to take off one of his socks to do the math. "But there's four of us," he muttered finally.

Peyton looked around. "Five if you include Precious Wescious."

Precious made a hah-like noise and tossed her phenomenal nose up in the air. Plainly, she was tired of humans not counting her. Peyton's little affection name addition wouldn't do the trick, not unless he backed it up with her favorite type of Milk-Bones.

Ratchley dropped an empty, recently sucked Strawberry Kiwi Kick Go-Gurt on a table. "I didn't eat the cupcakes—" she burped in an eloquent fashion— "but I think I'm going to ralph anyway." She scrambled into the kitchen.

Bubba ran to the doors that led to the hall. "DAVID!" he bellowed. "CYBIL! DOC!"

The only answer was the sound of Ratchley emptying her insides into the kitchen sink, which only made Bubba want to throw up, too.

•

"Now the sun's up," Tandy said, pointing with her cigarette. "It seems like it should all be better because the sun is up, but it isn't, is it?"

"Are you asking?" Peyton asked. "I don't think it's better unless the National Guard comes prancing up to the front door armed with bazookas and Sherman Tanks." He'd made Bubba and Tandy a cup of tea after locating a stash of mint tea in one of the cabinets. He'd even made himself a cup, pausing to inhale the soothing fragrance.

"You ain't seen our local National Guardsmen," Bubba said. More questions meandered through his head. Why blow up the Mercedes Benz? Distraction for the people or perhaps a way to get people to separate from each other? Furthermore, why were there five cupcakes and not just four? Did cupcakes have anything to do with anything?

Ratchley sipped water and stared at the pile of snacks that Peyton had persuaded her to give up.

Bubba took some more pills because he had such a headache. He considered finding another Coke in the kitchen because the mint tea wasn't giving any kind of caffeine assistance that he desperately needed.

The bomb had to be a distraction, he told himself. Someone wanted to get a few more witnesses out of the way. The person on the outside planted the device on the Mercedes and blew it up, then waited to cull the herd.

Bubba, you stupid fool, he thought. *Should've known.*

Should've never left David alone.

There was a sick feeling deep inside Bubba. He wanted to think it was the sympathetic pregnancy symptoms he was feeling, but it wasn't that at all. It was the thought that David, Jesus, and Thelda might very well be dead, killed by some kind of psychopath preying on the hospital.

And what had Bubba done? Why, he'd put a fire out from a Mercedes Benz and a Volkswagen Rabbit instead of keeping three people from vanishing into the ether. Wasn't that just ducky? How many points was that going to get him in the long run?

Bubba's hand constricted around the mug. It wasn't about points. It was about the people he knew and liked and what had happened to them.

Somewhere there was an answer to all of this madness, but Bubba wasn't thinking all that well. There was nary a nap to be found in the pressing crush of homicidal insanity. He would have to hold on until help was to be had. He glanced at a wall clock. It was just after eight a.m. The sky was blue. There were some clouds to the west. It didn't seem like the kind of morning where murderers were prancing around doing evilness with impunity. Not twenty-four hours earlier, Bubba had been sitting in the boat, eating a Moon Pie, holding a fishing pole, and considering the J names in a baby name book. *Jude. Judd. Jules. Jun. Julie. Justine.*

He looked about. Peyton, Tandy, and Ratchley (Should he ask what her first name was at this point or just pretend the last name was fine?) sat around him.

Tandy had suggested locking themselves in their

rooms until the cavalry showed up. The problem was the bad guy (or guys) wasn't going to stop there. Not at this point. There wasn't any motivation to stop. In fact, things would probably escalate until he/she/it/they got what they wanted.

And Bubba had never been the kind of person to sit down and take it. A few ideas trickled through his brain. He thought about that Agatha Christie novel again.

Bubba drained the mint tea with a compulsive swallow. "We're goin' to the doctor's office. Ratchley, you still got your keys?"

Ratchley held up her keys attached to her scrubs by a retractable reel. "I wrestled them back from David. Can I have a Ding Dong first?"

"No Ding Dongs," Bubba said. "Do you really want to barf again? Or make me barf again?"

"No, but a bag of Fritos would make me feel so much better," Ratchley said.

"Why are we going to the doctor's office?" Peyton asked. He rubbed his eyes and then abruptly seemed to recall that he was wearing eye makeup. "Crudcakes on toast," he said, "did I mess my wings up?"

"There's just a little blur on that side," Tandy said as she pointed.

"Because I think there was only one dang way that there's two of them out there," Bubba said.

Precious nudged the cafeteria doors open with a loud bang and everyone jumped. She trotted happily up to Bubba and laid something down at his feet. He bent over and picked it up, ignoring the copious amount of dog saliva. It was the calabash pipe.

"Isn't that..." Tandy said and trailed off. There was only one person with a pipe in the hospital, and it wasn't her.

"Yep," Bubba said morosely. He carefully used the edge of his t-shirt to wipe the drool from the pipe. Then he stuck it in his pocket. "Keys, Ratchley." He held his hand out.

Ratchley disconnected the reel and dropped the lump of jangling steel in Bubba's hand. "Some Smarties then?" she asked hopefully. "Just to take the edge off?"

"Sorry," Bubba said. "You'll feel a lot better when the sugar gets out of your system. Which way to the doc's office?"

●

Bubba had also been in Dr. Adair's office before. He'd given it a cursory glance before closing and locking the door. The doctor had a smaller desk than Blake Landry. He had a single window that looked out on a row of air conditioners. He had a few framed degrees on the wall. It didn't really look like what he imagined a psychiatrist's office should look like. "What do you know about the doctor, Ratchley?"

"He was divorced. He was bitter about it. He didn't have children. He didn't have a girlfriend. I don't think he had a boyfriend," Ratchley said with a distinctly monotone voice.

"Peyton?"

"Adair, Adair, Adair," Peyton said. "I don't know any Adairs. I don't think he was related to any up-and-coming socialites, and he wouldn't have been on my marital radar at all. So I've got nothing."

"Tandy?"

"He preferred behavioral counseling," Tandy said. "We discussed some aversion therapy in relation to the weed. He smelled like peaches sometimes."

Bubba sat in Dr. Adair's leather-backed chair and looked at his steel desk. He touched the laptop and then flipped it open.

"You know, there's probably a law against that," Ratchley said, "which I would happily ignore if you gave me some sort of snack food. In fact, I would take pork rinds right now, and I hate pork rinds. Most people keep some kind of snack food in their drawers, you know."

"Mebe pork rinds with some redeye gravy and fried zucchini," Bubba suggested while he turned the computer on. He was stopped as soon as it powered up because it demanded a password. None of the typical passwords worked. Bubba tried god, God, GOD, password, Password, PassWord, and PASSWORD. Then he tried Adair, adair, and ADAIR. He shut the computer with a sigh. Then he looked at the doctor's brass inbox on one side of the desk. He pulled the pile of papers out of the box and put them in front of him.

"Why are we digging through the doctor's stuff?" Peyton asked. "I got sidetracked before."

"You remember how Blake died," Bubba said.

"Strangled. Awful for the eyes. I bet makeup artists for morticians are seriously badass," Peyton said.

"Well, why did his body up and leave?" Bubba asked.

"Someone moved it," Peyton said.

"It didn't walk away," Tandy said.

"Mebe it did," Bubba said. "I was thinking about Agatha Christie and all, and in that one movie, someone did pretend to die. Guess who helped the fella do his pretend death? Guess which person no one would question until it was too late?"

"That would be the doctor," Peyton said.

"Betcha." Bubba shifted through papers. He saw memos. He saw some medical paperwork relating to patients. There was an electricity bill for a house located perhaps ten miles from the hospital. It was past due, and it was the second notice. There was a bank statement showing where he had bounced checks several times. Finally, he stopped and pointed. "Bankruptcy proceedings. Dr. Adair is about to go belly up and not in a dead way."

Tandy peered over Bubba's shoulder. "Dah-am. How does a person get into debt for almost a million dollars?"

"Three houses," Bubba read. "One is on the beach in Pensacola, Florida. One divorce with alimony in the thousands per month. Sixteen credit cards. Five cars including a 1980 Mercedes Benz 500SEL, which was the cheapest of the lot. That one had sentimental value on account that it belonged to his uncle, who was a retired colonel from the U.S. Army. That explains how it ended up in the states." He glanced up at three confused faces. "That model of Benz didn't come to the states."

"So he was a financial dud," Tandy said. "What does that have to do with the price of tea in Guatemala?"

"Do they grow tea in Guatemala?" Peyton asked.

"Mebe someone done came up to him and asked him does he want to make a buck or two, mebe enough to get him out of the debt he's in," Bubba said. "Mebe that gives the not-so-good doctor a motive." He glanced at the bank statement again. The bottom line didn't really reflect what a man in the throes of bankruptcy should have. He frowned.

"Precisely, Watson," said a woman from the door. She was about David's height and weight. She wore a pink polka-dotted dress and white heels. Her hair was dusted gray. Her face was powdered with flesh-colored foundation. Her lipstick matched her polka dots. However, her face was David's.

"Great Caesar's ghost," said Peyton.

"No, just David," Tandy said dryly.

"I am Mrs. Penhallow-FitzGibbons," announced David. "I have come to assist you and also chew bubble gum. However, I am freshly out of bubble gum."

Bubba leapt out of the chair and was in front of David in a heartbeat. He grabbed the former Purple Singapore Sling and gave him a fierce hug. "I ain't bin so happy to see a loonie in all my life," Bubba said.

David pulled back slightly and asked, "Is that a calabash pipe in your pocket or are you just happy to see me, Watson?"

Chapter Nineteen

Bubba and the Horrendous Hunt

Sunday, April 7th

Bubba was happy to see David but not in that way. The question made him back away from the other man faster than a bell clapper in a goose's butt. He tugged the calabash pipe out of his pocket and pushed it at David, who took it with his fingers revealing a pristine set of carefully manicured nails. (Pink like the lipstick and the polka dots. Bubba didn't care to look closely at the nails, but it didn't look like there were a lot of mistakes. He was certain he couldn't quickly apply pink fingernail polish without making a lot of mistakes. He shuddered before making himself stop that particular train of thought.)

"Nice dress," Tandy said, puffing on a fresh cigarette.

"A lady always dresses for the occasion," David said grandly. He expertly swished the bottom of his skirt in demonstration. (A little too expertly if one asked Bubba, but no one did.)

"Then we should all be wearing camouflage, right?" Peyton asked. "That's the occasion here. The one where we should all be hiding."

"Mrs. Penhallow-FitzGibbons," Ratchley said, "do you happen to have a snacky-poo in your clutch?"

Bubba hadn't noticed the white clutch. It could have been one of his mother's. In fact, the entire outfit could have been one of his mothers. In fact, Bubba became

240

increasingly certain that it *had* been one of his mother's outfits. She liked to wear it after Labor Day so that it would irritate the ladies at the church socials with the blatant rule breaking. (No white after Labor Day. It was a rule to be remembered in the same league with never take a cooler to church and never let the dogs eat at the table no matter how good their manners are.) (Precious always ate *under* the table, although she never did excuse herself after burping.)

Mrs. Penhallow-FitzGibbons dug in the clutch. "I have peanuts from Eastern Airlines. I think I flew on them in 1989 just before the Berlin Wall fell. I sat next to the most interesting man from the German Democratic Republic. He had a delightful accent. All those V's and W's. He swore that all Americans would love communism." He made a noise, withdrew a little silver package, and then held it out to the nurse.

Ratchley took it with obvious trepidation. If Bubba had to guess, he would say it was because the nurse expected someone to yank the peanuts from her before she could eat them. Privately, Bubba thought that if Ratchley really wanted to eat antique peanuts from a defunct airline, then it was on her own head.

"So what happened to you, Da-er, Mrs. Penhallow-FitzGibbons?" Bubba asked.

"Once the explosion occurred, I took the opportunity to freshen up," David said and withdrew a compact from the clutch. He opened it up and powdered his nose. Peyton made a noise and quietly asked to borrow the compact to check his own makeup.

"When I came back from the facilities," David went

on, carefully adjusting his dress by doing a little hip shimmy, "the cafeteria was empty. Imagine that. I knew that you, Peyton, Ratchley, and Tandy had gone out to view the explosion, so it was simply Dr. Adair, Cybil, and myself." He waved a hand in front of his face. "I blame myself. If only I hadn't left my brass knuckles and sap in my room."

"Does the murderer think he's going to kill us all off?" Tandy asked. "I mean, if there's only one person left when the police show up, they're just going to blame that person for the crime."

"Yep," Bubba agreed. "I reckon that's the plan." Thinking about the unknown murderer's plan gave rise to a plan of his own. If it came down to it, that was what Bubba would do.

"You mean the murderer doesn't care if he or she is caught?" Peyton asked. "Where in the name of Saint Hubert of Leige does he hide them all? Is there a place where all the bodies are piled up?"

There was a pop of electricity from above Bubba's head. He glanced up to see that the fluorescent lights were flickering madly. Why hadn't he thought about that before? It was because he couldn't just leave all the people unprotected. He had tried that once, and it had turned out horribly. But he should have come back to it. If his head wasn't throbbing and his eyes weren't burning with fatigue, perhaps he would have. It might not be too late.

"I got tied up in the next building," Bubba said. "Let's mosey over there and check things out."

Ratchley rattled the package of nuts in her hand.

She tipped it upside down and watched a few grains of salt spill out. Then she licked the bits of salt. "That only had four peanuts in it," she complained.

"Well, it was a wretched airline," Mrs. Penhallow-FitzGibbons said. "There were strikes galore by the union workers."

"What if the guy has a gun?" Tandy asked. "I mean, all these people don't just go with him or her, right? He has to have a way of...persuading them to go with him. I wouldn't just walk off if someone walked up to me."

"That would depend on who it was," David said, "now, wouldn't it?" Mrs. Penhallow-FitzGibbons had an upper crust accent as if she had gone to an Ivy League school and graduated to take over the management of her family's mansion. She was the kind of woman who knew exactly what kind of hors d'oeuvres to serve at a breakfast meeting on the north lawn with the Federation of International Polo. (Not pigs in a blanket.) Bubba couldn't help but wonder where David dug up his personas, but of course he was still Sherlock Holmes, albeit Sherlock Holmes in the guise of Mrs. Penhallow-FitzGibbons.

"No, she's right," Bubba said. "Ain't no one just goin' to go by themselves especially when they be knowing what else has happened. For example, the doc ain't a fool." Bubba wasn't sure about Cybil, the dupable Daphne.

"We should bring whatever weapons we can," Tandy said, "and go and look. If they tied you up, then they might have tied them up, therefore they might be still alive."

"I can see the headlines now," Peyton said. "'Wedding Planner Solves Mystery and Saves Victims From Certain Doom.'" He grinned broadly and handed the compact back to David. "Also the subtitle would be 'His Wedding Planning Was Kick Ass.'" He thought about it. "Do you think they would put kick ass in a headline title?"

"Maybe," David said, putting the compact back into his clutch.

Everyone flowed out of Dr. Adair's office, and Mrs. Penhallow-FitzGibbons lingered long enough to mutter into Bubba's ear, "I have a gun." He eyed Peyton, Ratchley, and Tandy and quickly gave Bubba a peek into the clutch. Inside was a small revolver. If Bubba wasn't mistaken it was a J-frame revolver with a black grip.

"That's Ma's Smith & Wesson 642," Bubba whispered.

"Miz Demetrice said it went with the outfit," David whispered back.

Bubba's mouth opened, and if a couple of dozen of flies had thought to fly inside, he wouldn't have been able to do anything about it. There were a number of things he would have liked to say to his mother at the moment. One was that he couldn't comprehend where she was putting all of her illicit weapons on the property. Two was that her registration with the Pegram County Sheriff's Department must read like Tolstoy's *War and Peace*. Three was that his mother had absolutely no business giving a loaded weapon— "Is that loaded?"— to a resident of a mental institute.

"Of course, it's loaded," David said, snapping the

clutch shut. "An unloaded gun is like walking with a stone in one shoe and a pebble in the other."

"Did my mother say that?" Bubba hissed.

"She might have said that," David admitted.

"Do you know how to use that revolver?" Bubba demanded. He knew how to use it, but the 642 was a lady's weapon, and his big fumble fingers could barely squeeze into the trigger guard. He might not be able to even hold it without dropping it.

"Of course I do," David said loudly. Tandy glanced back, and David's mouth snapped shut. When Tandy turned back to say something to Ratchley, David whispered, "She gave me lessons. Well, one lesson. We shot at the old oak tree in the back. Pull the hammer back, point, and shoot."

"Did you hit the tree?"

"Once."

"It's only got five rounds," Bubba said.

"That's a twenty percent chance of success," David confirmed happily.

"Can you walk in those heels?"

"Sherlock Holmes is a master of disguise," David said indignantly. "What kind of master of disguises would I be if I couldn't walk in heels?"

Bubba couldn't think of an answer for that, so he didn't say anything.

●

It took Bubba a little bit of time to figure out where the building was located. After all, he was thinking with a majestic headache, and his caffeine meter was depleted. He needed quarters, and none were to be had.

Not much was making a lot of sense. He wanted a nap, but he didn't want to wake up to find another missing person.

After turning left and right, Bubba made a noise and sighed.

Ratchley said, "You mean the old office building?"

"There's an old office building?" David asked.

"It was inconvenient, so the administration discontinued using it. The last I heard they were trying to convert it into offices for insurance companies and such, but who wants to be all the way out here? And besides, most insurances can do their business over the phone." Ratchley shook her head. "Originally it was staff headquarters for the first hospital here. I hear it's haunted. One of the first administrators shot himself. He couldn't make the hospital profitable and bit the big one. I think they're going to demolish the building soon."

"That's just wonderful," Tandy said and lit a second cigarette. She didn't bother putting out the first one. It was an indication of how nervous the movie actress was getting. "Thank God it's not dark anymore." She stopped in the middle of a grassy area and checked all of her phones. "Where's my Samsung?"

"Whoever hit me took it," Bubba said. He glanced at his sock feet. "Took my boots, too. I stepped in goatheads. I think I ruint the socks Willodean gave me. I'm a mite put out about that."

"And you've got a baseball-sized bump on the back of your head," Peyton said. He tilted his head. "No, it's about the size of a grapefruit now. The photographer can totally work with that. Besides it should go down in a few days."

Bubba had thrown away the rapidly melting bag of corn, so he'd have to hit the cafeteria's kitchen for something else for the swelling, but nothing was to be done about it at the moment.

"Do you know anything else about this building, Nurse Ratchley?" Mrs. Penhallow-FitzGibbons inquired as if she was asking about what colors were trending in New York this spring.

"Three stories. They store a lot of crap there. I heard there were rats. There are no snackies there," Ratchley said. "I'm really wanting the snackies now. Those peanuts didn't last long."

"Did you know you have an eating problem, Ratchley?" Tandy asked.

"Did you know that a bear poops in the woods while wearing a pope's hat?" Ratchley snapped back. "People in glass houses shouldn't smoke two cigarettes at once."

Tandy rolled her eyes and put the shorter cigarette out.

"It's this way," Ratchley said.

Bubba and the rest followed her. It turned out there was a nice well-appointed path, one he'd missed altogether when he'd been fleeing earlier. There was nary a goatshead to be found on the path.

"Did you mean that you think the doctor might have done it?" Peyton asked Bubba as they walked.

"I mean the doctor might have helped," Bubba said grimly.

"You think they watched that movie?" Peyton asked.

"I think they dint watch that movie," Bubba said. "I think they think they're smart, but they ain't nearly as smart as they think they are. I think I need a big cup of coffee."

Peyton frowned in obvious concentration. "It's been twenty or more years since I've seen it. I don't really remember it except for the singing rhyme." He began to sing, "Ten little Indians standing in a line. One toddled home and then there were nine..." He paused. "Every time someone died or vanished, one of the statues got broken." He pursed his lips, and Bubba realized he had applied raspberry-colored lip gloss. "We don't have a statue of ten little Indians around here."

"We've got cupcakes," Bubba muttered grimly.

"You mean someone eats a cupcake every time someone dies," Peyton said. Then he laughed. "That's coincidence. Someone doesn't want to admit they've got the midnight munchies and are scarfing the goodies."

"There are five cupcakes left."

Peyton looked around. He muttered aloud. "You. Me. David Sherlock Penhallow-FitzGibbons. Ratchley. The movie star. That's five." He glanced at Precious, who had stopped to pee on a rabbiteye blueberry bush. "And your dog, of course. But what about the someone else?"

"Mebe the someone else decided to cut back on his possible exposure," Bubba suggested. "Eliminate the middleman so to speak."

David fell back, carefully treading on his heels so that he didn't trip on the gravel of the path. "Good show, Watson," he said. "We route out the villain in his own lair."

"What do you think, Sherlock?" Peyton asked. "Was it the doctor, or rather, is it the doctor?"

"The doctor had a motive, to be sure," David said with an accent that was part upper crust New York and part British and altogether odd. "The implication is that the plans were laid before Hurley Tanner was put into this place."

"Mebe," Bubba said. "I reckon if we looked or asked we would find out that someone steered Hurley to this place and then picked a time. After all, he wasn't killed during the time where most of the residents and employees were gone. Even if there hadn't been renovation of the place, he would have been murdered. I figure all this—" he waved at the hospital, the people, and the building they were walking toward— "was cover up. Mebe the killer would have been happy ifin Hurley's death was recorded as an accidental overdose or a suicide. But he still covered up. The plan was to frame someone. The plan was to make sure no one else was looked at but..." Bubba's gaze settled on David. "And then you had to go and open your mouth, screaming to everyone that both Mrs. Ferryjig and Hurley Tanner had been done in by means most foul."

Peyton hmphed. "You don't always sound like a redneck, mendacious redneck groom of mine."

David leaned close to whisper into Peyton's ear, but Bubba heard the words anyway. "That's because he isn't really. He's truly Dr. Watson."

"So David precipitated the whole Agatha Christie

ensemble?   Blowing up the cell phone tower and covering the only road in? Everything?" Peyton asked. "Where did they get the explosives? I would think that was a question that people would want answered."

"They're going to demo the other building," Ratchley called back. "There's an explosives shack on the other side. I heard some of the orderlies talking about it. It's locked."

"I reckon it ain't locked now," Bubba said.

"Okay, then," Tandy said, "what now? I mean, if we all know, then the person, or persons, can't let us go. This is actually bad news unless the police show up right the eff now." She looked eagerly heavenward as if expecting a police helicopter to appear.

"We could hide," Bubba suggested.

"I say we look in the building for those other people," David said. "Who knows what clues we might locate? Besides, the killer will not recognize me, as I am cleverly disguised as Mrs. Penhallow-FitzGibbons."

"You're not really—" Peyton started to say, but Bubba interrupted him, "Just give him his moment, Peyton."

Peyton nodded.

●

The other building was pretty much as Ratchley had said it was. It was mostly locked, filled with various boxes, and dusty. There was one door that had been used; they could tell by all the footprints in the grime.

"It's like a treasure map," Tandy said, "except with dust and footprints."

David produced a flashlight out of his clutch. Bubba

secretly wanted to know what else he could magically fit into such a tiny bag. There was probably a safe in there, too.

They found the room that Bubba had been in by virtue of observing the door lying on the hallway floor.

"I dint feel like using the knob," Bubba explained. "But also it was locked."

"Look, the straitjacket," Ratchley said, pointing to the twisted garment on the floor. "You know we don't actually use those anymore. These must have been left over from the time that the criminally insane were held at the hospital in 1978. There was a brief period where the hospital only held psychopathic prisoners from Huntsville." She looked at the expressions on the people around her. "What? There's a plaque in the foyer that talks about it. Also a picture. Did you know the Foghorn Ripper stayed here for six months? He did sculptures made with matchsticks. One of them is mounted by the plaque. It's amazingly complicated."

They looked over the entire building floor by floor and found evidence of people being there. There was one room with empty Pepsi bottles and a pile of empty Hormel Vienna sausage cans. "Are you sure they're all empty?" Ratchley asked despondently. The room also had a single aluminum chair by the window with a cheap set of binoculars sitting on the sill.

Bubba held up the binoculars and looked out the window. "You kin see most of the entrances of the hospital from here."

"But there isn't a signed confession about," David said with clear frustration. He swung his white clutch around as if he wanted to hit someone with it.

Bubba put the binoculars back on the windowsill. "Let's go take a gander at the explosives shack."

He paused on the way out, shooing Ratchley from where she was checking to see if there were any remaining unopened cans of Vienna sausage. On one of the other windowsills was a single little doodad – a stylized oil derrick no bigger than the palm of his hand. On the bottom it said Amarillo, Texas.

Bubba said, "Hmm."

Chapter Twenty

Bubba and Explosive Potential

Sunday, April 7th

The explosives shack had a broken lock on its door. The actual shed sat within a chain-link box that was supposed to further protect it. The gate to the small enclosure had been twisted off and broken by someone with a determination that Bubba couldn't quite envision. Neither Bubba nor David were surprised considering that a cell phone tower and a cliff had been blown up. Nor were they surprised that there were clearly explosives missing inside the shack. The neatly aligned bricks sitting within the shack were askew and had gaps.

Bubba took a moment to look closely at the explosives that were left. A company name had been imprinted on the plastic. Nunngesser's. He gave a little sigh. It wasn't a big world when he recognized things like that. He'd run into the Nunngesser company before, but he quickly dismissed it.

"Should we take some?" Tandy asked. "I mean, a little Semtex would be just the thing if someone tried to cap my ass." She fingered a small box with a skull and crossbones emblazoned in red across it.

Precious nosed a stack, dismissed it, and went outside to pee on the exterior of the shack.

"I don't reckon they'll hold still long enough for you to put the device on them and then wire it to a detonator," Bubba advised. "And I wouldn't try it except as a last resort." Pegram County had had entirely too many people running about helter-skelter with explosives, his mother included. Who knew what would happen if he let the famous actress have some. Furthermore, Bubba didn't want to mention that there was more than plastique explosive in the shed. He also saw a box of dynamite half hidden underneath a tarp.

"Is the building already wired?" David asked Ratchley.

"I don't think so," Ratchley said. "They wouldn't just leave it that way. We've got no security out here. Wouldn't they have put up a chain-link fence or something around the building to keep people out?"

David rubbed his closely shaven chin and accidently smeared some pinkity-pink-pink lipstick off. Peyton did a little motion with his index finger and his thumb. "You've got a lipstick smear there, fella," he whispered loudly. "Also you might want to reapply your guyliner."

"Your manscara is starting to wear," David said promptly.

"Awk," Peyton said and looked around frantically. David gave him the compact before reapplying his lipstick.

"Ifin we lock it again, then someone might just break it open," Bubba reasoned. "I don't think the fella or gal is planning to blow us all up, or he-she-it would have done it already."

"You don't want to make it easy for the murderer," Tandy said. "I say we hide the stuff."

"I know what to do with it," Ratchley said. "Pick it

up, and we'll take it to the cliff. We toss those suckers off and problem solved. Someone would have to have rappelling gear or be related to a spider to get the stuff back."

There was little argument to that.

Bubba carried about half of the explosives that remained, putting them into a sackcloth bag that had been left in the shack. The rest of the bricks were divided among the other four. Tandy was surprisingly reluctant to carry one considering that she had just suggested taking some with them for protection or possibly for offense.

"What if it blows up while I'm holding it?" she asked, holding a yellow package of the explosive material between her thumb and her index finger. "It looks like Play-Doh. How can something that looks like Play-Doh blow so much stuff up?"

"It requires a detonator to blow it up," David said. "It's like they say in the North, 'You can hide the fire, but what will you do with the smoke?'"

"What does that have to do with explosives?" Tandy asked with a grimace.

"I don't know," David said, "but it sounded like something Mrs. Penhallow-FitzGibbons ought to say at the moment."

Ratchley motioned to them. "This way." She led them back down the trail and cut to the north. They threaded through tall piney woods and scrub until they ran into the rim of the mesa. Bubba was surprised how close it was and how deep it appeared to be. "There's a bench down that way," the nurse elaborated. "The staff and some of the patients use it as Make Out City. I'm married, so I wouldn't know."

Bubba edged up to the brink while Precious whined uneasily at him from a safer locale. The cliff dropped away fifty feet into a sea of oaks and pines. The Sturgis River had chipped away at the mesa until it was a steep step for anyone to cross. The finality of the rock face was the reason why no one could leave the back way. He might have tried because there were always ways to and fro, but the precipice was a solid "No!" shouted in his face at a very close interval. "Now why don't the hospital have a fence around this?"

Ratchley shrugged. "Most patients stay in the hospital or the yard. We have a ropes course around one side but we only use that in really good weather. It's never been a problem."

"Will the stuff blow up when we toss it over?" Tandy asked hopefully. She had actually stubbed out her cigarette before accepting one of the explosive packages.

"It shouldn't," Bubba said. He took the package from Tandy and motioned for everyone to back up. "Keep going," he added. Then he pitched the single package over the edge. He jumped back and covered his ears, waiting for the possible kaboom.

A long minute later, Bubba uncovered his ears and looked at the other people. He raised his eyebrows in a see? way. David shrugged and aimed his package for the side. He threw it like it was a football. They heard it ten seconds later as it crashed through the tree limbs below. No explosion ensued.

Bubba shrugged the bag handle off his shoulder and put it on the ground. He withdrew a yellow wrapped brick and shucked it like a baseball, hoping there weren't deer or other animals below that he would hit. Peyton threw his and hit the edge of the cliff. He winced when it bounced and then sallied over the edge.

He waited for the sound of branches being hit before he said, "I always did throw like a girl, which is why I played volleyball in college."

Ratchley handed her package to David, who skidded it across the granite of the cliffs like it was a stone on water, until it hit free air and dropped away.

"Mebe you shouldn't do that," Bubba said nervously.

Tandy brushed her hands together. "So the murderer can't blow us up now. That's good, right?"

"Makes me happier than a pig in poop," Bubba said. He threw three more bricks over the side and listened to each one as it hit the canopy of leaves far below. "Or at least as happy as a fella can get at the moment. The only way I'll be happier is ifin the po-lice stick their faces in the front door of the hospital and I wake up in the morning with Willodean by my side and Precious lying on my feet."

"There's one more brick," David pointed out.

Bubba brought it out with a sigh. "This isn't how I expected to spend my Sunday. I should have been going to church with Willodean. Then we'd be eating breakfast with Ma and Miz Adelia. Miz Adelia's family is coming today. I was supposed to make my special biscuits and gravy. My gravy is a secret passed down from my father's side, which was about the only good thing passed down from my father's side."

"Biscuits and gravy," Ratchley drooled out of the side of her mouth.

"I was planning on sleeping in," Tandy said, "with the potential of smoking three packs of cigs later. I'm reading a script for the sequel to *Bubble People,* which is really an issue since they killed off my character in the first one."

"I was going to watch a Basil Rathbone film festival," David sighed.

"Wedding planning research," Peyton said, "but the biscuits and gravy sound divine."

Bubba hefted the last brick. He inhaled the spring air and found just the scantest moment of knowing that not *all* was wrong in the universe. "It ain't bad right this minute, but I wish I knew where Jesus, Thelda, and the rest were. I hope they ain't dead because I'll be angry. I just cain't imagine someone doin' something bad to a nice fella like Jesus or a gal like Thelda. Just for what? Money?"

"It's a lot of money," Peyton said. "The Tanner family has billions. I don't know what the details of Hurley's will are, but I would imagine most of it would go to his wife and daughter."

"All that from oil," Tandy said. "I make a pretty good living as an actress, but I don't have to show up in a board room, and I don't have to take every job anymore. I don't think my mother would kill me for my money, but then I just bought her a house in Tarzana, and she gets a big allowance every month. I also just bought her a car with one of those fancy GPS units built into the dash. She still gets lost anyway."

"GPS unit," Peyton said. "There's a GPS unit in the Charger. Once they figure out that I'm missing, too, all they have to do is call Avis and ask where the car is at. We're so saved." He clapped his hands together.

"They have to figure out that you're missing first," Bubba said, balancing the last brick in his hand.

"I'm sure they've figured out that you're missing," David said to Bubba, "so it's not a stretch that the wedding planner is with you, Watson."

Bubba nodded. "Shore hope so." He cocked his head. "Do you hear music?" If he wasn't mistaken it was "Sweet Child O' Mine" by Guns N' Roses. ("Whoa-oh-ah-ah.") The wind had died down, and he could swear Axl Rose was crooning immortal words of heavy metalness.

Ratchley's head came up and she muttered, "I smell popcorn...and tequila."

Bubba tossed the last brick. Because his head was still aching, and he was tired like a dog, he didn't pay attention to what he was doing, and it bounced on the edge of the cliff. He saw the spark as rocks ground into other rocks when the brick pushed them together. He ducked even while he pulled David and Tandy to the ground. The thought of Precious, Ratchley, and Peyton crossed his mind but there really wasn't anything he could do about them in that last instant.

Then everything went boom and not in a good way.

•

There was a lot of dust and grit in the air. Bubba sat up from a prone position on the ground and brushed bits of debris from his shirt. He could hardly read the "Bun in the Oven" part because it was so stained and dirt covered. He shook his head and looked around. "Precious?"

An extraordinary nose bumped into his arm, and a tongue licked him wetly, leaving a clean trail after the swipe. Bubba hoped that it was his dog and not David before he saw a very dirty canine sticking her nose under his arm and her tail weakly wagging. *Not David, unless his disguises have gotten really good.* He checked his dog and was relieved to find that she seemed uninjured.

The vast cloud of dirt stirred and swished away as a wind gently dispersed it over the cliff edge, but the cliff edge was a lot closer than Bubba remembered. In fact, he could reach out and touch it, it was so close. As the wind pushed more of the dust away he could see that it was like a giant had taken a tremendous bite out of the side of the cliff. A forensic specialist would have tittered with glee at the fantastic half-round shape that had been left behind.

David groaned from nearby. "I broke one of my heels," he said. He had lost both of his fake accents and sounded like plain old David again.

"I lost my cigs," Tandy said, "again."

Peyton said, "Way to go out with a boom." Then he giggled weakly.

"Did I do that?" Bubba asked.

"I didn't see anyone else throwing explosives off the cliff," Tandy said.

"I did," David interjected. "I guess I was wrong

about them blowing up."

"Wait, so should we just leave them at the bottom of the cliff like that?" Bubba asked. "What if a troop of Boy Scouts comes by and decides they *are* packages of Play-Doh?"

"That's an isolated area," David said. "The likelihood of children happening past and causing a fatal explosion is improbable."

"Well, I caused an explosion," Bubba said, patting Precious awkwardly. He thought about it. The Semtex wasn't supposed to go off if simply dropped. There had been the dynamite, and he winced at the thought of having left it in the shack. Most importantly, the dynamite tended to leak drops of nitroglycerin, which in its pure form was highly volatile. (Odd facts that he could thank his mother for imparting to him.) If some of it had gotten onto the blocks of explosive plastique, then...

"It wasn't fatal," David explained, "so it's all gravy goodness."

"*Gravy*," Ratchley said longingly.

"You don't suppose that someone heard that from out there?" Tandy asked. "Maybe they might call the sheriff's department?"

"Then they would have called when the cell phone tower and the cliff, the other cliff that is, blew up," David concluded.

"Oh," Tandy said. "It was a thought. Maybe after the third one they might get a little curious."

"Was that music I heard before?" Bubba asked. "I thought it was a blast from the heavy metal past."

"My ears are ringing now," Tandy said. "The only music I heard is the sound of my heart racing. You know this would make a great movie. I should talk to some screenwriters; I'm not going to be a popular actress for much longer and getting the good zombie-movie parts. I don't want to be stuck doing Lifetime's movie of the week for the next decade." She shuddered.

Precious whined and put her nose on Bubba's knee. He glanced at the semi-circle of air that used to be part of a cliff. "Mebe we shouldn't tell this part to the police," he suggested, "but I guess we do need to tell them about the Semtex lying down there. I mean the ones that dint blow up."

Tandy inched up to the new side of the cliff and looked down. "Some of it is probably covered with about three tons of cliff face now. I'd say it was moot except possibly to the construction company who will have to pay for the missing explosive materials. Hey, you made a ledge about ten feet down."

Somehow that didn't make Bubba feel better. "What do we do now, David?"

"Mrs. Penhallow-FitzGibbons," David corrected. "A lady always knows what to do in situations of ill repute." He took off one shoe and efficiently broke off the heel. It then matched the other one. He replaced it, a bright smile appearing on his grimy face. The pink lipstick was pretty much the only thing visible.

"I'm thinking we go back to the hospital," Tandy said, "and lock ourselves in a room until the police come, just like I wanted to do to begin with. That way four of us and one dog make it just fine."

"Mebe we should hunt around for that music," Bubba said. "I'd like to know who was having a party and why we weren't invited. Wait, did you say *four* of us?"

"I don't really feel like crashing a party," Peyton said, "but it's better than hanging out here."

"Four of us. That don't sound right to me." Bubba sat by the edge of the cliff and patted his dog's head. "Um, I think my head is goin' to explode next. Where was the VIP lodge, Ratchley?"

There was a ringing in one ear. Bubba slapped it with one hand, thinking one knock deserved another. If he could blow up half a cliff, then he could get rid of a pesky ringing in his ear so that he could hear if Axl Rose was still wanting to know where he was supposed to go now. Bubba recognized the irony there but didn't want to concentrate on it. Instead of hearing the front man from Guns N' Roses, he heard...

Nothing.

"Ratchley," Bubba said again. "You said something about a..."

"Oh, crud monkeys," Peyton said with more perception than Bubba possessed.

Bubba finally looked around. There *were* only four of them. Tandy had made it to her feet and stood there with knocking knees, patting her pockets for her cigarettes. Peyton sat near Tandy's feet. His eyes were like the brightest pair of moons on a starlit night. David crawled to his feet and checked out his newly altered shoes.

"Ratchley?" Bubba asked. He looked at the cliff. He

looked back at the other three people. He glanced back at the cliff meaningfully. "Did she—?"

"She was behind us," Tandy said. "She was in the tree line. When you said back up, she backed up. She must have run off. Possibly to find snackies."

Bubba certainly hoped Ratchley had run away to find snackies. In fact, he hoped she was up to her elbows in Twinkies, Lay's Potato Chips, and chocolate-covered cherries, if that was what she was into, as long as she was alive and kicking. (Vanilla ice cream with broken-up Lay's Sour Cream & Onion-flavored chips on top popped into Bubba's head. He made himself think of England.)

David offered Bubba a dusty but well-manicured hand. Bubba took it and helped himself up. Precious scooted away from the cliff edge as more rocks began to fall. "Perhaps a judicious retreat," David suggested. Bubba concurred.

Tandy jerked a thumb over her shoulder. "There was a trail back there. It probably goes to that bench Ratchley talked about."

They found the trail without trying too hard and stumbled on their way. No one was singing, "Lions and tigers and bears, oh my," or skipping. Precious didn't look like Toto in the least. Bubba wasn't about to put on a gingham dress even if he would have been able to find one that would fit him.

Bubba dry swallowed the rest of the aspirin he'd been given by Dr. Adair. He did check to make sure the package hadn't been tampered with. He looked around the woods and shook his head. He wasn't just out of ideas; he was completely dumbfounded and flabbergasted. His mother would have called him a nonsensical nincompoop and that was only if she was in a good mood. He would have agreed with her.

There had to be a way to catch the murderer or murderers without losing any more people. Bubba was plumb tired of looking up to see another person missing, or even worse, dead. All he could think of was a plan that involved two people left, and he didn't want it to come to that if it could be prevented.

They came around a curve in the trail, and David stopped in front of Bubba. Bubba bumped into him and said, "Sorry, Dav-er-Mrs. Penhallow-FitzGibbons, I'm a little put out. In fact, I'm would up tighter than a two-dollar watch what been dropped in a group of overwrought yard monkeys." He waited for David to say something, but David didn't say anything and Bubba added, "I'm like a bear with his head caught in the hive?" Still nothing. "You cain't even drive a needle up my butt with a jackhammer?"

Bubba finally looked up and saw that Peyton, Tandy, and David were all stopped in similar positions, standing shock still with their eyes on the bench ahead. Precious had paused to pee on a nearby oak tree.

Of course, Bubba's eyes followed theirs and saw the person sitting on the bench as if they were watching the distant clouds floating away. However, they weren't really watching anything because they were really dead.

The knife sticking out of their chest was the big giveaway clue.

Chapter Twenty-one

Bubba and the Fact That He Don't Go to Jail in This Chapter

Sunday, April 7th

The person was dead. For a split second, Bubba had a sudden thought that it was Ratchley sitting there. The nurse had run off in search of the ultimate snackie-poo to make her feel better. Alternatively, she had discovered a knifey-poo and death. But the split second passed, and he realized abruptly it wasn't Ratchley sitting on the bench. There was not even a single detail that remotely resembled Ratchley. Also, the corpse didn't have a pile of snackies sitting beside them ready to be consumed in a fit of nervousness.

No, it was Dr. Adair. Bubba took a moment to decide that he needed to ensure that the psychiatrist was really, really dead. (Bubba had previous experience with corpses not being dead or not being murdered that he didn't care to share with the rest of the group again.)

"Well," Peyton said while spreading his hands palms-up in the air. "I'm going with...the doctor didn't do it. It's just a little thought I had."

"This is important. Really, truly important, people, so listen up," Tandy announced. She put her arms akimbo and contemplated the dead man on the bench. "Did he have any more NicoDerm patches on him? Was he holding out on me?"

Bubba walked around David and approached the

266

doctor's body. He stopped beside the bench and systematically looked around. As he turned toward the direction of the hospital, he realized he could see the building where they had just been, the same building where Bubba had been held captive for a brief time. He looked, and he thought he could see a glint in the same window that had the binoculars in it.

Reluctantly, Bubba touched his index and middle fingers to the doctor's neck. He was momentarily repulsed when he realized that Dr. Adair's flesh was cold. He'd been out here for some time. Rather he'd been out here long enough to be coldish to the touch. Once Bubba got past the whole flesh-not-warm-thing, he ascertained there wasn't a heartbeat. As for the knife, Bubba wasn't going to mess with it. Finally, he could say that he wasn't going out on a limb by announcing, "Yep. Really dead this time."

"What do you mean, this time?" Peyton asked.

"Isn't it obvious, man?" David pronounced. Judging on the poor British accent, Bubba guessed that Sherlock Holmes had returned even while still wearing Mrs. Penhallow-FitzGibbon's dress and shoes with broken heels. "The first death yesterday was not a death at all, you barmy nitwit."

"While you're over there, Bubba," Tandy said, "do me a solid and check those suit pockets for NicoDerm packets."

"Don't you have cigarettes already?" Bubba asked.

"I'm going to need them later because I'm going through them quickly." She held up the two she had lit as an example.

"You should get his keys," David said.

Bubba agreed with that. Ratchley had the other set, and no one knew where she was presently located. While he found a set in the doctor's jacket and quickly inserted them into his pocket, he thought about what was happening. His glance went over to the cliff. Why leave a corpse where someone could find it? Why not chuck it over the cliff like they had done with the Semtex? Someone wanted someone else to find the body and probably for the reason that had brought Bubba out to Dogley to begin with.

"David," Bubba said quietly, "did you touch a knife like this today?"

David glanced at the knife and his mascara-adorned eyes went very big in obvious realization. Bubba looked at the knife, too. It was a standard 8-inch chef's knife. The brand was Henckels. Bubba recognized the Gemini logo on the handle's heel. It looked like one of the many knives Miz Adelia had in the Snoddy kitchen; Miz Adelia had about as many knives as Miz Demetrice had guns. (No one looked askance if one was a cook with that many knives, even if some of them weren't exactly used for the culinary process.) In fact, Bubba had a touched a knife like that earlier when he'd made a sandwich.

"I do remember a sandwich earlier," David admitted. "I like the crusts cut off. Then a diagonal cut is best for the roast beef. Exposing the grain enhances the flavor, you see?"

"And what did you do with the knife?"

"I put it into the sink."

"Did you wash the knife?"

"I did not wash the knife."

"I see."

"You mean, someone went and got the knife he used on a sandwich and then used it on the doctor?" Tandy asked. "What if he hadn't had a sandwich?"

"Then it would have been something else that David had touched," Bubba concluded. "A lamp. A statue. A rock. A flashlight. A toilet seat. Something. The knife was providence for the murderer."

"Lucky murderer," Peyton said weakly.

"Unlucky doctor," Tandy added. "Was the doc in on it?"

"Prolly," Bubba said. "We ain't apt to know today. The po-lice will have to fill in the blanks."

"Bubba," David said, "I have an urge to wipe off the knife's handle."

"Don't matter," Bubba said. "There's something else with your fingerprints handy. Don't you fret, David. Sheriff John will clear you right up. He ain't convicted me yet, and look at all that I bin through."

"Watson," David protested, "I have boocoodles upon which to fret. I shall be *the* villain in this horrid affair. Especially if none of you are no longer here to say that I am not *the* villain in this horrid affair. Why couldn't you be *the* villains in this horrid affair?" He paused and looked at Tandy and then added, "and *the* villainess."

Tandy shrugged in an unconcerned fashion.

Bubba thought about it. He could be the villain if someone looked at it, if someone had used the knife he'd used on the bologna sandwich, and if someone wanted to point the finger at someone besides David.

"You're the one who liked to play games with all of the people and especially Hurley Tanner," Bubba said defensively. "Ain't fair, but it is what it is."

David stomped up and down the path. The act didn't come across the way it was supposed, considering that he was wearing large-sized pumps without heels. But then, Bubba didn't have any shoes on and it was okay.

"So let's forget that, and the cigs," Tandy said, "and figure this out. The doc got up and walked out of the cafeteria when we rushed out to see the Mercedes Benz burning up the Rabbit. Did he get kidnapped along with Cybil, or did he kidnap Cybil, since you're suggesting that the doctor had the most motive to kill people off? Which, by the way, I don't understand because, unless the doctor has been doing some underhandedness, he wouldn't be in anyone's wills. I think rich people would suddenly notice if their loved one kicked off, and he or she left money to the doctor who was in charge of their care. That would be *suspicious.*"

"It was the other murderer who was paying the doc off," Bubba said. It was actually a theory, but he bet the police would figure out where the money came from that had recently been deposited into his formerly bereft bank account. In the midst of bankruptcy, an account didn't go from $17.32 to $100,017.32 without some significant explanation. "I reckon the doctor was smart enough to ask for a deposit up front or no can do. But he didn't can do. He can didn't. Once the murderer dint need the doctor anymore, he was history."

"$100,000 wasn't going to pay off all his debt," David reflected. "Furthermore, it's not so smart to deposit a blackmailing slash murder payoff into your bank account where the IRS will be privy to anything over $10,000." He paused for a moment to allow that to sink in. "So the doctor was expecting a large payoff." He glanced at the corpse. "But not *that* kind of payoff."

Tandy crossed her arms over her chest and said with two cigarettes hanging out the side of her mouth, "Do I understand this correctly? So the bad guy or girl has an accomplice. Then the accomplice needs to be eliminated. When that's done, does he or she go after us? Is that what happened to the rest? Did this person just winnow the gaggle, or did all our brethren take an opportunity to beat feet into the woods? He couldn't have gotten to all of them. He can't get all of us, right? Right? Right?" The last part started to elevate in tone, showing that Tandy's typically equable exterior was beginning to break down.

"I hope not," Bubba said. "It would prolly be best ifin we went back to the cafeteria."

"I vote we climb down the newly created ledges and haul ass for Farmer John's barn where there will be cell phone coverage," Tandy said. "Or Farmer Pete or Farmer Fred or whichever farmer who doesn't have a collection of chainsaws and/or sharp knives that were touched by David-freaking-Sherlock Holmes."

"I'm sticking with Bubba," Peyton said. He brushed back locks of multicolored hair from his face. "The client is always right."

"I say the client is only right if one isn't about to be murdered in an icky fashion or mysteriously disappear," Tandy said.

Bubba decided that if his head were to suddenly explode it wouldn't be so bad at that very moment in time. People were vanishing pell-mell. There were at least two murders. He was surrounded by individuals who had been, and were, certifiable, with the exception of Peyton, and Peyton might as well be certifiable. (To be perfectly frank, the people in Pegram County who weren't certifiable were the minorities.) The only thing that kept him going was that he was going to stumble around enough to figure out why this was happening and who was responsible.

"Why didn't they kill you, Bubba, when they first got to you?" Tandy asked with obvious doubt in her words. "No one saw you get hit in the head, and furthermore, how could they have dragged you off? No offense, but you're a big boy."

"240 pounds," Bubba admitted sourly, wishing he had something unwholesome to eat at the moment. Had Ratchley rubbed off on him, or was it still the sympathetic pregnancy? (Popcorn covered with salsa, the hot kind of salsa, sprang to his mind. He'd need a spoon with that one.) "I think someone used a cart with me, and I don't know why they dint kill me. I figure that one of them two killers isn't really a killer or is just enough of a killer to kill off the person or persons that counted. I dint count. I hope that some of them others don't count neither." An insidious thought occurred to him. Perhaps they needed Bubba for something. *For what? That would be the insidious part.*

"I miss Thelda," David said. Then he whispered, "Thou villainous, full-gorged lewdsters."

"And Jesus likes to lay hands on," Tandy said. "It didn't make me want pot or cigs less, but he meant well."

Bubba looked at Dr. Adair again. They could cover him up, or they could carry him to the hospital, and hopefully he wouldn't vanish like Blake Landry. But then Bubba had a pretty darn good idea that no one was going to vanish like Blake Landry. He bit his lower lip and looked around again.

"What are we goin' to do?" he asked himself.

"'I say we take off and nuke the entire site from orbit,'" David quoted, and it was a second before Bubba realized it was a quote. Then David added, "'It's the only way to be sure.'"

Peyton tittered. "I just love Sigourney Weaver. She should be an honorary transvestite."

"We don't have a spaceship or a nuke," Tandy said acidly. "And really, how do we know it's not you, Bubba? You were alone most of the time. You had the opportunity."

"Same as the doctor," David said. "Who was going to write Bubba into the will?"

"Maybe it's not money at all," Tandy said slowly. "Maybe it's because he's addicted to dead people. Dead people are falling all around about him. I mean, the dead probably rise from the grave to come and see him."

"That's not my fault," Bubba protested. "It was a movie with zombies. You were there. There wasn't really any dead people except the one guy."

Tandy took a step backward. She dropped one of

her cigarettes and mashed it with her foot. "I don't know anything. I'm tired. I need a hit of blue mystic pot. I got a stash at home in the base of my Olmec head statue." She paused. "I did not tell you that. I don't have an Olmec head statue." She paused again. "Just in case anyone is listening. I don't have a stash at home."

"I brought Bubba into this," David said with a reasonable tone as if he was talking to a child. "He didn't know anything about it before yesterday. He was fishing on a lake, looking at baby name books."

"How do I know you're not all in on it?" Tandy asked, taking another step back. "You could be all be murderers. A Sherlock Holmes murderer. A wedding guy murderer. A redneck murderer."

"Wedding *planner* murderer," Peyton corrected helpfully.

"Peyton isn't a murderer," Bubba said sharply. "He's just a fella that done got caught in the wrong place at the wrong time."

"I don't know that," Tandy said cuttingly. "I think I've been a pretty good sidekick up until this point." She motioned at Dr. Adair's body with her remaining cigarette. "Sarcastic, biting, humorous. Yep. All there. But this is murder. Really murder. I should have realized that when we saw Blake's body. I don't know what was wrong with me, but my eyes are open right the eff now."

"What did you think it was?" David asked gently.

"It's all surrealistic. This kind of crap doesn't happen to normal people." Tandy waved at Bubba. "No one named Bubba goes around finding dead bodies all the time. Furthermore, Pegram County is becoming the murder capital of the world. How many murders have you had here in the last two or three years?"

Bubba had to think about it. There was his former fiancée, Melissa Dearman, the realtor, Neal Ledbetter, and Steve Killebrew and Mrs. Smothermon were victims of the Christmas Killer. That murderer had also killed Robert Daughtry who'd worked at a driver's license bureau, but Bubba didn't think it had happened in Pegram County. Then there was poor Mary Posey, but that hadn't happened in the last two or three years. Of course, Justin Thyme had been done in by the same person who had done in Mary Posey. Then the movie director had died but that turned out to be a case of creative coverup-a-cide.

"Five," Bubba said. "And I only found the first one, the second one, the third one, and the fifth one, but he vanished." He brightened. "Just like the people keep doing around here." It wasn't anything to be happy about. He wished he could vanish. First, a meal, then a nap, and conclude with vanishing.

Precious whined sharply and sat down next to Bubba's sock-covered feet. He hunkered down next to her and scratched the part under her jowls she liked. He wished he had some more Milk-Bones or even a ragged tennis ball to throw for her. Sometimes it seemed as though all the problems in the world could be solved by throwing a tennis ball for a Bassett hound.

David said, "Uh, Tandy, don't get all paranoid. You know one of the symptoms of chronic marijuana use is paranoia. In fact, cannabis use can exacerbate schizophrenia."

Bubba glanced up. Tandy was all the way to the edge of the woods with one foot inside the tree line. At least she wasn't pointed toward the cliff. Her face was wild; her eyes were large. She was twitching and not in a good way. The cigarette in her mouth went up and down as her head jerked.

"Just because chronic pot use can cause paranoia doesn't mean that people aren't after you," Tandy shrieked. She twirled and ran off into the woods.

David started after her and Bubba said, "What are you goin' to do ifin you catch her, David?"

"If she's alone, she might run into the killer," David barked. "She's not safe, Bubba."

"And she won't trust him anymore than us," Bubba said. "Cain't tie her down. Cain't lock her in a room. Hopefully she'll lock herself into a room until we can get her some he'p."

Peyton glanced into the woods. "Miss North!" he yelled. "Don't trust anyone! Lock yourself in a room! We'll come looking for you when the police come!" He sighed. Then he looked at David and Bubba. "What? She might get married one day, and she'll think of Pure Love Weddings, LLC, and then I'll be in clover. Although I should say I'm not entirely sure which way she swings. She might very well marry the Olmec head she talked about."

"That's the bass calling the trout fishy," Bubba muttered.

"I heard that, dear redneck groom," Peyton said calmly. "I am entirely heterosexual. Ginger is my goddess. She will come to the wedding, and you will see. She's got more woman in her little finger than all the women in this county have in their bodies." He looked David up and down. "Of course, your disguise was all that, Sherlock."

David raised his eyebrows. "Of course," he agreed. He looked after Tandy. "We can't just let her run off."

Bubba stood up. "No, we cain't. Come on." He strode into the forest and winced when he stepped on a pinecone. "I hate pinecones," he mumbled.

"Precious," he said. The canine bounced up, having found some energy from somewhere that Bubba wished he could find. "Find the lady. She's got Milk-Bones. Hunt, girl. Hunt." He carefully picked up Tandy's ground out cigarette butt and let his dog inspect it.

Precious sniffed around the butt and then into the air. She swung her head about. Bubba wasn't sure why she had been a miserable failure at being a hunting hound. With the right motivation she did just fine. Usually food had to be involved.

Precious stopped to bay at the skies.

David winced and whispered, "The hound of the Baskervilles is among us once more."

Chapter Twenty-two

Bubba and Nefarious Noodleheads

Sunday, April 7th

"We shouldn't have let her go," David said, looking at Bubba. They had hunted through the woods for Tandy North for an hour and hadn't found anything but a telltale smoking cigarette lying on the trail nearest to the hospital. They had reluctantly returned to the cafeteria. Bubba had helped himself to more coffee before he noticed that there were three cupcakes left in the cupcake stand. *Three. Three cupcakes. Three people left.* How obvious was that?

Bubba glanced at David, who turned away and gazed out the large windows. Bubba looked away from David because he felt guilty. Then he stared at the cupcakes. The cupcakes didn't appeal to him and not because there was zucchini and carrots hidden within the recipe. No, it was because they represented something evil and warped.

"Did you eat those cupcakes?" Bubba demanded of David.

David had changed back into man clothes to include the deerstalker cap and Inverness coat. He chewed on the end of the calabash pipe and apparently contemplated the idiosyncrasies of murder. Sherlock Holmes was no longer in disguise; he was large and in charge. He also shook his head. "Chocolate gives me the volcanic whoopsies," David said sadly. "Plus, I wouldn't be able to fit into that dress that your mother gave me. It doesn't matter how much zucchini and carrots Leeza put into the recipe. It all goes to my hips. I don't know how some women do it."

Bubba thought about the Smith & Wesson in the white clutch purse. The purse had gone the way of the white heelless pumps and the dress. Bubba wanted to assume that the weapon had gone into one of the deep pockets of the Inverness coat along with the brass knuckles and the sap, but everyone knew what happened when one assumed.

"Did you?" Bubba asked Peyton.

Peyton delicately wiped the corner of his mouth. "I wouldn't know what to tell you, Bubba."

Bubba glanced at the wall clock. It was close to ten a.m. He didn't want to think about his mother and Willodean going through the agony of wondering where he was, but he hoped they were close to figuring out that all was not well in Happytown and that also he was at the Dogley Institute for Mental Well-Being, anxiously waiting for assistance. He didn't want to think about the fact that a murderer might be getting more and more antsier about his extra guests. After all, if it had been up to the killer, David would be the only one left and consequently the only one to blame. Problem solved. Case closed.

But there was the problem of Bubba and Peyton. The case was *not* closed.

I'm smarter than this, Bubba thought. *I'm smarter than this other fella. This other fella don't know exactly when the po-lice are coming. He don't know and neither do I. It could be in five minutes. It could be in five days.* Bubba grimaced. It wouldn't be five days. The hospital's employees were due to show up on the following day, and surely they would want to say something about a big mound of rocks and dirt blocking the only road in or out of the hospital proper. The construction crew would show up at the landslide the next day. They would report it to the police or to someone.

Normally Bubba would sit in a chair, maybe one of them plastic Adirondacks on the lawn, put his feet up, and wait for someone to take care of business. But someone else *was* taking care of business, and Bubba didn't want to wait to see what that someone's next plans were.

Bubba stared at David and then at Peyton. First, he was going to have to get rid of the wedding planner. That was a given. But how? There were all the traditional methods of making someone disappear; shallow graves, rivers, old abandoned mines, and whatnot. (There was also a nearby conveniently located cliff that Bubba had to consider.)

This was probably an all-time new low for Bubba. It had been building and building, growing like an ignoble blackhead on the day before the wedding, but here it was. (Or should that be that it had been descending and descending, dropping into the earth like a dastardly sinkhole sucking down a McMansion in Florida?)

Bubba stomped back and forth in front of the table with the cupcake stand. Trudging was easier than giving in to fatigue. He knew that if he put his head down and closed his eyes, he would wake up hours later or possibly not wake up at all. Or even worse, he would wake up and David would be gone by reprehensible means. Who wanted to explain that one lost a loony while taking a nap? Who wanted to explain that one lost any loonies at all, period?

Plus his head was throbbing. Aspirin, ibuprofen, and acetaminophen hadn't put a dent in the pain. He was a little afraid to throw some other chemical additive to the mix in case something ugly and unwarranted happened. (Glowing in the dark would be bad. Growing an extra arm would be bad. Having his penis fall off would also be bad. No more pills.)

"What if we set up a big fire?" Peyton asked. "We could put lots of green leaves on it so it would smoke. We could make it huge, and people wouldn't be able to ignore it. I know a recipe for homemade sparklers. All we need is bleach and a salt substitute. I've used it in weddings before. You can make them different colors."

"A bonfire is like the explosions," Bubba said. "People prolly heard them before and dint do anything about it. This is out in the country, and folks think it's jelly because jam don't shake like that."

"What does jelly have to do with anything?" Peyton asked.

"Smoke won't work because we're too far away," David said.

"Folks sometimes use dynamite to go fishing 'round here," Bubba explained.

"That's hardly sportsmanship-like," Peyton protested.

Precious yawned widely and fell over onto the floor with a thump. She put a paw over her eyes and adjusted her body so that she was comfortable. It made Bubba wonder what to do with her. After all, she would likely be all right. She couldn't very well announce to all and sundry who the murderer was, so there wasn't any point in killing her. Although she had been known to go after people with shovels and metal detectors with impunity, she didn't typically go after local murderers. (Which was a shame in Bubba's opinion, but who knew how to train a hound to do that? Teach her all the sociopathic and psychopathic tendencies and then alert on that? Precious would be pointing to half the people in Pegram County which would get old fast.)

Bubba finally stopped stomping and looked at Peyton. "You seem like the easy going sort, Peyton," he said with a voice that sounded a lot calmer than he felt. "You've bin proper about this whole murder and missing people business. You haven't even cried once, which is something I truly appreciate. How would you like to play a game?"

"A game?" Peyton repeated. "I can play games, although I don't think I want to play dominoes with David, er, Sherlock. Things tend to happen to the people he plays games with."

"Hey!" David protested. "It was only a few, and I didn't do it."

"A game," Bubba repeated. "It's sort of like hide-and-seek."

Peyton said, "Can we make electric smurfs? That's a frou frou cocktail. It's got coconut rum and blue curacao in it. I think it comes with a splash of Sprite and some pineapple juice, too. I just love a little blue umbrella in it. Sometimes you can get it with dyed blue olives."

"I don't think they have any alcohol around here," Bubba said.

"Oh, there might be some about," David said.

"Mebe later," Bubba said.

"Okay, then," Peyton said gleefully. "Let's play."

●

"What if someone comes along and finds Peyton?" David asked fretfully.

"There's a lock on the door. There's a lock on the inside. I tole him to use the stuff inside to barricade the door." Bubba rubbed his chin. "I stuck Precious inside with him. He's got the best hound in Pegram County around. We gave him three knives and a baseball bat, plus he's still got that baton. You know, that wasn't just any baseball bat but a Louisville Slugger with a lizard skin grip. Ifin he cain't protect himself with them things, then I don't know what is what. Besides he cain't plan the wedding if he ends up dead. That's the right motivation."

Peyton had been pushed inside one of the interior offices that had no windows. Bubba had locked the outside with a key from Dr. Adair's ring. The inside had a sliding catch. "Do all them doors lock that way?"

"It's a double locking procedure for security issues," David said. "You should know that, Watson. These particular offices are used for violent patients when there is an overflow, not that I can recall that happening. You remember Nancy Musgrave, the social worker who introduced us?"

Bubba remembered Nancy Musgrave, her and her big gun, too, and her little Santa Claus cheese knife, also. (Actually it hadn't been her knife, but she had been the last one to use it.)

"She often threatened us with locking us in these offices. There's no surveillance here like in the bubble-wrap rooms."

"The bubble-wrap rooms?"

"That's where they put the ones with DTs or when someone is undergoing a psychotic break. The walls are padded, and there's a little camera in one of the ceiling corners to make sure no one dies in there. Your fellow resident of Pegramville, Newt Durley, has been in one three times. I think he received special dispensation on account that he doesn't have any money. I don't think operating an illegal still nets him a significant profit." Newt Durley was a local alcoholic who often spent time in the Pegram County Sheriff's Department's jails. Sometimes he spent time in the city's jails, too. He was an equal opportunity drunk.

"It don't make a profit ifin you drink all your proceeds." Bubba looked at the door again and sighed.

Peyton hadn't been all that willing at the last moment. In fact, he had complained vociferously.

Bubba hadn't been paying attention to Peyton. He'd been looking around the hallway and ascertaining that no one could see the office door from an exterior window. To be perfectly honest, he didn't want the person spying on them to be able to tell where Peyton had gone. Before he had shoved Peyton inside, Bubba had also turned off the security system in the long hallway and covered up the lens with pieces of masking tape just to be sure.

"Bubba," came Peyton's voice through the door, "I don't like this game. Neither does Precious." The sound of claws raking against the door came next.

"I know, I know," Bubba said soothingly. He wasn't sure if it was more to Peyton or to his dog, but then he made up his mind. It was to his dog. "This'll be safe for ya'll," he added for Peyton's benefit. "Just don't open the door until you hear me or Willodean. Not for no one. No matter what they say. And stay quiet, too. Ifin this fella don't know you're in there, then he won't try to kill you."

"What about David?"

Bubba looked at David and shrugged. "Hard to say about David. Several people might want to kill him."

"But if he's the one being railroaded, then shouldn't he be locked up in here with your dog?" His voice lowered for a moment into a consolatory tone. "Of course, I don't mind being locked in here with you, darling redneck hound." The tone went back to his normal, and Bubba could imagine Peyton tossing his mane over one shoulder and directing his voice at the locked door. "I could have your back, you know. I might be all about wedding planner, but you would be surprised how closely related wedding planning is to prevention of homicidal activities."

David set his shoulders in a straight line, emphasizing the cut of the Inverness coat. "I resent your saying that people want to kill me, Watson," he announced. "I say that you are…a noodlehead! In fact, you're all noodleheads!"

"We need to cover up the doc," Bubba said. He hesitated for a moment while he thought of an appropriate insult to return with. "And you're just a crazy fella."

"Is that the worst insult you can come up with, Bubba?" David whispered.

"Wait!" Peyton cried. "Why are you fighting? You're just tired, right?"

Precious yipped imperiously.

"Okay, then," Bubba said. "Let's get back there and make sure that body ain't vanished into thin air."

"Turnipface," David said.

"Is there a food theme?" Bubba asked.

"I'm hungry, Watson," David said. "You mushmouthed man with hepatitis breath."

"Yep," Bubba agreed. "I could go for collard greens with a peanut sauce but nothing spicy."

"I was thinking of Oreos," David said. "What's wrong with you?"

•

They trudged back out to the cliff. Bubba held a blanket. He was expecting that Dr. Adair's body had disappeared, but it still sat in the same place. The knife was still in the man's chest. The person was still dead, as far as Bubba could tell.

Bubba disregarded his roiling stomach and covered the former psychiatrist with a mint green blanket that had what Bubba thought were candy canes embroidered on it. (It was clearly homemade, and they might have been barber's poles.) It wasn't exactly respectful, but it was better than the Grateful Dead throw that he had first picked up from one of the patient rooms. The choices of what to cover up the recently dead had also included a blanket with the Eiffel Tower and the words "Do it in Paris!" on it, but Bubba had also dismissed that.

"Now?" David asked. "I have everything I need. We can even..."

"Wait," Bubba said and tilted his head as an odd noise registered on the peripheral part of his brain. The last cup of coffee (three actually) had given him a boost of energy, and he didn't feel quite as poorly as he had. The ice cream sandwich that he had snatched and gulped up had helped, too, even if it had been Neapolitan.

"Perhaps we should switch roles, Watson," David went on. "I would imagine your affianced one will likely kill me in a gruesome fashion should one hair on your phenomenal head be harmed. Did you know that she can shoot the wart off a hog's nose at a hundred feet?"

"Willodean is goin' to kill me if something happens to me," Bubba confirmed. "Ifin I should get kilt, she will find a voodoo priestess who will bring my sorry ass back to a zombie-like life and then kill me again on account that she will be that mad at me."

Bubba turned a little toward the hospital. He heard something he shouldn't have heard, considering that they had just locked up a wedding planner and a Bassett hound.

His dog was baying. Precious let a mournful howl go, and it echoed across the woods to them.

"That doesn't sound like she's still locked up," David said.

Bubba didn't think so either, so he ran for it.

•

The door was open. The locks had been thrown from the inside. The exterior lock had been broken. Bubba looked at it and decided it had been broken from the inside. Peyton had gotten himself out.

It took David a minute and the extraction of his large magnifying glass from his pocket to come to the same conclusion. The dragonflies and butterflies on the handle and rim of the glass did not detract from his deduction. "He planted his foot here," David said and pointed to the large footprint next to the door handle. "Then he kicked it three times. Maybe four times."

"How is a lock like that supposed to keep a psychotic person inside?" Bubba asked. "It couldn't keep a fella like Peyton inside. He don't look like the type to lift weights."

"He does yoga and super Pilates," David said. "I inferred this from the books he had about yoga and super Pilates in his car. There was also an exercise DVD. Also there was a program on Pilates on his iPod. Plus, he discussed it once with me. In addition, he talked to your mother about it, who complained that the only way she would do yoga or super Pilates was if someone held a gun to her head, and she wasn't sure about it even then. I think that's all."

"Why would he do this?"

Precious yowled again, and Bubba turned to see her charge down the hallway toward him. She power slid into his leg and nipped his ankle. Then she plodded off to a nearby corner and licked her paw. She sat down with a loud thump and glared at Bubba.

David took a deep breath and looked over the door with his magnifying glass. "I deduce that his girlfriend has left him for a WWE wrestler named The Shadow Reaper. I deduce that his business is secretly going down the potty because his partner took all of the money and escaped to Rio de Janeiro and now lives with an exotic Carnaval dancer named Papaya. Papaya was once hooked up with King Momo, who is the central figure in Brazilian carnivals. Peyton, however, came to get money from killing off rich alcoholics and addicts to keep from going under financially. It's a terribly diabolical plan. Secretly I admire him, but I would never admit that elsewhere."

"There ain't a WWE wrestler named The Shadow Reaper," Bubba said. "I ain't sure about the rest."

"There were the remnants of a bug found only in Rio de Janeiro and some sparkly glitter used for body decoration which was only made in Brazil," David explained, "or possibly it was a mummified house fly with ordinary craft glitter." He looked closer, angling the magnifying glass for the best look. "Yes, it is a regular house fly. Forget I said all that other stuff."

"Are you suggesting that Peyton is in on all this?" Bubba asked. He waved his hands around in explanation of "all this."

"Why else would he break out?" David asked. He

straightened up and replaced the magnifying glass in one of the Inverness coat's deep pockets. "Surely, even a man such as he should realize it's safer in there than out here."

"But Ma and Miz Celestine dint know they were goin' to hire him until a week ago. They were lucky he was free." Bubba chewed on his lower lip. "Plus Peyton's so...wedding planner-y."

"A clever ruse," David inferred. "The makeup, the ambiguous sexual orientation, the deep interest in all things wedding. It threw me off the track. In fact, perhaps the real killer took Peyton's place. He discovered that he would be coming to Pegramville and killed the real Peyton."

"That's really a stretch," Bubba said.

"So is what we're planning to do."

Chapter Twenty-three

Bubba and Impending Peril

Sunday, April 7th

"Peyton dint do it," Bubba said with certainty, "any more than you did. Ifin you think about it, David, that's too many what-ifs, even for Pegramville."

Bubba insisted that they look for Peyton. They searched the hospital, careful to bring the Louisville slugger that Peyton had left behind. (Apparently, Peyton *had* taken two of the three knives, so he wasn't exactly helpless.) They went from top to bottom, opening all the doors and leaving them open in their hunt. Instead of dead or missing people they found a diorama depicting the march of Hannibal the Carthaginian's army over the Alps. (The elephants were the kind from a craft store and wore battle armor constructed of aluminum foil.) They discovered that Thelda had a secret cache of extra sweaters in a closet down the hall from her room. The cache included the crème de la crème of Christmas sweaters with Rudolph constructed from brown felt and a battery operated nose that glowed a brilliant red. Two ornate wreaths were placed in strategic locations. They also discovered a collection of empty bourbon bottles lined up by size and color inside one of the attic access doors.

"That's Timothy's," David commented. "He's an orderly and likes to collect bourbon bottles, but only after he's consumed the bourbon."

"Of course," Bubba said. He had tried to get Precious to hunt for Peyton, but she wasn't having any of it. She had clearly been reluctant to follow them as they went from room to room, as she was still ticked off at her master for locking her into a room with the wedding planner.

They checked every room and under the hospital, as well. The crawl space wasn't really a crawl space at all, but a place where the floors had been finished with concrete, and boxes had been piled up along every free wall.

They didn't find anything remotely resembling a body or a missing people. There wasn't even a dissected bloody ear or other dismembered random but creepy digit to give them a case of rampant goose bumps.

They didn't find a third cupcake. Bubba couldn't help but notice that there were only two cupcakes in the tree. He didn't really want to think about how the third one had disappeared, so he dismissed it for the moment and kept searching.

"I don't get it," Bubba said as they came back into the main foyer. He perched on the corner of Cybil's desk and rubbed the bump on his head. It felt like someone had hit him and then he remembered that someone *had* hit him. "The only one we done found was Dr. Adair. Well, we found Blake Landry but then he up and cut a chuggy. How do eight people, nine if you count Blake, just vanish into thin air?"

"The most logical answer is always the simplest," David said. He threw himself down into Cybil's chair with a loud humph. "They're here somewhere."

"How is that simplest? Ifin we can't find them, it ain't simple," Bubba said irately. If he was any more irate he'd likely pop like a loose balloon in a pin factory.

"If they're not here," David said gently, "then they are somewhere else. Since we know that all these people cannot leave the hospital area because of the avalanche, then they are still here." He motioned at the entirety of the area with one hand.

"David," Bubba said, "we don't have a lot of time. What happens ifin the po-lice show up?"

"Willodean kicks your tuckus, and I get blamed for murder," David pronounced solemnly. "Possibly you get blamed for co-conspiracy or accessory. We both go to jail. We buff up, or in your case, buff up even more so that you can't bend over to tie your shoelaces. We spend the rest of our lives in prison. I might get the death penalty since this is Texas, but I have a whole bunch of previous mental health issues, so they would likely offer me a plea bargain where I admit to the crimes and get life. I start a collection of toenails while in prison and make toenail sculptures with homemade glue. The sculptures get a showing at MoMA in Manhattan after I die. It becomes a Lifetime movie of the week. Tandy gets to play herself." He looked at Bubba expressively as if silently adding, "Duh?"

"No, the person's got to wrap this up," Bubba said. He was so tired, and his head hurt so much, he was beginning to doubt his own reasoning. It had started off as a practical plan, and now it was beginning to sound like a parody of a bad mystery movie. "*We've* got to wrap this up."

"What if the person kills you?" David asked seriously.

"It's a chance I got to take," Bubba said. "Ifin we don't, we might miss our opportunity."

"What about Precious?" David asked, looking at the canine. Precious woofed softly at the sound of her name. Then she turned her nose away to show her disdain. (Milk-Bones were not raining from the heavens into her mouth, so naturally she was disdainful. Anyone who's ever owned a pet would understand that.)

Bubba glanced at the dog. "Cain't be helped now. Ifin we tie her up, she'll find a way out. It's best to leave her in the afeteria-cay ith-way ome-say ood-fay. Ome-say *ood-gay* ood-fay."

"There's hot dogs," David said. Precious's right ear twitched tellingly. She might have eaten a hot dog before upon occasion.

A few minutes later, Precious was gobbling down hot dogs. She received a bounty of three all-beef wieners. Bubba had calculated that it would take them the time that she would eat two to get out of the cafeteria and block the doors shut. By the time she had the third one down, they would be out of room and hurrying down the hallway.

Once they had accomplished their despicable dogly deed of bait-and-switch, they heard a startled bark, and then Precious began to bay. She had cottoned to their treachery and was responding in kind. The baying sounded distinctly like "YOOOUUU NOOOBS!"

"However do you go anywhere without her?" David

asked.

"It's a knack," Bubba said. "A fella gets used to it."

They went outside via the front doors of the hospital, and Bubba looked around. For a very tiny moment he thought he heard music drifting to them. (AC/DC's "You Shook Me All Night Long.") He shook his head, and the sound was gone. Someone was around somewhere. (The killer? Unrelated would-be victims hiding behind a varied array of machetes and chain saws in the old broken-down barn down by the cemetery by the nuclear plant that was haunted by an alien-murdered pedophile? Possibly. That's how befuddled his brain was acting.)

"Remember," Bubba whispered, "someone's got their eyes on us."

"How do I know it's not you?" David said loudly.

"You came to me for he'p," Bubba said back just as loudly. He gestured toward the cliff-side path. They threaded their way through the trees. Bubba glanced back several times. He didn't think it looked abnormal. After all, they didn't know where people were or where the murderer was or where the police were. Pretty much they knew a lot of nothing. Looking cautiously over one's shoulder seemed like the smartest thing anyone could do in the situation.

"It was a heinous strategy of wretched malevolency!" David bellowed.

"I need a dictionary!" Bubba yelled back.

A few minutes later they reached their destination. It was the spot where the Semtex had blown up a huge semi-circle resembling a terrific bite taken out of a granite cookie.

"What are we doing here?" David asked. They stopped at the edge of the cliff.

Bubba resisted looking over his shoulder. "You should just confess, David!"

"I AM NOT SHERLOCK!" David screamed. He winced. "I MEAN, I am not David!"

"I'm not Captain Koala!" Bubba yelled back.

"Captain Koala?"

"Comic book character," Bubba explained. "Very cool. Brownie likes him."

"Future reference," David muttered. He fumbled in his coat pockets and brought out...

The calabash pipe. He inserted the end into his mouth and pretend-puffed. "I wonder why Tandy didn't want to smoke my pipe. I have tobacco. It's black bourbon flavored, although the thought of smoking it myself makes me want to blow chunks. I had no idea it was so foul."

"I don't know why she didn't want to smoke your pipe!" Bubba shouted.

David sighed. "I should have gotten the soap bubble pipe! You're a big...JERKFACE!"

"Is that a British insult?"

"No, no. My ex-wife used to call me that. Also needlenuts and microbrain when she was feeling particularly perky." David shook his head sadly. "She's not a very nice person. I think she's on her fourth divorce now. I wouldn't know because my daughter won't talk about her anymore."

"David?" The question wasn't just David's name but

rather, "Is it *you* again, David?"

"Yes, Bubba?"

"You okay?"

"No, I'm worried about Thelda and Jesus. To a lesser degree, Tandy and Peyton. That wedding planner guy really grows on you. He kind of fits right in around here."

"I know. I'm beginning to think that fingernail polish on a guy isn't so bad."

"It's because you've only slept about two hours."

"Prolly."

"Should we yell some more?"

"I'm not sure." Bubba waved his hands up and down angrily and paced back and forth on the edge of the cliff. He bounced to one side when it seemed as though a chunk of the cliff might fall. "Be careful here, David."

"Are you waving your arms up and down for a particular reason?"

"I figure ifin someone is watching, they cain't really hear us," Bubba said.

David casually glanced over his shoulder. He gestured wildly. "I don't understand all of this!" he yelled.

"I think you did it!" Bubba roared. He pointed at David. "I think you mean to kill me next!"

"I was thinking strangulation," David remarked, "but you've got such a thick neck."

"Mebe you should use...a weapon at hand," Bubba suggested. He waved one of his hands meaningfully at David's coat.

David looked at the pipe. "I suppose I could stab you

with the end of the pipe, but it's not very sharp."

"Remember what my mother gave you, fully loaded, and it's something for which I intend to discuss with her at a later, and safer, time and date."

"Oh, the white clutch purse," David said. "That's hardly lethal. Perhaps as a sap?"

Bubba took a deep breath. It didn't really help. "The gun, David," he said after a long moment. "The gun?"

"Oh, of course," David said. He put the pipe into a pocket and withdrew the Smith & Wesson. For such a small revolver it had a very large barrel. Or at least it seemed big when Bubba was on the wrong side of the business end.

"There ya go," Bubba breathed. "I still think you're the bad guy, David! It was all them dead bodies before! It was the association with the Christmas killer! It was all them nasty triglycerides the FDA warned us about! There were special chemicals in all them letters you delivered while you was in the Postal Service! Please don't shoot me!"

"I've never eaten a triglyceride," David protested vehemently. He waved the gun around.

"Don't point that thing at me!"

"You did it, Bubba! You planned this all! You killed poor Mrs. Ferryjig by making her have a fake heart attack! You made Hurley Tanner commit suicide! You made all those people vanish! Did you throw them over the cliffs, for God's sake? You stabbed poor Dr. Adair, and all he really wanted to do was psychoanalyze people! You strangled the social worker! Or was that a cheap ploy to get back at the last social worker who tried to kill you and most of your family?" David wildly waved the end of the Smith & Wesson about.

Bubba inched as close as he could get to the edge. His face twisted. He wasn't really up to this. It churned up his insides something fierce to think badly of people he had come to...should he say it? Should he even think it? Yes. He liked David Beathard. He liked Jesus Christ. He even liked Thelda. He liked her Shakespearean insults, too. They might be crazy, but they weren't bad people. Unless, of course, one armed them with a lethal weapon.

"You should just give me the gun, David," Bubba said. "It might go off and shoot someone by mistake, you know."

David cocked the hammer. It was a particularly deadly sound that Bubba didn't like even when it was himself doing the motion. Everyone knew that his mother kept a few guns around the house. Bubba had fired in some contests once upon a time. In the military he'd scored relatively well on his Army weapons qualification test. (Thirty-nine out of forty shots had hit the targets. He swore that the missed shot was because the target malfunctioned, but the result had been the same.) He never got used to the noise, however. In recent years he'd begun to actively dislike it on account of all the dead bodies that kept appearing. After all, guns were fine for hunting, but he wouldn't have wanted to be the person who shot someone by happenstance. Not that shooting someone for the express purpose of murdering them was happenstance.

David swung it around and pointed it at Bubba.

Bubba's stomach clenched up. Bile rose in his throat, and for a split second in time, he wondered if he had made an abysmal error of judgment. The entire previous twenty-four hours suddenly seemed like one mistake after another. Although he wasn't responsible for peoples' murders, there seemed like there was always something that could have been done. Hindsight was always twenty-twenty as they said.

There wasn't anything else to be done. It was time to pee on the campfire and call the dogs. The problem was that there wasn't a campfire, and the only dog around was locked up in the cafeteria with the cupcakes, which boded poorly for the remaining two cupcakes.

"We going to do this?" David asked.

"I reckon we ought," Bubba said. He lunged at David.

David bellowed furiously. "You'll never persevere, foul beast!"

Bubba enveloped David into a bear hug and swung him around. Bubba could see off the cliff. He could hear the rattle of loose granite being shaken loose by their weight on the brink of the precipice.

They struggled. Bubba could see they were too close to the edge of the cliff. He couldn't help trying to pull away, but David wouldn't let go of the weapon. Bubba started to say, "I don't think we should—" and there was a loud crack.

The sound of the bullet being fired from a Smith & Wesson 642 was loud enough to make anyone freeze up. Bubba stared into David's eyes, and he could suddenly smell the distinctive aroma of gunpowder.

There was a wisp of gray smoke before the wind whipped it away from them.

David's eyes seemed so large in his face. He didn't look like Sherlock Holmes anymore. He looked afraid, more like an ex-postman whose mind had slipped a gear once upon a time. Some terrible price had been paid.

Bubba's mouth opened to say something else, but the words dried up on his tongue.

"Bubba," David said, "I don't feel so great." Then he fell backward, slipping over the edge.

Bubba initially let go because his hands seemed to be unable to do anything else, but as David fell, he reached out. His huge fingers touched the material of the Inverness coat, and he grasped it within a finger and a thumb. David's fall hesitated in mid-air, his back was over the abyss, his feet balanced on the cliff's threshold. His heartfelt pain-filled eyes stared into Bubba's. Was a plea contained there?

Bubba held the strip of material for the longest second imaginable. It was as if time had stopped. The sound of ripping came to him, and he had to wonder if it was his pants splitting before he realized it was David's coat separating under the tremendous stress placed upon it.

"Bubba," David said again. His tone was oh so serious, the very epitome of solemnity. "I have to ask you something."

"Anything," Bubba breathed, trying to get a better grip. His fingers slid helplessly against fabric, unable to clutch anything.

"Does...if a woodchuck could chuck, would he really

chuck wood?"

Then David was gone, and Bubba was left holding a segment of plaid cloth in his fingers.

Bubba was alone.

●

Bubba stood on the brink for a long time. He didn't know how long it was. He simply stared down and held a bit of checkered fabric. Finally, he shook his head when Precious nudged his ankle with a wet nose. She whined softly and he said, "Okay. Okay, then."

He turned back toward the hospital and stumbled when his feet chose not to cooperate. Precious trotted after him, keeping to his heels, and rumbling quietly in a dogly fashion.

Abruptly, he stopped and the canine bumped into him. "You were locked in the cafeteria," he said, glancing back at her.

Precious yipped softly.

"Either you opened the door yourself," he said quietly, "or—" It wasn't unknown for the dog to be an escape artist. She knew exactly for what a doorknob was used. She knew how to open a refrigerator until Miz Adelia had placed a child safety lock on the door. Precious hadn't yet figured her way around that one, but it was probably only a matter of time.

Bubba started forward again. All alone. All he could hear was the sound of the wind whipping branches around above his head. Precious started to pant once he hit his full stride. He was all alone, as alone as he had been the day before while he was fishing on the lake.

Not quite alone for there was a man, his dog, and a

murderer.

The man had lots of questions to be answered.

Bubba came out of the woods without pause. If a person had been watching him at that moment, they wouldn't have guessed he was tired and longing for a good meal and a good woman, not necessarily in that order. He had an urge, no, an imperative need, to put his head to Willodean's still mostly flat abdomen and worship it.

The door to the hospital was open. It wasn't merely unlocked. Bubba hadn't locked it on the way out; he hadn't even thought about locking it. But now it stood wide open. He stepped inside and heard the clacking of Precious's nails on the marble behind him.

The receptionist's area was as it had been before. The desk was the same. The marble the same. The seats were still metal and attached to the floor. What wasn't the same was the noose hanging from the second floor landing of the staircase to one side of the foyer. Attached securely to the railing was a large thick rope with a hangman's knot on the end, just the right size for slipping over a man's head and tightening up.

There was only one thing that Bubba could think to say. "Let's put some lipstick on this pig."

Chapter Twenty-four

Bubba and the Murderer

Sunday, April 7th

Bubba stood in the foyer looking at the noose. It hadn't been there before he'd left with David or before David had fallen over the side of the cliff or before Bubba felt like the winning heel in the heel of the universe contest.

This was what every path led to in the crazy world that Bubba was presently residing within. If something new had appeared in the loonaverse, then there was also someone there who hadn't been there before.

"You're not goin' to hurt my dog, are you?" Bubba asked politely. "That would make me madder than a Maine Coon cat in a room full of rocking chairs." For a single moment that dangled in time, there was only silence as a response.

"Now why would I do that?" came the answer after the suspended pause. The person swung around in Cybil's chair and looked frankly at Bubba.

Bubba wasn't exactly surprised at the person's identity. "I dint think you had walked away," he said.

"Sure I walked away," the person answered.

"I reckoned the doc was in on it," Bubba said. "Left all his financial problems all over the place. He was clever enough to demand money up front."

"$100,000 was a small price to pay," the person said. "It can't be traced. I gave it to him in cash. He was stupid to put it into his bank account. The bank has to report deposits over $10,000, but there's nothing to be done about that now."

"Funny how money can make up for a little murder and the complete annihilation of a moral compass," Bubba said. "I figure it was for the money, right?" He didn't wait for an answer. "You have a connection to Hurley Tanner. Hurley's got to have bin the original target. Everything else was just lagniappe."

"Oh, I'd love to hear your theory," the person said. "I think we have a little time, so go on."

"Well, mebe you're the daughter's boyfriend," Bubba said. "You've got an eye on the piggybank. Mebe the piggybank was goin' to cut you off."

"That would account for Hurley Tanner's death, but what about the rest?" the person asked.

"I don't expect you kilt everyone," Bubba said. "I don't think even you could explain a bloodbath out here."

The person giggled. "Well, I only really wanted to be expedient. Do proceed with your denouement. I'm all a-goggle."

"You needed a fall guy," Bubba stated. "David Beathard was the fall guy that you picked."

"David did have a lot in common with all of the objectives," the person admitted, "if you don't mind me calling people objectives."

"So David needed to be framed for your master plan. You shore waited for all the right cogs to fall into place. The demolition, the renovation, the patients and staff being mostly gone. That was a lot of variables that could have easily gone wrong."

The person leaned forward in the chair. Eyes twinkling with an unstated malevolency, the person said, "That wasn't waiting for opportunity, Bubba. That was all orchestrated to a fine degree. A well-constructed plan of master proportion."

Bubba pulled out the little oil derrick figurine he'd found in the empty building. He'd stuck it into his pocket. "This was one of the clues."

"I was wondering where I'd put that."

"And your accent which is clearly from Georgia."

"Marietta, Georgia to be precise. I went to college in Atlanta. Go Dooley."

"Which all connects you to Hurley Tanner, who was an oil man from Georgia. I seem to recollect that he lived in the same area. Stands to reason that would be a connection."

"Yet all of his oil came from wells in Texas and Alaska."

"There's still some I cain't figure out."

"Such as how I came to be at the Dogley Institute of Mental Well-Being, is that correct?"

"Either you're a social worker for real, or you kilt the real one and took his place, which would be a heck of a coincidence because that sort of thing has happened around here before." Bubba frowned briefly. "Though it wasn't a social worker that time. Ye gods, Dogley needs to be a lot more circumspect in hiring social workers."

Blake Landry nodded solemnly. "It's hard to decide which is the real scenario. Shall I give you a clue?"

"Shore. A fella like me can never afford to turn down an offer of he'p, no matter where it comes from."

"I *am* a real social worker. I have an MSW. That's fancy letters for a master's in social work. I also have some other initials, but who wants to brag?" Blake smiled brightly. "Isn't that just peachy pie?"

"But to come here to Dogley is a stretch."

"Blessed serendipity," Blake confirmed. "I actually came here because I had a relative in the area. A relative I love very much, although she's not here anymore."

"You claimed credit for Mrs. Ferryjig," Bubba said. What relative? It was present tense, so it wasn't someone he'd killed. Who could Blake be related to, and what did the relationship have to do with the present set of circumstances?

"Mrs. Ferryjig actually had a heart attack," Blake said. "It could have been poison, if one wants to try being creative. It certainly helped David along the track of his downfall. One death is unfortunate. Two deaths is suspicious. I think I might have tipped him over the edge of delusion into his Sherlock Holmes persona. It's convenient for me that he wasn't a very good Holmes. He had a horrible British accent."

"So you drugged Hurley, tied him down with duct tape, and poured barbiturates down his throat."

"One of the biggest advantages of being a licensed social worker is that you learn a great deal about medications, whether you want to know or not. I was always interested in the field of recreational chemicals."

"You planted the searches on David's Xoom,

knowing that sooner or later your subterfuge would be discovered."

"I couldn't believe the police ignored the signs of the duct tape," Blake said. "I bet if it had been the sheriff or your fiancée looking at Hurley's death, it wouldn't have been ignored. But again, serendipity was hard at work. I hear she's a real bitch. Not your fiancée, but serendipity. Though I wouldn't want to be on the wrong side of your deputy's mace can."

"So once you had the hospital emptied out, you went to work. First the cell phone tower and the road were taken care of through the explosives from the shack. The doctor and you faked your death. That left you with a certain freedom of movement."

"Who is going to double check a medical doctor's statement? All I had to do was stay still for a few minutes," Blake said. "Then who was going to come back and make sure the body was still in the same place? Besides you, of course."

"I was looking for clues."

"That gave me plenty of time to set everything up. You forgot that I took out the main phone trunk line, too. That was a PITA, I'll tell you. It's not for the average criminal to do."

"I thought it had something to do with the avalanche."

"No, it's quite separate. Kudos to me."

"And the cupcakes?"

"Not me. I think it was the wedding planner. Or Nurse Ratchley. She's a compulsive eater, in case you hadn't noticed. She's not going to admit she ate all the cupcakes." Blake giggled. "I think your dog ate the rest. So no cupcakes left." He motioned with both hands palm-up in the air. "Very apropos."

"So how did you get work at Dogley so conveniently?"

"I was working here before all of this happened," Blake said. "The truth is that you're right about the order of things, but you've got the why all wrong. It doesn't have anything to do with Hurley Tanner per se."

"And the oil derricks in your office?" Bubba asked as he glanced down at the stylized one in his hand.

"I've always liked them. Collected them for years. I suppose I should stop. You know, all of my relatives give them to me for Christmas and birthdays. I have about two hundred in my home. It's hard to tell your loved ones to knock it off. It really is a coincidence that I like oil derricks and that I'm originally from Georgia. I never even heard of Hurley Tanner before he checked in here."

"So what makes you think I ain't goin' to tell the police when they come a-knockin'?" Bubba asked. He put the oil derrick on a side table and shook his head.

"Because I have a big gun," Blake said and removed a large revolver from his waistband. It was the grandfather to Miz Demetrice's Smith & Wesson 642. If Bubba wasn't mistaken it was a .45 Colt Peacemaker. A third-generation model based on what he knew from his mother's collection. It wasn't his mother's, however. Hers was all nickel. Blake's model was blued. In either case, it was still a big gun. It wasn't as big as the Christmas Killer's gun on the fateful night of the end of her reign of terror, but it was big enough.

"Yes, you've got a dang big gun."

"And your choice is to hang yourself or get shot," Blake said. "You did shoot poor David. It looked to be right in the gut. Lucky he fell off the cliff because if he hadn't, he'd still be writhing in agony with a gut shot like that. I don't think the authorities will accept an excuse of rampant paranoia."

"You did want him out of the way," Bubba said. "What ifin he had bin the one to shoot me?"

"That would have worked, too," Blake said cheerfully, "but I prefer you. After all, it is all about you."

"All about...me?" Bubba's mind worked furiously. "If this wasn't about Hurley, then it isn't about money. If it isn't about money, then it's about something else."

Blake nodded. The end of the gun nodded, too.

"I think we can dismiss a domestic argument, since it was so well planned, and I don't reckon you're having a relationship with all these folks," Bubba said.

"Other than a professional one," Blake said and considered, "and I'm not sure what you really call the relationship between victim and murderer. It was professional in the case of Dr. Adair. I simply couldn't have him blabbing later on. After all, the authorities are bound to look into all the financial affairs as a matter of course. They would have asked him about a certain deposit. He would have waffled. They would have pressed. He would have cracked. He wouldn't have been able to stand it."

"Not a drug or alcohol deal," Bubba said, "unless

you're connected to Ralph the Potman."

"No, no, no," Blake said. "Ralph sells his own stock. You should try his homemade brownies. He makes them for his aunt who has cancer. Delicious. Oh, wait, you won't have a chance to try them, will you?"

Bubba figured that was a rhetorical question.

"So money is out," Bubba reiterated. Blake nodded again. "And this don't smack of something you're doin' for kicks, am I right?"

"Goodness, no. I'm having the worst case of the trots for all the anxiety this causes. All the nerve-racking planning I've had to do and all of the events that had to have been coordinated. It wasn't easy getting the place mostly to myself. I couldn't even count on David staying here for my big finale. That's why I had to feed him a few clues before he could leave. He was going to see his daughter, you know. I had to convince him to stay without actually using the words. His presence was critical. I needed him to get to the real McCoy."

Bubba thought of the last reason. It was the one that motived other murders in abundance. There was the top five. Money, for-the-hell-of-it, domestic argument, alcohol/drugs, and...da...da...dah...revenge. If David was the impetus, then Bubba was the target.

"I'm it?" Bubba asked, dumbfounded. A thought came to him like a lightning bolt. *Nunngesser.* It was the name he'd seen on the explosives. Once upon a time he'd known a woman named Constance Posey nee Nunngesser. She had been in the Olympics, and she'd been the wife of a judge. She'd also been a murderer who had done her level best to eliminate Bubba from the face of the Earth. At the time Bubba had seen the name printed on the explosive packages, he'd thought it was coincidence. Apparently it was not.

"You happened to be working here," Bubba started slowly, "when Pegramville's First Annual Murder Mystery Festival took place?"

Blake nodded.

"You're related to someone who used to live here? Someone you love and who ain't here no more. And by that, I mean, she's not dead, just in another place." *Like in a women's prison not far from Donna Hyatt AKA Lurlene Grady, for example.*

Blake nodded again.

"And her name would have been Nunngesser at one time," Bubba stated.

"Oh, you've got it!" Blake cried cheerfully. He would have clapped his hands together, but the big .45 Colt got in the way. He immediately sobered up. "It took you long enough, but of course I threw in all those red herrings, so it must have been difficult." He considered Bubba for a long moment. "You're not really a dumb redneck, are you?"

"Redneck is as redneck does," Bubba said. "I reckon it was you who threw the Nunngesser company at the hospital for the demolition of the building."

"I might have leaked a lowball number for them to bid," Blake admitted. "It just meant that I had access to all the explosives I wanted. Did you know I worked at Nunngesser's during my college summers?"

"I didn't," Bubba said, "but I ain't surprised. You're also the one who broke into the explosives shack, on account that would look like someone like me had done it."

Blake nodded eagerly.

"And that's why I wasn't kilt when you knocked me out. You needed me to be alive for the big ending."

"That's right. You're pretty good at this. Too bad you didn't think of all of this *earlier*. Well, too bad for you."

Bubba sighed. "Was Miz Constance your cousin?"

"On my mother's side. Connie's mother and my mother are sisters." Blake shook his head sadly. "You wouldn't believe how angry my mother is right now. After all, Connie is a pillar of the family. A former Olympian and married to a judge. Why, a woman like that couldn't possibly be a murderer. Consequently, all of the witnesses must be fools or out to gain financially."

"So this isn't really about revenge," Bubba said. "You killed Hurley to get David all riled up. You wanted him to see the searches so he would come to me for he'p, on account of how we're friends. Mebe you even found a way to suggest it to him. You came to see me to make sure I felt guilty enough to follow up. You waited until you knew I was coming and blew up the cell phone tower and the road. You set us all up."

"Yes, I killed Hurley. I killed Dr. Adair after he helped me pretend I was a victim, too. Yes, this was a frame-up job on top of a frame-up job. You and David are completely, utterly innocent of any wrongdoing. Good Lord, do we have to go through everything?"

Bubba scratched the side of his head. "And after I'm dead?"

"There will be no one to testify against dear cousin Connie. The news will fixate on Pegram County's murderer du jour. They'll have to let her go. My mother will be happy. Aunt June will be happy. I can go back to being a social worker with a much larger trust fund than I had before." Blake sighed gustily.

"How do you explain all them other people who vanished?" Bubba asked.

"I couldn't kill everyone," Blake complained. "I'm not Super Killer Man. I think each of the rest ran off into the woods to hide until the fuzz appears. That's fine as long as they're there and not here."

"And how will you explain that you died already?"

"I wasn't dead, silly," Blake said. "I was merely unconscious. I woke up with the garrote around my neck and disoriented. I went to hide in the woods, too. If any of the rest says differently, then they'll still be loonies, and I'll still be an upright social worker with respectable credentials."

"You do know I ain't the only witness against Miz Constance," Bubba stated.

"Of course, but you're the one who heard the worst of it, you and that other big fella, Daniel Gollihugh. I'll take care of him in a few months. He's been in so much trouble that no one will blink if he gets shot in the back of the head in some dirty alley. The police will hardly blink." Blake sighed with a hint of anticipation.

"I wouldn't make Dan angry," Bubba said. "He don't do well when he's all upset-like."

"I'll keep it in mind," Blake said. "Now, you. Rope or gun?"

314

"Ifin you shoot me, how will you explain that?"

"I'll have to go climb down the cliff and put the gun in David's hand, of course. I don't think anyone will notice the difference between times of death. Besides, it'll take a while to find David's body, and I won't be directing them to it anytime soon." He clicked his tongue. "But then you and the loonies had to throw the explosives over the cliff, so the authorities won't want that just sitting down there. By the way, however did you get one to blow up without a detonator? Well, it doesn't matter. I'll have to redirect the authorities for about a day or two just to muddy the waters. Perhaps a manhunt in the opposite direction. Another potential murderer on the loose. If I hide the doctor's body, then he could have escaped to the north, and he's truly the mastermind. Yes, that could work very well."

Bubba grimaced. "You got just about everything planned out. A fella like you rolls with the punches, don't he?"

Blake sighed loudly. He waved the end of the weapon. "No more prevaricating. If you won't hang yourself, then I will shoot you."

"Wait," Bubba said. "Was that everything? You planned this all to a t. You accounted for certain variables. You wanted me to be dead, so I wouldn't be able to testify."

"Not just dead," Blake said. "Also painted with a tarred brush so that nothing you ever said would be taken seriously. You see, you'll be the killer at the insane asylum. I should think of a clever name for you. The Asylum Killer. The Loony Murderer. Something catchy. What do you think?"

"Bubba at the booby hatch."

Blake stared at Bubba. "Not quite there. But it has potential. Anyway, you've got to be smeared. Several of the others will testify that you were gone for critical points in time. You even made several of them suspicious of you. Miss North, for example, was terrified. Then your wedding planner was skeptical, especially when you locked him in a room."

Bubba frowned. "You have other cameras hooked up."

Blake nodded. "Yes, I needed to keep an eye on everything. It's all connected to the main security cameras. That's on the second floor in the back. You went in there twice, but the cameras are concealed behind a set of whiteboards. I had the monitors turned off. All I have to do is a massive erasure when you're gone and ta-dah, I'm all done. My mother and aunt are happy. I'm happy. Connie will get out of prison within a few months once the lawyers have their field day. I might even get a bonus out of it. Who knows? I may decide that I no longer enjoy the field of social work and retire to a South Pacific island."

"I figured that there had to be more cameras," Bubba said. "I also figured you watched that one Agatha Christie movie one too many times."

"It was inspiration," Blake admitted. "Ms. Christie was a master at planning a damned fine mystery."

Bubba smiled. "Gotcha."

Chapter Twenty-five

Bubba and Another Big Bada Boom

Sunday, April 7th

"What do you mean, gotcha?" Blake asked.

"I mean you've bin duped," Bubba said firmly. "You might as well put the gun down and put your hands in the air." Assertiveness occasionally worked when nothing else did. Miz Demetrice would have bellowed, "Screw fear, and do it anyway!" Sometimes his mother was correct no matter how much Bubba didn't like to admit it out loud.

Blake responded by putting both hands on the weapon. He braced his elbows on Cybil's desk. The .45 Colt must have been getting heavy. He steadied his aim and frowned at Bubba. "How?"

"Blake," came a voice over the loud speakers, "you've been a very bad social worker. And with all those extra qualifications, too. Advanced practitioner, huh? For shame."

Bubba glanced upward at the speakers in the corners of the oversized foyer. There were also camera mounts next to the speakers.

"No," Blake breathed. "I saw him. He was gone. I mean he was *gone*." His face screwed up in concentration. "How in holy hell did that..."

"The shot went into the ground," Bubba said and smiled. It wasn't a good idea to smile at a man who didn't have anything else to lose and who was also

317

holding a large revolver in a way that suggested he was used to it, so Bubba stopped smiling. "That explosive made a ledge down below there. I guess you dint have the time to go look at it. He hid there until I was back at the hospital door. Then he snuck in the back way and made it to the security room. Unlike me, David knows all the nooks and crannies in this hospital. He already knew about the cameras. He knew that he could record whatever you had to say to me. Even if you killed me, he could get that, too. For a loony, he shore is a smart fella. You might say it was very Sherlockian."

"No matter," Blake sighed. "I'll kill you and then I'll kill him. Then I'll find whatever it is that you think you've done."

"You can walk away now, Blake, while you have a chance," David said from the intercom. "I've got the whole thing on disc." There was a loud click and then came Blake's voice from the speakers in the corners, *"Yes, I killed Hurley. I killed Dr. Adair after he helped me pretend I was a victim, too. Yes, this was a frame-up job on top of a frame-up job. You and David are completely, utterly innocent of any wrongdoing. Good Lord, do we have to go through everything?"*

"So?" Blake asked. "It's easy enough to get that disc and just as easy to destroy it."

"You're not listening, Blake," David said, and his voice was triumphant. "Pay attention to the details."

"Listen to what?" Blake snapped.

Bubba tilted his head to better hear. There was a faint noise that was growing louder. It was a chop-chop-chop of something cutting through the air. There couldn't be a mistake as it came closer and closer. He knew that in another minute if he looked out the front doors of the mental institute he would see it.

It was a helicopter.

"You goin' to kill all them people, too?" Bubba asked. "I don't think that revolver has more than six rounds in it. There's me, David, whoever's in the helicopter, and a few other people hiding in the bushes. I'm assuming you kin hit a moving target and them folks in the helicopter will prolly have a gun or two or more. They won't like you shooting at them. Or us, for that matter. If Willodean, that's my affianced one, is in it, she'll shoot you out of spite. Don't you dare shoot at her, or I will come back from the dead to pound you into little itty-bitty pieces of social worker mincemeat."

The sound of rotors increased. The helicopter was right on top of them. Bubba had an idea that it would be landing on the side lawn where the patients had been playing with foam darts.

Precious inched behind Bubba's knees and leaned her head there. Bubba watched Blake Landry attempt to make a decision. Various expressions surged across his face like the vacillations of a powerful thunderstorm.

Bubba took a foot and nudged Precious away from him toward the still-open door. "Get the ball, girl," he whispered and jerked his thumb toward the exit. Her head shot up and she looked for the nonexistent ball. After a moment, she trotted toward the opening and went outside.

Blake watched the dog go without moving the weapon away from Bubba. Bubba nearly sighed with relief. Blake really didn't have to do anything to Precious, so he didn't. It was even possible that all the others were okay because he hadn't really needed to do anything to them either.

"Come down here, David," Blake said, "or I'll kill Bubba."

"Don't come, David," Bubba said. "He's just goin' to kill us both."

Blake said, "Well, it was worth a shot." He paused. "No pun intended."

"You can run now," Bubba said, repeating what David had told Blake. "Mix in with the people. Leave while you can. I'll promise not to say anything until you've had a chance to go."

"Oh, really?" Blake said. "I can't see that happening." He sighed again. "You can tell I don't really like hurting people. The only one I really wanted to hurt was you, of course, because of what you did to Connie."

"Do I need to point out that no one made Miz Constance murder the judge's first wife or the fella who'd bin blackmailing her? She dint have to blow all that stuff up? Does that company *ever* take an accounting of all them explosives?" Bubba inched closer to the door. He wasn't going to make it easy for Blake by standing still. He could still hear the rotors slowly as the helicopter powered down. There was a chance, albeit a slim one, to get away before the social worker decided to make him look like an oversized colander.

"Sorry, Bubba," Blake said. "You seem like a decent enough fellow. Sure Connie made mistakes, but you know how it is. Family comes first."

"That's right," came a new voice. Peyton stepped into the foyer, holding up something in his hand. His streaked hair was badly mussed. His wings were blurred. The manscara and manstick were nearly gone. His pants, shirt, and Gucci loafers were covered with dirt. Even his manicure was chipped. Bubba wouldn't have noticed the man's fingernails except that they were on the ends of the fingers wrapped around the stick of dynamite he was holding up.

"Family comes first," Peyton repeated. "A very important tenet."

"Uh," Bubba said. He thought of the brick of Semtex which shouldn't have blown up when thrown off a cliff even if it had bounced against the rock face. He thought of the box of dynamite in the explosives shack. He thought of the previous week when an arctic front had slid all the way to the south and caused some lows in the teens. He thought about how if dynamite is frozen, it sometimes destabilizes. (Another factoid obtained from the idiosyncratic mind of his mother, which popped into his head when it wasn't really wanted.) If dynamite has been destabilized then it sweats. It sweats nitroglycerin, which crystalizes on the outside. He thought that he could see bits of twinkling matter on the stick that Peyton was holding.

"And this boy has a wedding to go to," Peyton went on. "A wedding that will take place even if I have to drag his dead body to because I planned it. A wedding by Pure Love Weddings, LLC *always* goes on and in spectacular fashion, no matter how many murders, felonies, or conspiracies have occurred."

"A wedding," Blake repeated. "Can I go? Never mind, I'll just shoot you, too."

"And wiiill you shooooot the Soooon of the Loooord, as weeeell?" Jesus asked, stepping in beside Peyton. He also held a stick of dynamite. There were two more sticks in his rope belt, and Bubba winced.

"Let's see. I've got four of you now, so yes," Blake said, "yes to all of you. Line up beside Bubba."

"And thee, thou beslobbering, plume-plucked maggot-pie?" Thelda asked. She stepped inside the foyer and sidled to the left to give herself a little room. She still wore several sweaters and also held a stick of dynamite in each hand.

"Five," Blake said. "I can shoot five. I'll have one to spare if I miss one of you."

"Uh, dynamite," Bubba choked. In the wide world of Snoddys, he had been around dynamite before. He had a second cousin who did, in fact, like to fish with it. He once took Bubba to a lake. They'd managed to fill three coolers with fish before the authorities had appeared. (Fishing by dynamite was not an inconspicuous business.) Bubba had been detained but only until Cousin Artemis had admitted it was his dynamite, thirty years old, and obtained from Mexico on a dark and stormy night. That had also been the occasion when an elite team from Dallas had been flown in to dispose of the sweating sticks of dynamite with a specialized chemical that burned it. The team's leader had lectured Artemis all the way to the back of a departmental vehicle. Bubba hadn't thought to mention that the box that his cousin had used was only one of five that he had in his shed.   But then Bubba hadn't gone around Artemis's shed ever again.   Somehow his cousin managed to get rid of the rest of the dynamite before anyone was disintegrated via the explosive method. Artemis always had seemed to have a lot of fish in his freezer.

"JESUS!" David yelled gleefully as he appeared at the top of the stairs. "THELDA! Peyton, too! I thought you were all DEAD!"

Blake's gun wavered between David, Bubba, Jesus, Thelda, and Peyton.   Clearly, he couldn't decide who to shoot first.

"So just put the weapon down," Peyton told Blake. "I mean, just because you get paid a measly $40,000 a year is no reason to be a mass murderer."

"It's a little more complicated than that," Blake said.

"Where have you been?" David asked.

"There was a party in the VIP house," Peyton said. "It was sick!   Apparently, it's been going on since yesterday morning. Can you believe they didn't invite us? When I escaped I followed the music and found it. You shouldn't have locked me up.   I'm slightly claustrophobic. I've had five Irish kamikaze Jell-O shots. I think they used the 140 proof vodka."   He stuck his tongue out.   "Ithh yy onnggg eeen?" which Bubba translated into "Is my tongue green?" It was.

"Thou guts griping malcontent," Thelda said, but it was with an affectionate tone.   Then she stuck her tongue out. It was about as green as a leprechaun's underwear. She giggled.

Jesus grinned broadly and stuck his tongue out. It

was also green. He retracted his tongue to say, "Iiiit was a veeeery good paaaarty. There waaaas a baaaand. They plaaaayed techno, reeeeggae, hip-hop, aaaand the bluuuues. It was bitching."

"Just how many people are over there?" Bubba asked.

Ratchley stuck her head in the door. "They've got food!" She held up a plastic tray of pigs in a blanket. Fortunately, she did not have more dynamite.

Cybil yelled from behind Ratchley, "And no danged murderers, those poopy Peters!"

Abel yelled, "I've got some more Jell-O shots!"

"And I've got a bottle of Everclear!" cried Leeza.

"Cigs, too!" Tandy yelled. "Also some damn fine weed! Did you know Ralph is here? He brought in a bunch of people to party before the cell phone tower and the cliff got blown up!"

"How did you know to bring dynamite?" Bubba asked.

"That was purely coincidental," Peyton said. "We were going to throw the dynamite over the cliff to see if it would blow up, too, when we saw you and followed you. With the door open, we heard everything. It worked out well."

"Blake," Bubba said seriously, "you don't have enough bullets to kill everyone."

Blake's face fell. "I obviously didn't plan for this. Do you know they're holding dynamite?"

Bubba sighed loudly. "No one plans for Pegram County."

Blake put the oversized revolver on the desk and

leaned back in Cybil's chair. "I know when I'm licked. Someone call a lawyer."

Just then the sun came out from behind a cloud. Rays of purest light shot into the foyer and created a spotlight of crystalline magic. If Bubba's heart had been stopped, it would have miraculously begun to beat again.

Willodean pushed through the crowd and held her gun out, unsure about who to point it toward. She stood in the middle of the sunlight rays and positively glowed. Bubba smiled at her and indicated Blake Landry.

Blake had his arms wrapped around his head and was muttering, "What am I going to tell ma?"

"Whoopee!" yelled Peyton shaking the dynamite in the air.

Bubba's heart nearly stopped. For a split second he'd forgotten the next most imminent danger, and Willodean was standing right next to it. She was surrounded by six sticks of dynamite, all of which were covered with bits of crystalized nitroglycerin. "EVERYONE FREEZE!" he roared.

Surprisingly everyone did.

Blake peeked between his arms and froze when he saw Willodean in her neatly pressed uniform with her smartly shined Glock pointed at him.

"They got dynamite," Bubba said, indicating Peyton, Thelda, and Jesus. "It's sweating. That is very, very bad. Big bada boom."

"Everyone out," Willodean ordered, "except anyone who is holding a stick of dynamite." Blake went to rise, and Willodean moved swiftly. She threw him around as if he was half her size and put the cuffs on him with economy of movement that Bubba found enthralling. She pushed him up and toward the door, pausing near Bubba.

"Ya'll need to put the dynamite on the desk," Bubba told Peyton, Thelda, and Jesus.

Peyton stared first at Bubba and then at the dynamite. "It's...sweating. But it isn't hot."

"It don't work like that," Bubba said. "You remember that little explosion we had before?"

"That was Semtex," Peyton said. "Even I know the difference between plastique and dynamite."

"Yeah, I reckon it had been right next to the dynamite," Bubba said. "Must have sweat some of that nitro right onto those blocks. It's the crystals there that are dangerous."

Peyton looked at the stick in his hand and paled. "You mean, it could just blow up?"

Bubba shooed Willodean toward the exit, and she frogmarched her prisoner out the door. He heard her say, "Everyone needs to get away from the building right now!" Then she yelled, "Bubba! That means you too!"

David scurried past all of them with the disc in his hand. "Just let me give this evidence to the police, and I'll be right back."

"Theeee Son of Gooood cannot diiiie," Jesus said. "Except that one time. A minor thing, really."

"Jesus, don't move," Bubba said. "Mebe you cain't die, but you could blow up. And you could blow up the rest of us."

"I seeee your pooooint," Jesus capitulated.

"Thee art an artless shard-borne death token," Thelda said, holding her sticks of dynamite as far away from her body as she could.

"I was just trying to help," Peyton said. "Do you know how poorly Pure Love Weddings, LLC would look if the groom got murdered right before the wedding? I take my job very seriously." Then he hiccoughed and giggled at the same time.

Bubba looked around. "Just very carefully put the dynamite on the desk."

Peyton stepped forward and softly placed the single stick of dynamite atop Cybil's desk. He sighed and said, "I need some more Jell-O shots. Outside, people. Ratchley might have left some pigs in a blanket if we're lucky."

Jesus put the stick in his hand on top of the desk as tenderly as he could. The two in his belt followed. It was a gentle, careful movement. He stopped and patted the last stick. Bubba cringed. "Father," Jesus prayed, "pleeeease do not aaaallow the dynamite toooo explode preeeematurely." He backed away, and Peyton guided him out the door.

"Thou crusty botch of nature," Thelda told her sticks and put them on the desk. She let out a deep breath and looked at Bubba. "I'm never touching dynamite again."

Immediately, Bubba twirled the woman and shoved her toward the door. Thelda didn't need a lot of motivation. Her personal nitrous oxide kicked in, and she shot out of the building.

Bubba was right behind her. There was a noise, and

he looked back. One of the sticks rolled slightly. It hesitated as if held by the tip of an invisible finger, and then it rolled again right to the side of the desk. Just before it started to tip over the side, Bubba looked forward and jumped out of the door. Still in movement, one hand pulled it shut behind him. The last thing he heard was the click of the latch.

Epilogue

Bubba and the Ignoble Ending

?

Bubba opened his eyes. He saw a white ceiling with ugly off-white drop tiles. He looked around and saw a hospital room. Without thinking about it much, he knew he'd been in that particular hospital room before. He might have even been hooked up to the very same IV before. It definitely looked like the same hospital gown he'd worn before; no one could mistake the baby puke-green color.

He began to take an accounting of himself. Everything hurt. From the top of his head to the tips of his toes, it was all a dull ache. If someone had entered the hospital, announced he'd been hit by an out-of-control Mack truck hauling coconuts to Outer Mongolia, he wouldn't have been surprised. Regardless, everything seemed to be present and mostly operational.

"There you are," came a voice from his side. There was an inordinate amount of relief in the tone. He turned his head and saw bright lights exploding. It was a burst of rainbow kaleidoscopes careening in midair. Then he blinked, and it was all clear. Willodean sat in the chair beside the bed with her hands resting lightly on her abdomen. She had changed out of her uniform into a baseball jersey and jeans, but she still looked like a million bucks.

"It wasn't my idea for them loonies to get the dynamite," Bubba said quickly. He also quickly regretted it as his tongue hurt, too.

Willodean shook her head sadly. "No more explosions this year, huh?"

"I swear," Bubba said and reached out with his left hand. She took it and wrapped her pinky around his pinky.

"Pinky swear," she said.

"Pinky swear," he affirmed. They shook pinkies, and then the pinkies stayed connected.

"Blake Landry confessed everything," Willodean said. "I'm beginning to think that murderers are so stupid that they're attracted to Pegram County. Why would he think that no one would notice that a bunch of people at the institute suddenly died? Why would he think he could frame you by framing David Beathard?" She rubbed her belly thoughtfully. "I just don't understand criminals. Plus Landry is as loopy as a cross-eyed cowpoke's lariat, just like his cousin. Must run on their mothers' side."

"I reckon David gave you the disc," Bubba said.

"It takes 2nd place in the evil monologues category. I think Donna Hyatt's monologue was better." Willodean grinned crookedly. "At least it wasn't me that hit you this time. No, it was a heavy oak door. Good thing you shut it behind you."

"Constance Posey's monologue wasn't bad," Bubba said, "but we dint get that one on something like video or digital. Mebe I should start wearing one of them body cameras. I could avoid a whole lot of this. And mebe a helmet."

"I started looking for you right away," she said.

"How did you find us?" Bubba asked.

"Lloyd Goshorn said he told Peyton where you were and then Miz Demetrice remembered what you said, but she said she thought you'd been joking." Willodean smiled weakly. "Once we found the blocked road, I dragged the National Guard's pilot out of a sleep-in and made him start up his Huey. You know the rest."

Bubba laid his head against a mostly flat pillow and sighed. He could look at Willodean Gray all day long and never get tired of it. "I hope you weren't too worried."

"Of course, I was worried," Willodean snapped. "You were missing, doofus. And you didn't come home. Your truck was nowhere to be found. Your dog had vanished. I had visions of you driving off into a canal and us finding your skeleton and Precious's in a rusted-out Chevy carcass one hot and dry summer twenty or thirty years from now. Then we'd say, 'I knew he didn't run away to Madagascar like all those people said he did.' I was sick to my stomach. I drank milk straight from the carton. Miz Adelia nearly slapped my hand."

"I love you," he said.

Willodean leaned her head down and touched her forehead to his hand. He brushed his fingers across her silky flesh. "I love you, too. Stop doing this."

"I dint..." Bubba stopped speaking and then wound up to try again. "I'll do my best," he promised.

"I know. I know," she muttered. "Try to do better than your best."

"Anyone else hurt?"

"Thelda got a little singed. The glass windows blew out and cut up her left arm, but it wasn't anything that even needed stitches. I had no idea there were so many Shakespearean curse words. Somewhere Brownie is saying, 'Hey!' There was a lot of damage to the building. The administrator is having fits, saying he's going to sue you, sue me, sue everyone who was there, but he doesn't really have a leg to stand on since Nunngesser was so negligent with their explosives. Let him sue Nunngesser's. They've got some serious whack jobs in their family, so I don't think that's going to be an issue."

"Ma okay?"

"She's around here somewhere," Willodean said. "So is mine. This is suspiciously like the last time you woke up in the hospital, except that I didn't put you in here this time."

Bubba let his right hand drop over the side of the bed. A wet nose immediately brushed itself over his fingers, and a whine issued from the depths down under the bed. Precious licked his fingers and he sighed.

"I feel a little beat up," Bubba said, "but don't look like nothing is broken. I kin wiggle my toes and my fingers. Ain't nothing wrong with you or...the baby?"

"We're fine." She stood up and let him touch her stomach with his fingers. He stroked it over the t-shirt she wore and sighed with relief.

"Wedding still on?" he asked hopefully.

"If you can get out of that bed, cowboy," Willodean said. There was a return of the sauciness he enjoyed so much.

"It won't be the only reason I get out of this bed," he shot back with a smile that reminded him that the muscles on the sides of his head hurt, too. It was all bark and no bite, but it didn't hurt to say the words.

"I have a strange longing for cookies covered with spaghetti sauce," Willodean said. Bubba had an idea that she was serious. The problem was that cookies covered with spaghetti sauce sounded good to him, too. Should he tell her about the sympathetic pregnancy thing? *Naw.*

They heard voices from the hallway. Miz Demetrice wailed mournfully, "Poor, poor Bubba!" Peyton waited for Miz Demetrice to pause before asking loudly about wedding photographers and how would Bubba look if they made him wear a hat and makeup. David Beathard said, "Quiet, you. Dr. Watson needs his rest. He's bound to be abominably knackered. All this rubbish has likely knocked him arse-over-tit." There was a pause and then David said, "Oww. You didn't need to smack my head, Thelda. You knocked my deerstalker cap on the ground." Jesus said, "Iiii will heeeal Bubba!"

"We're about to be swarmed," Willodean warned.

"I kin take it." Bubba paused. "Brownie dint visit?" He touched his face. "Last time, it took a week to get all the Sharpies off."

"No, it's just bruised." Willodean smiled down at him. "Hey, I brought you something."

Bubba was instantly suspicious. "You dint bake again, did you? Baking's prolly bad for the baby. You should be sitting down with your feet up or something. Mebe I need a pry bar to get my feet out of my mouth."

"Haha," Willodean said dryly. "No, it was something David brought yesterday. This is Monday, by the way, in case you were wondering."

"It was on my list of things to ask."

Willodean reached beside the bed and brought out a small plate. One item sat on it all by its lonesome covered with a swatch of plastic wrap.

It was a single cupcake. It was the last cupcake Leeza had made. A chocolate zucchini carrot cupcake. The last one of twelve which Precious apparently had *not* eaten. The rhyme that Peyton had sung came to his mind and he smiled, unable to help himself, singing the words that slipped into his head. *"One little Indian livin' all alone. He got married and then there were none."*

Mr. and Mrs. Evan and Celestine Gray

and

Mrs. Demetrice Snoddy

formally request the honor of your

presence at the marriage of their children

Willodean Gray and Bubba Snoddy

Saturday, April 27th

The Snoddy Mansion * Pegram County, Texas

No dead bodies allowed.

The End.

Note from the Author

I have been fortunate in my indie work to be successful enough to be happy. I cannot thank enough the people who help me out. My husband and daughter top the list. Thanks to Mary E. Bates, freelance proofreader of ebooks and printed material. Contact her at mbates16@columbus.rr.com. Sometimes when I get the corrections back from her, and I see what I have done and done and done a few more times, I don't quite understand why she hasn't ripped all her hair out in frustration. Any mistakes made are mine, however, not hers. Thanks to all the readers who keep buying my books. You rule! I can't say enough that I really appreciate your support.

Finally, I need to say that I played around with wedding invitations for Bubba and Willodean and then posted them on Facebook to see what people thought. However, it dawned on me that people thought this book would be about the wedding, and it is, kind of, but it isn't. The wedding is definitely next, I swear. Would I lie to you? Besides all ya'll are invited to the big event.

In other bat news see me at www.clbevill.com or on Facebook at https://www.facebook.com/pages/CL-Bevill/135805749827314?ref=hl or email me at clbevill@clbevill.com.

Sincerely, Caren

About the Author

C.L. Bevill has lived in Texas, Virginia, Arizona, and Oregon. She once was in the U.S. Army and a graphic illustrator. She holds degrees in social psychology and counseling. She is the author of *Bubba and the Dead Woman, Bubba and the 12 Deadly Days of Christmas, Bubba and the Missing Woman, Bayou Moon,* and *Shadow People,* among others. Presently she lives with her husband and her daughter and continues to constantly write. She can be reached at www.clbevill.com or you can read her blog at www.carwoo.blogspot.com.

Other Novels by C.L. Bevill

~

Mysteries:
Bubba and the Dead Woman
Bubba and the 12 Deadly Days of Christmas
Bubba and the Missing Woman
Brownie and the Dame (3.5)
Bubba and the Mysterious Murder Note
The Ransom of Brownie (4.5)
Bubba and the Zigzaggery Zombies
Bubba and the Ten Little Loonies

Bayou Moon
Crimson Bayou

Paranormal Romance:
Veiled Eyes (Lake People)
Disembodied Bones (Lake People)
Arcanorum (Lake People)

The Moon Trilogy (Novellas):
Black Moon (The Moon Trilogy 1)
Amber Moon (The Moon Trilogy 2)
Silver Moon (The Moon Trilogy 3)

Cat Clan Novellas:
Harvest Moon
Blood Moon
Crescent Moon
Hunter's Moon

Shadow People

Sea of Dreams
Mountains of Dreams (Dreams 2)

Suspense:
The Flight of the Scarlet Tanager

Black Comedy:
The Life and Death of Bayou Billy
Missile Rats

Chicklet:
Dial 'M' For Mascara

Urban Fantasy:
Deadsville

CPSIA information can be obtained at www.ICGtesting.com
Printed in the USA
LVOW06s1623080715

445461LV00014B/227/P